MAZE OF DESTINY

Hussin Alkheder

1

Mullah Abdullah

An ear-piercing whistle, followed by an earth-shattering explosion nearby, interrupted Mullah Abdullah's recitation of afternoon prayers in the Shagoor mosque, which was down a narrow alley in the heart of old Damascus.

What would the target be this time? he wondered.

Every day now, mortar shells took their toll indiscriminately. The victims might be a man doing errands for his family, a woman buying food for her children, or students returning from school. The target might be a house, a restaurant, a school, or even a church or a mosque.

Oh no. The revolutionaries are fighting for the sake of Islam. They would never target mosques.

He shifted his thoughts back to reciting the prayer. As an imam leading prayer, his reciting of the Quranic verses needed to be audible to the congregation behind him. Deep inside, he was glad his voice was not very clear to the congregation because with each explosion he was shaken to the core; terror caused his mouth to go dry and added an unwanted tremor to his voice. Today there were only ten men behind him, unlike before the war, more than a year ago, when worshippers filled half of the mosque during daily prayers. In those days, the mosque had always overflowed for Friday's sermons and prayers. Still, it didn't prevent him from leading prayers five times a day, seven days a week.

He paused his reciting again as another piercing whistle approached, even louder and sharper than the last. He squeezed his eyes shut as he stiffened in anticipation. The ensuing explosion didn't move him.

Good. If any of the men behind were watching me, they wouldn't think their mullah was scared.

The truth was, he was terrified. The floor vibrated and the crystal chandeliers jangled. He continued to recite.

His stomach growled, reminding him of the rich lunches he shared daily with his daughter Zahra and his wife Amani after afternoon prayers. But first he fetched Zahra from school. He prohibited her from walking home alone. She waited for him with her high school friend Zakiya. This year would decide what her university major would be. He wanted her to be a doctor, and this major would require top grades in high school.

She didn't get them last year. Hopefully she will this year.

He shifted his attention again to the supplication of the third kneeling, then raising his head, lowered himself to a prostrate position. Afternoon prayers comprised four raka'ats. Each raka'at comprised a standing, a kneeling, and two prostrations.

The war had fallen on Syria like a witch's spell. Two years ago, Damascus was one of the safest cities in the world. Now, every day when he left his house, he said goodbye to Amani as if it would be his last time seeing her. Every time he dropped Zahra at school, he looked up at the sky and begged Allah to protect her in case he died. Now Damascus was one of the most, if not the most, dangerous cities in the world. During this cursed war, Syrians were unfortunate enough to be eyewitnesses to the kind of violence they thought only existed in horror movies. Killing had become a daily occurrence. Most adults and children alike had seen at least one body lying in a deserted alley or at the edge of a neglected garden. Masked men broke into apartments and killed residents in full sight of their neighbors. Gangs specialized in looting property from cars, apartments, and factories to the point of tearing the electrical wires from under the tiles. Kidnapping had become a profession earning billions. The lucky ones would be exchanged for ransom, but the unfortunate ones ended up supplying either the illegal organ trade or human trafficking. The devil poured out his wrath on the Syrian people and left suppurated wounds in the heart of humanity that will never heal.

I must focus on my reciting. It's a sin to keep thinking about earthly matters while praying. I seek refuge with Allah from the accursed Satan.

He raised his head from the fourth kneeling, then went down for the last two prostrations.

As he turned his head to the left to greet the angels and end his prayer, a tremendous explosion sent him flying. His face struck the *mihrab*, the marble niche that faced Mecca. Lightning exploded behind his eyes as he fell to the floor. The pain was unimaginable. An agonizing scream tore from his mouth, raw and fierce, like a furnace erupting with heat. His moans mixed with the cries and screams of the injured worshippers and the crashing of falling wood and stone. He writhed and twisted on the floor under the blinding pain. The pain in his head was a hammer pounding his skull from within. His eyes were squeezed shut, and when he opened them and raised his head to look, a searing pain erupted in his neck. He quickly gave up trying to raise his head and turned his body to the side to look. Clouds of thick dust swirled in the shaft of sunlight streaming through a gaping hole in the roof. The ceiling, once supported by enormous cedar beams, lay in ruin. Shattered chunks from the ceiling were scattered on the floor among the wreckage. Some still dangled from one end, while the other ends pierced the floor like huge spears.

Flesh and blood spattered the floor and walls, and bodies were scattered across the floor like slaughtered carcasses. The number of onlookers increased as people rushed into the mosque through the enormous hole where the wall had been moments ago. Everyone was trying to help the injured. Several men came to the mullah's side to talk to him. He was having a hard time understanding them due to the noise around them and the buzzing in his ears. He struggled to get to his feet as many hands stretched out to help. Then his view of the people around him rotated, as his legs turned to putty, and he tumbled into the arms of his rescuers. They carried him out and laid him on the pavement outside the mosque to wait for the ambulance. He tried to speak, but a lump was blocking his throat. Every breath was like sucking air through a clogged pipe.

Zahra, I am coming. Wait for me. Don't walk home alone, I promise I will protect you; I will not let the impurity of this war touch you. I will not allow anyone, or anything, to hurt you. Wait for me, I am coming.

As he struggled to raise his head, blood filled his mouth. He coughed, the blood spurting down his white beard, choking him as it ran into his windpipe. The

coughing became more intense, then...
Everything went dark.

2

Amani

For a fraction of a second Amani thought a volcano had erupted from under the courtyard. Windows shattered, jars and stainless-steel cookware and utensils crashed to the floor in the kitchen. Vibrations from the ground traveled through her body, reaching the very marrow of her bones. She had been watering the plant pots in the courtyard using a plastic kettle. She put it down quickly and leaned against the wall, breathing deeply with her eyes squeezed tightly shut. Amani felt as if a needle had pierced her heart. She gasped for air and thought for a moment she might vomit, but there was nothing in her stomach to come up.

The explosion was different this time. Not only did it feel as if the mortar shell had hit right outside the door, but she had a feeling something else was wrong. Her instincts rarely betrayed her, and she was sure something bad had happened to the mullah or to Zahra, or both of them. The very thought sucked the strength from her legs, so she moved to the *liwan*–the shaded open space between the two rooms at the front of the house connected to the courtyard–and sat on the sofa.

People's screams rose in the alley. She couldn't tell how many there were, but it seemed like a lot. The sound of their running steps alarmed her, so she ran to the outside door to listen. From behind the door, she could hear what they were saying as they ran. It was what she'd been most afraid of; the explosion was at the mosque. She hastened to her bedroom, threw one of her husband's cloaks over her shoulders, tied on her headscarf, then, still in her rubber house slippers, took off at a run.

Slamming the door behind her, she rushed toward the mosque. By the time she arrived, bodies of the dead and their blood were strewn everywhere. The wooden roof of the mosque was in tatters, allowing in beams of sunlight now thick with dust. Rushing inside, she looked one by one at the dead bodies, but none was her beloved husband. She headed to the *mihrab* where her husband always stood to lead the prayer. The mullah's body was not there, but his red velvet fez lay crumpled as if someone had stepped on it. As she picked it up, the touch of wet blood brought fresh tears. Looking around, all she could see was a blur. She wiped her tears. One man was removing debris from over a dead body. She asked him urgently, "Have you seen the mullah?"

He answered without raising his head or even looking at her, "They took him to City Hospital."

"Is he...?" She couldn't say it.

One of the men recognized her, maybe because she was wearing her husband's cloak. He jumped over two shattered roof beams before reaching where she stood. With downcast eyes, he said, "Oh sister, don't worry, the mullah is ok. He has only a few injuries."

Fresh tears streamed from her eyes and without replying, she stumbled outside. It would be impossible to find a taxi in the alley unless they were called in, so she hurried toward the street, still wiping her tears with her sleeve.

No one stopped to ask if she needed help. No drivers asked if she needed a ride. Even the passing pedestrians avoided meeting her eyes. People's sorrow changes them. The appearance of a distraught woman screaming and crying while wearing her husband's cloak has no effect. They were used to seeing people slaughtered at the roadsides every day. A crying woman was nothing by comparison.

With a sinking heart, she halted on the sidewalk, realizing she had no money and couldn't pay for a taxi. Gasping for breath and still wiping her eyes, she thought, *I should be stronger than this. I must not act like a bereaved woman. The mullah isn't dead, he was only injured. But what if he had died? He's all I have in this life.* She turned her eyes skyward. "Oh Allah, I leave the mullah in your hands." Then she went back home to change into proper clothes and get some money.

After she'd changed and left the house again, she jogged through several alleys until she reached the main road, breathless. She waited a long time, but there wasn't a taxi in sight. So, she squeezed herself onto a green bus packed with passengers, most of whom were men wearing army attire. The horror of war tainted their faces. This was the first time since the war started that she'd left the house alone. She felt vulnerable riding a bus with so many men.

Zahra will be worried, waiting at the school for her father to pick her up. But I shouldn't worry about her, she's old enough to come home alone. But she doesn't have the house key. Well, she can stay at Zakiya's apartment until we get back.

Zahra had spent a lot of time with Zakiya and her three sisters, whose mother Hadiyah had died. Amani didn't object to that. Hadiyah's daughters were like sisters to Zahra.

Amani stared wide-eyed at the number of soldiers swarming around the hospital. At the gate, there were three soldiers, one sitting behind a metal table and two standing behind him. The one sitting was in charge. He took her ID and asked her a few questions irrelevant to the purpose of her visit, but she didn't mind, she just wanted to get in and find the mullah. He informed her he would call her when entry was granted.

Hundreds of people were outside of the hospital. Most were squatting, some lying down, and the rest standing. Their relaxing positions showed they had been waiting for some time. She prayed she wouldn't have to wait long. Unfortunately, her prayers were not answered. She waited almost two hours before they called her name.

Once inside, the smell of blood caused her to gag. The scene was more like a morgue than a hospital. Injured people covered every empty space in the reception area. She didn't care. All she wanted at that moment was to find her husband.

She found him in a ward crammed with extra beds, all occupied by injured people, many with family members gathered around them. He had an oxygen tube up his nose, wires attached to several parts of his body, and a saline drip in his arm. The beeping monitor beside the bed showed that his heart was beating normally. His head was covered with blood-stained bandages. She didn't know whether to laugh or cry. Walking to the left side of the bed, she took her husband's hand between hers and squeezed. Then she let her tears flow once more. Her main purpose for living was still alive.

She imagined the beeping sped up a little when she squeezed his hand.

3

Zahra

Zahra couldn't remember her father ever being late. At the end of every school day, he would be waiting for her and Zakiya to escort them home. Today Zahra went out, and he wasn't there. Fifteen minutes passed and still no sign of him. She used to make the fifteen-minute walk from the school to her house by herself, but ever since the war began and the horrible events that followed, her father refused to let her walk home alone.

Zakiya, her neighbor and best friend, waited with her. Zakiya's mom was dead, and her father lived in Dubai. Zahra's father took care of Zakiya and her three sisters as much as his time and clerical responsibilities would allow.

Since the beginning of the war, kidnapping had become a trend. Her father insisted that corrupt government forces were the kidnappers. Her teacher told her class that the kidnappers were rebels who needed money to buy weapons to fight the government. One of her cousins claimed the kidnappers were extremists who considered anyone not with them must be against them. Some people swore the kidnappers were a criminal organization that not only demanded ransom money but also sold human organs for profit.

For Zahra, who might be responsible for such wicked deeds, wasn't clear. The only thing clear to her was, because of the astronomical ransoms, more than half of the hostages ended up dead.

Thirty minutes later, the school was empty. The last to leave was the janitor, who locked the school gate, threw a scrutinizing glance at her and Zakiya before he hurried away.

Zakiya's pale face was so vacant it seemed to Zahra there were no muscles in it. She could, however, read Zakiya's eyes. She had the most expressive eyes Zahra had ever seen. Now those eyes radiated anxiety. Zahra couldn't blame her. Nowadays, people never went out of their homes unless they had urgent errands. Two young females standing on an empty street were as vulnerable as a deer among the leopards.

Zahra grabbed Zakiya's hand. "Let's go home."

Zakiya's only answer was a nod. Her school attire was loose and saggy, reminding Zahra of a skeleton wearing clothes.

The school was on a separate lot on Naser Street, surrounded by three-story buildings. They walked to the end of the street then crossed over to enter the Medhat Basha market, a busy street, especially at this time of the day. They reached an alley called Dakaken and from there they entered the Shagoor alley, which was narrow, dark, and empty. Zahra's heart raced as she quickened her pace. Zakiya did her best to keep up.

Old Damascus houses are famous for their spacious interiors. They're connected by narrow, intertwining alleys, and were built at a time when mules were used for transportation. Thus, only compact cars and scooters can pass through them, forcing pedestrians to step aside to allow them to pass.

As Zahra and Zakiya reached the long narrow alley

called Zukak Tanyus, they heard a car engine, so they stopped and pressed their backs to the wall, allowing the car to pass.

As Zahra contemplated the silent alley, her mind went back to a time before the war when, during the day, window curtains were always drawn aside, revealing rooms occupied by happy families. Doors were always open, exposing courtyards filled with the chatter of kids playing. Neighbors talked to each other from rooftop to rooftop, or window to window. Passersby could hear the murmuring of the fountains in the courtyards and catch a whiff of fragrant jasmine and the aroma of the citrus aurantium or bitter orange planted around the edges of the courtyards of every house in old Damascus. These days, everywhere you looked, there were locked doors and barred windows. Nothing to hear but silence, and only the smell of fear in the air.

A dirty old, pale blue Volkswagen van with its unique engine noise approached. Zakiya and Zahra stopped and pressed their backs against a closed door, waiting for the van to pass, but as the van got to them, it stopped, and the side door slid open. Two masked men jumped out and quickly threw black canvas bags over the girls' heads. Zahra screamed and kicked out, hoping Zakiya was doing the same.

4

Ward

Ward knew he was different from his brother George. First, his appearance; his face flatter, his eyes almond-shaped and slanted, his ears exceptionally small, his neck thick and short, his fingers short and plump, and his tongue sticking out of his mouth most of the time, testing the air according to his brother George. Second, people didn't understand his speech like they understood George. Fortunately, George always understood what Ward was saying, and sometimes even what he wasn't.

Ward was sitting in the liwan, waiting for a beep from the digital clock. Five beeps had sounded so far since his brother George left the house. He folded the fingers of his right-hand one by one with each beep until it became a fist, while his left hand remained open, ready to fold his pointing finger when the sixth beep sounded. That would mean George would arrive home shortly, and Ward must start preparing the table for lunch.

The clock beeped, and he folded the pudgy index finger of his left hand. He was supposed to go to the kitchen, bring out the utensils, and arrange them on the table. First, he wanted to be sure it was the sixth beep. He started counting the fingers, starting with his right hand, "Wa, To, Te, Fo, Fi," then looking at the only folded finger on his left hand, and counted "Tik." A wide smile plumped up his cheeks, turning his eyes into slits for a moment. It was almost time for George to come home.

The table was in the liwan, so he went to the kitchen and got two forks, two spoons, two plates, and two glasses. He went back to the table and arranged them opposite each other, so he could sit across from George. Then he brought a jug of tap water and put it on the table. A last glance at the table caused him to smile in satisfaction.

Ward went quickly to the door and squinted through the peephole. Like every day, he would surprise George by opening the door before he could insert his key. Just thinking about the smile on George's face made his heart flutter.

Through the peephole in the front door, he saw two girls standing outside the door. He was about to open the door to tell them they were blocking him from seeing when George arrived, when a van stopped out front "Hoony Moony," Ward snapped. He decided he had to ask both the van and the girls to move out of the way.

Ward grabbed the doorknob without taking his eye away from the peephole. The side door of the van slid open and two masked men jumped out. The men covered the girls' heads with canvas bags and started to wrestle them into the van.

"Hoony Moony," Ward yelled, "bat met steenin girns." The thrashing limbs of the girls reminded Ward of chickens trying to get away from the butcher and his slaughtering knife. He had to do something to prevent the bad men from stealing the girls.

Ward opened the door, grabbed one of the girls by the wrist, and pulled with all his strength. He didn't step at the threshold, though. He couldn't let the door close, because he didn't have the key, and he would end up waiting for George on the street.

"A'n 'o bi'," Ward yelled in the face of the masked man who was pulling on the same girl as he was pulling. He thought calling the man a son of a bitch would scare him and cause him to loosen his grip on the girl. But the masked man only pulled harder. Ward bit his lower lip, and grabbing the girl with his left hand, he let fly with his right hand, clouting the masked man in the head. The pulling eased only for a second, but it was enough for Ward to yank the girl through the door, like throwing a sack of potatoes. When she landed on the floor, her head banged on the tiles.

Ward wanted to rescue the second girl, but the masked man leaped after the girl, so Ward yelled and jumped back, trying to slam the door. The kidnapper put out his hand to prevent the door from closing, but Ward threw his entire body weight against it, and the man screamed like a wounded ox. Ward pushed harder. The man screamed louder. Voices erupted from the far end of the alley. Ward heard the masked man in the van calling for his friend to leave the girl and just get in the van. Ward pushed even harder until he heard the cracking of bone. The man shrieked so loudly that people peered from the windows of the nearby houses.

A forceful shove on the door pushed Ward back a few inches. The hand jerked free, and the door banged shut. Ward looked through the peephole again to see the driver who had come to his friend's rescue hurrying back to his seat. The other man, cradling his injured hand and cursing a blue streak, jumped into the back, and the van rocketed away, with only one of the girls.

Ward looked down at the girl on the floor. He leaned

against the wall, his head spinning. The girl wasn't moving. The canvas bag still covered her head, but now there was a puddle of blood beneath it.

Ward burst into tears.

5

Zakiya

Zakiya wriggled as much as the tight space on the floor between the seats would allow. The filthy canvas sack still covered her head. The man pulled it back just enough to shove a foul-tasting gag into her mouth. Her arms and legs were bound tightly, causing her hands and feet to go numb because of the lack of blood circulation. The man who had pulled her into the back of the van was resting his feet on her tiny body. She couldn't see his shoes, but she decided they must be army boots due to the severe pain she felt every time he kicked her to stop her from wriggling or making noise. She did her best to choke back her cries, but when he kicked her in the kidneys, she almost passed out.

The trip was taking a very long time. More time than it took for her grandfather to drive them to his farm at the far end of the Damascus countryside, a trip they made once a month.

Finally, the van stopped, and the door slid open. Strong hands grabbed her feet and dragged her out. Her head hit the hard ground first, and she nearly blacked out. The canvas bag prevented her face from being scratched, as she was dragged a short way, then carelessly tossed like a trash bag. The bag was snatched off suddenly, causing her head to bounce on the ground. The gag remained in place. The air was heavy. Odors of sweat and urine assaulted her nose. She realized she was in a tin barn and there were other girls with her.

She was scared to look into the man's eyes, the one who snatched the canvas bag off as he checked her face, turning it right, then left, then raising her chin. She stared at his hands covered with calluses and scars, and fingers as fat as sausages. His skin was badly sunburned. Maybe he was a porter or a farmer or some other job that kept him out in the sun a lot. Now he was a kidnapper. He removed the gag and forced a finger in her mouth, prying it open to look at her teeth, then pushed the gag back in. He stood and walked out of the barn, closing the gate behind him.

Zakiya sat up and looked around. The other girls around her were tied and gagged as she was. Some of them were looking at her, some were lost in their own misery. Two of them were moaning, and a couple of them crying out in pain. The ground beneath them was damp and the smell of urine told her she shouldn't expect to be given any bathroom breaks.

Since the war had started in Syria, thousands of families had been forced to flee their homes in hundreds of villages across the country. Many of them ended up in Damascus, but those who couldn't reach safe cities like Damascus were forced into refugee camps on the borders with Turkey, Jorden, and Lebanon. Many people lost their homes, cars, shops, factories, and everything they owned in this life and were forced to live in a tent in the middle of nowhere that couldn't protect them from the piercing cold of winter or the burning heat of summer.

As Zakiya lay there wondering what her destiny would be, she recalled some of the horrifying stories her sisters had told her about things that happened to others during the war, but she'd never thought something like this could happen to her.

One of her classmates had cried while telling how a group of thugs from the army forced her father out of his expensive car at gunpoint. Luckily, they only took the car and didn't kill him. Zakiya had thought at the time, *I don't have a car, so such a thing could never happen to me.*

When her friend's aunt, who was originally from Mezzeh but lived in Doma, and her entire family were killed when Doma was taken by the rebels, Zakiya had thought, *I have lived in the heart of Damascus all my life, and no one will dare to kill us.*

When one of her cousins who was in the army, got killed by a colleague just because he disagreed with him about defecting from the official Syrian Army and joining the free Syrian army, Zakiya had thought at the time, *I will never face such a fate because I'm female and will never serve in the army.*

When their rich neighbor Ziad was kidnapped and his family paid a fortune in ransom to his kidnappers, he came back missing all his fingers. Zakiya had thought, *that would never happen to me or my sisters because we're poorer than church mice.*

When one of her schoolteachers lost her will to live and became a walking zombie, because her son was stopped at an inspection point and arrested. For several months, no one knew where he was, or if he was alive or dead. Zakiya had thought, *that could never happen to me. I stay away from inspection points.*

Her best friend Zahra always warned her not to go out alone for fear she would be kidnapped and raped. Zakiya had thought then, *I'm just an ugly witch. Who would think of touching me?*

An approaching engine disturbed the eerie silence of the tin barn. The vehicle stopped out front and its sliding door opened. The metal gate clanged open, and two men came in carrying two new girls over their shoulders, depositing them on the ground like sacks of trash, causing one of them to yell out in pain. Pulling the bags off the girls' heads but leaving the gags in their mouths, the men left the barn. The newcomers were so young, but the stresses of life already showed on their faces. A few minutes later, an argument erupted between the men outside. Apparently, there was a misunderstanding regarding payment.

One of the men came back into the hangar and looked the girls over, one by one, not only at their faces but head to toe. He finally chose one and pulled her to her feet. The girl screamed and kicked, but her voice was muffled by the gag in her mouth. Zakiya felt guilty for exhaling in relief when the man didn't choose her.

The monster didn't take the girl too far. Zakiya could hear desperate moaning as if the poor girl was being poked with a sharp instrument. With each poke, a scream left her throat but didn't go far because of the gag.

It was a sound Zakiya would never forget.

When he brought the girl back, her face was red and wet. Her dark blue dress was smeared with dirt and vomit. The man hadn't bothered to pull her underwear back up for her and she couldn't do it herself because her hands were tied behind her back. She couldn't stop crying.

Zakiya couldn't help crying when she saw her. A few

of the other girls also cried. One of the men came in and barked at them to shut up. Zakiya swallowed her tears and closed her eyes tightly. She could block out the sorrowful sight, but she couldn't block out the stench of vomit and urine. She was grateful she hadn't had her breakfast. She felt nauseous, but there was nothing in her stomach to bring up.

Zakiya had never expected to find herself in a more miserable situation than her family was already in. Her mom was dead, and her father living a life of luxury in Dubai. Her grandfather controlling all their expenses made their lives worse than poor people. Poor already know they don't have money, so they find ways to make do with what little they have. Zakiya and her sisters knew their grandfather received a lot of money from their father in Dubai, but instead of being loving and supportive, he humiliated them instead. If they asked for more dish washing liquid, he instructed them not to use more than one drop per dishpan load. If they asked for toothpaste more than once a month, he told them the correct amount to put on their toothbrush was the size of a chickpea. One tube of toothpaste for four grown girls brushing their teeth three times a day was not enough, so when they ran out early, they would use salt to brush their teeth until the end of the month. Sugar was a luxury they could do without, and they were instructed to use only one tea bag per pot instead of one per mug. They were only allowed two eggs per week, and most of the time, they didn't even have bread.

"But that's a good thing," he told them. "You won't get fat."

She had long ago forgotten what the sense of ownership felt like. She shared underwear, bras, and outfits with her elder sisters. Because she was a lot smaller than her sisters, none of the clothes fit her properly. The last time she'd bought new clothes was before their mom died three years earlier.

Time moved at a snail's pace in the sweltering barn. The girls were still tied and gagged, but the men took away a couple of girls, including the one in extreme pain. The girl who had been crying was now leaning against the blazing hot tin with her eyes shut. *How can she sleep in this hell?* Zakiya tried hard to sleep, but the pounding of her heart and the nausea made it impossible. She wished God would send the angel Azrael to pull her soul out of her body.

6

George

When George finished teaching his last class in English reading at the Assieh Elementary School, he always rushed home to have lunch with Ward, then went to the church to do his daily volunteer duties. He was supposed to be in the army like millions of other young men serving their country during the war, but because his brother Ward had Down's syndrome and he was his only guardian, they had waived the compulsory army service. He still felt a duty to his community, though, so he volunteered at the Maryamian church on Bab Sharqi Street, helping families affected by the war, especially Christian families. Because Iran was supporting Shia families, and Saudi was supporting Sunni families. That left only the church to help Christian families.

He was surprised when Ward didn't open the door before he could insert the key in the lock. The smile he always had ready for Ward faded as he took the key out of the lock and entered the house quickly. "Ward," he called, as he walked to his bedroom door at the far end of the hallway. Still no response from Ward, so he didn't bother opening the door. Instead, he walked into the courtyard. The fountain was not running, not a leaf on the aurantium trees stirred, everything was still and silent.

Ward was sitting on the old sofa in the liwan, arms

wrapped around his raised knees. His eyes were red, his face wet with tears, his nose was running, and there was a bubble of saliva in one corner of his mouth. George put his work bag on the tea table and sat beside Ward, wiping away his brother's tears, mucus, and saliva with his sweater sleeve. Pulling Ward's face to face him, he asked, "What's wrong, genius?"

"Aad en steenin girns. I evd er. I elpd er. I dinin wan kin er," Ward's silent crying turned to loud sobbing.

George tried to process the details in his brain. Usually, he could understand what Ward said, but what he had just said sounded scary. Could it be possible that Ward killed a girl accidentally while trying to save her from bad men who were trying to kidnap her? "Where did this happen?" he asked.

Ward pointed in the direction of the outside door.

"Where is she now?" George asked. He didn't have to decipher Ward's words this time, he just followed his eyes. Immediately, he jumped up and ran to his own room and flung open the door.

The first thing George noticed was the girl was wearing a headscarf. *She is Muslim.* She was wearing a high school uniform; baggy gray pants, and a gray jacket three sizes too large for her. The pile of baggy gray clothes looked empty, as if there was no body in them. Her white headscarf was soaked with blood from a gash over her right eye, and part of her face was smeared with blood. Rushing forward, he put a finger on her wrist and exhaled in relief when he found a pulse. As he turned to go to the kitchen, he found Ward had come in right behind him.

"Quickly Ward, do you know where the onions are in the kitchen?"

Ward nodded. "Uh ya."

"Okay, get an onion, cut it in half, and bring it to me, as quick as you can now."

Ward sprinted off down the hall and in 30 seconds he was back with the onion.

George took one half from him and held it under the girl's nose. She gasped and opened her eyes. When she saw him and Ward standing behind him, she pulled her knees up to her chest and hugged them tightly, cowering at the far end of the bed.

He held his arms up, with open palms facing her, offering her a gesture of peace. He noticed she was looking at the big wooden cross hanging on the wall. Then a panicked look spread across her face. Her eyes darted left and right as she shrank back more, as if she was cowering before a predator.

"Calm down now," he said. "My brother Ward was just trying to help. I'm not sure what he did or why he did it, but I'm very sure he didn't have any bad intentions." George saw her eyes soften a little. "Let me help you clean your wound. After that, you're free to go. You can call your family to come and pick you up if you want." He waited for her response.

"I want to call my father," she said, looking right and left as if looking for something missing.

"We really need to clean your wound, otherwise it will get infected," George said. Ward was still behind him, watching without making a sound.

"NOW!" she snapped, "I need to call my father."

"Ok, ok, just calm down," George said, "You can call him, the telephone is on the dresser," he pointed to a dresser covered with cologne bottles, aftershave, shaving cream, hair clippers, and a cream-colored

Panasonic telephone.

She darted to the dresser, snatched up the phone receiver eagerly, pressed a few numbers, and stared at him and Ward while she waited.

George saw her eyes filled with doubt.

"Just let me clean your wound and then I'll drop you at your house." Not waiting for her reply, he turned and asked Ward to fetch the first aid kit. She was dialing numbers once more when Ward came back with the kit. George opened it and took out the bottle of iodine and some gauze. After pouring some iodine on the gauze, he approached her.

"Don't touch me," she snapped and moved back against the wall.

"It's Ok," George said, "I just want to help." He put the kit on the bed and moved back toward the door. Ward started to follow him, but before they left the room, George turned and said, "You can clean it yourself. We'll be right outside if you need anything." They left the room, and George closed the door quietly behind them.

7

Ward

Ward left the room right behind George, but he didn't follow George to the kitchen. He just squatted and peeked through the keyhole at the delicate creature he'd rescued.

She was standing next to the dresser, holding the phone receiver to her ear. Maybe she was trying to call her family again. Ward looked at her reflection in the mirror over the dresser, he held his breath for fear she would hear him and know he was looking at her. He used to peek at his stepmother like this, but not out of curiosity. It was just to be sure she didn't commit suicide as she threatened to do on the phone with their father, every time he called to inform her, he couldn't get leave to come. He was a lieutenant in the Syrian Arab Army, and he said she caused him more headaches than all his superiors caused him during his service.

Ward glanced at the reflection of the strange creature in the mirror again. She put the receiver down and moved next to the bed where his brother George had left the iodine and gauze for her. She picked it up, stepped in front of the mirror, and dabbed at her wound. She bit her lower lip, went back to the bed to pick up more gauze, then continued wiping the wound in front of the mirror. She tried to use a facial tissue to remove traces of blood, but the tissue stuck to the wound. She soaked another strip of gauze and carefully cleaned the bits of tissue from the wound. In the mirror, he could see that her face was tinted with the rusty color of iodine. She wasn't doing a very good job of it. She picked up the phone receiver again and dialed. Apparently, there was still no answer because she put it back down.

She sat on the side of the bed, staring at the blueish-green wall opposite, where a big, dark brown wooden cross hung. She got up and walked to the wall, touching the shiny cross with her fingertips.

She turned her head to look at the coat rack in the corner, mounded with clothes, giving it the shape of a small rocket. She glanced at the window above the bed. Before the war, George used to keep it open day and night, but now it was covered with black, adhesive-backed sheets to prevent the glass from shattering if a bullet or even a stone hit it.

Ward smiled. She was staring at everything in the room. Then she turned and looked at George's closet. The three doors of the closet were wide open, exposing stacks of clothes beneath rows of clothes on hangers. Open drawers at the bottom of the closet overflowed with socks and underwear.

"Awee," Ward's head banged against the door because George slapped him on the back of the neck.

"What do you think you're doing?" George demanded, with a serious face.

Ward swallowed.

George knocked on the door, then pushed it open slightly and peeked in. "Did you get through to your family?"

George entered the room, with Ward right behind him.

"No answer," she said. "I will just have to go home."
She stared shyly at the floor in front of her feet.

"I'll come with you," George said. "Make sure you get
there okay."

She didn't protest.

Ward said, "Wa uo aim?"

George smiled and without looking at her, said, "He is
asking what your name is?"

She smiled and looked at Ward. "I am Zahra."

She almost jumped when he yelled, "Ee too, ma aim,
Wad."

She looked at George, red-faced and bewildered.

George looked at Ward as he said, "Ward is the plural
of Warda, which is a synonym for Zahra," then he
turned to her. "I am George, and this is my little brother
Ward."

Again, she was startled when Ward yelled, "I wa co wi
uo."

"No, Ward, you stay here," George said.

"No, please let him come with us," she said. "But we
should hurry. I have to inform my father that they
kidnapped our neighbor Zakiya. I think Ward tried to
rescue both of us. But I was the lucky one."

On the way to her house, Ward told George about how
he'd rescued her. George translated for Zahra. Her house
was only two alleys away from where George and Ward
lived.

When they arrived, she knocked on the door, but no
one opened it.

"You don't have a key?" George asked.

"I've never needed a key because my father always
picks me up, and my mother is always home when I
return from school, especially since the beginning of

the war."

Ward watched sympathetically as she knocked again and again.

"Why don't you come back with us and keep trying to call? When your parents get back, we will walk you back over again?"

"No, I have to inform Zakiya's sisters about her," she said. "They live nearby. If you could just drop me in front of their building, I would be grateful."

As Ward and George walked with Zahra, she said, "I don't know how her sisters will take the news. They are already so unfortunate; their mother was murdered a few years back, and now their sister has been kidnapped."

Ward gasped.

Zahra continued, "To make matters worse, their father abandoned them, and they are extremely poor. No one would want to be in their situation."

On the way home after dropping Zahra off at her friends' building, Ward chattered on endlessly about Zahra, while George remained silent.

8

Amani

Three hours and twenty-seven minutes had passed since Amani arrived at the mullah's bedside. She hadn't let go of his hand the whole time. She gazed fondly at his rounded face, taking in his angelic features. His beard, a mix of gray and white, was always neatly trimmed but now smeared with blood – neither too long nor too short. His nose was long, slightly hooked, and perfectly complemented his full cheeks. At six feet tall and slightly overweight, her husband still moved with ease and agility, displaying surprising flexibility and strength. *What will I do if I lose him?*

The ring of his mobile phone pulled her back to the reality of the hospital ward. Letting go of his hand, she walked over to his pile of bloody clothes as the ringing was coming from there. She pulled the phone from the inner pocket of his long coat and looked at the screen, which said 'Haj Adel'. She exhaled loudly. *What does that old man want, other than making my husband a servant to his four granddaughters?* She didn't bear a grudge against the four lovely girls or their deceased mother. She loved them dearly. But their father and grandfather were nothing but hypocrites. The father lived like a prince in Dubai, and the grandfather had three wives in three separate houses, living lives of luxury while the granddaughters lived in poverty.

"*Salam Alaikum,*" she started with the Islamic greeting, even though she was the one answering. Her husband always taught her that the one who starts with the greeting gets 69 times the responder's *thawab* (reward).

"*Alaikum Assalaam,*" his voice was deep and genial. "Is this not the number of Mullah Abdullah?"

"Yes, Haj, it's Amani, his wife. The mullah is in a coma. They bombed his mosque during afternoon prayers." She heard him gasp. His surprise puzzled her. She had assumed he knew about the explosion and was calling to be sure the mullah was ok. This man never called without a reason. What he said next confirmed her suspicions.

"We belong to Allah and to him we shall return. They've kidnapped the girls on their way home."

The full weight of his words struck Amani hard. The phone slipped from her hand and clattered to the floor. Her wailing startled everyone in the ward. Dropping to her knees at the bedside, she took hold of the mullah's hand and pressed it to her face, sobbing inconsolably. Her husband was in a coma, and they had kidnapped her daughter. How many more calamities could this day hold for her?

The beeping of the heart monitor sped up, causing her to raise her head, but she couldn't see anything, her eyes were so full of tears. Raised voices were all around her. Someone running. She turned her head, and a figure dressed in green rushed in. The nurse spoke soothingly to her, pulling her up from the floor by one arm and leading her out of the ward. Sitting her on a bench in the hallway, the nurse brought her a paper cup of water in an effort to calm her down. But Amani refused the water and was not listening to anyone, as she continued to wail.

"Amani," the voice was weak. Amani recognized her husband's voice instantly and rushed back to his bedside. She could see the questions in his eyes.

"They've kidnapped Zahra," she blurted out as fresh tears streamed down her cheeks.

9

Mazen

The driver opened the back door of the Bentley as Mazen stepped out of the car, still talking on his Vertu mobile. Standing next to the car, looking at his reflection in the passenger window, he adjusted his beige silk necktie, checked his shiny black hair, and clean-shaven face. "Annie, my office manager, is on her way to pick up the ring," Mazen said, then hung up and dropped the phone in his pocket.

He bounded up the steps to the main entrance of Burj Khalifa, the tallest tower in the world. Julie stood up to greet him as he entered the luxurious circular lobby. She wore a plain, dark blue, knee-length dress that complimented her white skin and blond hair. She kissed his cheek. "Hi love." Her voice was like a cool breeze to his ears.

He smiled, took her hand, and they walked to the elevators. Entering one of the fifty-seven fastest elevators in the world, Mazen and Julie were whisked to the 163rd floor in seventeen seconds. Today was Julie's birthday, so Mazen wanted to kill two birds with one stone by celebrating her birthday and proposing marriage at the same time. Annie would deliver the diamond ring shortly.

Two attractive young women greeted them at the entrance to the Royal Lounge.

"I am Porcia, at your service, and this is Nadia, my colleague, here to serve you as well," Porcia said, her words carrying a trace of a Nigerian accent.

"Thank you, Porcia," Mazen said.

"Maldives awaits you," Porcia said.

Julie gasped and looked at Mazen's eyes, her own eyes getting a little misty. She had wanted to go to Maldives to work on her tan, but because of the new fractional laser machines they were in the process of launching on the market, they were both too busy to even leave Dubai. He raised the hand he was still holding and kissed it while looking directly into her eyes.

Porcia said, "Please follow me."

Mazen, still holding Julie's hand, followed Porcia, with Nadia taking up the rear. They entered a tunnel where the milky way surrounded them as if they were floating in space. He looked at Julie and they both giggled, because only two steps into the tunnel, they had both flung their arms wide as if they were falling.

"Don't look down, just focus your eyes on Venus over there," Porcia said and pointed to the planet without turning her head.

Porcia stopped and snapped her fingers at a glowing red planet that looked like Mars. The planet turned black, except for a tiny spark of light glowing in the center. The spark became a ring of sparks, then it widened out like a magic ring, and the center opened like a camera shutter. Porcia tilted her head and walked through the expanding circle as if she were entering a time machine. As Mazen and Julie followed her, they found themselves aboard a yacht surrounded by turquoise blue water. The sun was bright but not too hot; the yacht swayed gently, seagulls flew overhead, and a dolphin popped its head out of the water, making chirping noises as if greeting them. Cool breezes ruffled their formal clothes.

"After a few minutes you'll forget everything is virtual reality, and the desire to touch them will be very strong, but please don't touch anything behind the fences," Porcia said.

"To avoid electric shock?" Mazen asked.

"No, don't worry, the screens are safe, but they are very sensitive. Everything you need is available on the yacht. Simply snap your fingers, and we will be at your service."

Nadia said, "Please, follow me and I'll show you where you can change your clothes." Her voice was soft and soothing.

A few minutes later, Mazen and Julie were stretched out on beach lounges. He wore only shorts, and she was resplendent in a yellow bikini. Mazen looked at Julie lying back with her sunglasses on. He thought how lucky he was to have her in his life. The cool breeze and the soothing melody of the waves slapping the sides of the yacht were intoxicating. Mazen shut his eyes and let out a long sigh of contentment.

Nadia appeared pushing a trolley, parking it in the middle between Mazen and Julie. The press of a button on the side of the trolley converted it to a low table. On the table was a gorgeous cake covered in pink frosting. Centered atop the cake was an open oyster shell. The diamond ring that Annie had just delivered sparkled from where it lay in the bottom half of the shell.

Julie was still lying back with her sunglasses on, totally relaxed. Mazen was glad she hadn't noticed the cake yet.

He nodded thank you to Nadia as she was leaving, then stretched out his arm to pick up the ring. His Vertu mobile rang. He was about to press the red button to cancel the call, but then he noticed it was his mother's number on the screen. He would never ignore a call from his mother, no matter what he was doing.

"Salam," Mazen said. Julie raised her head, removed her sunglasses, and looked at him.

"Salam papa," one of his daughter's voices replied.

"What's wrong?" He had left the country when his children were extremely young. Now, they were adults, and he was always too busy to spend enough time with them to be able to distinguish their voices.

"We are so sorry to bother you, papa, but it is an urgent matter. Something you must know about right away," she said.

"What's wrong?" He held back his temper, trying not to explode.

"They kidnapped Zakiya."

"What?" He said, still trying to figure out which daughter was talking without hurting her feelings by asking. "How do you know this?"

"Zahra was with her."

"Wasn't her father supposed to be with them?" Mazen asked.

"Zahra doesn't know why he didn't go to fetch them, but when she got home, neither of her parents were at home, so she came to our apartment to tell us what happened. Then I went with Marwa and Ro'wa to inform grandfather. He insisted I shouldn't let you know about Zakiya."

"Did you...?" He paused, deciding on the spot he would ask them face-to-face if they had gone alone to their grandfather's shop. He knew it was 2013, and the girls didn't have a phone or TV. People would think he was still living in a time of ignorance when people lived in tents and wiped their asses with stones. He didn't care what people thought, he told himself. He would not allow Satan to enter his home. If his young daughters had a telephone, men would start stalking them, calling them all the time and dragging them down the path of sin. "My dear Farah, you did the right thing by telling me. Now listen to me. You must go back home with your sisters and stay there. Don't leave until I arrive."

Julie was staring at him. He forced a smile, closing his eyelids slowly, like a cat showing its love.

He hung up and dialed Annie's number. "Hi Annie, please book the next available first-class flight to Damascus." He hung up and dialed his father's shop number.

"Salam Haj," Mazen said.

"Salam Abu Khaled," Haj Adel said. In his neighborhood, people don't call each other by their names. They either call the elderly who had gone on pilgrimage to Makkah, Haj, or they call them Abu (the father) of the eldest son. If the man had only daughters, they would call him the father of a future son.

"Haj, what has happened to Zakiya?" Mazen asked. Only silence on the other end. "Haj, are you there?"

"Who told you?" Haj Adel asked with a voice drier than a cactus plant.

"It's not important who told me. I am concerned about my family's well-being."

"Boy, you couldn't be more concerned about the family than me," Mazen's father called him boy to emphasize his superiority. That's one of the things that pushed Mazen to leave the country and move to Dubai in the first place. When they had worked together in the same shop, his father always made him feel inferior. No matter how much profit he generated, his father still complained that the shop was not big enough for two bosses.

"No Haj," Mazen said, softly, "You are the tent that covers the whole family. I always ask Allah to grant you the energy and long life to be able to protect us. I just don't want you to be under pressure. I know you have plenty of responsibilities. Isn't it enough that you must take care of your own families? Why should you be bothered by my daughters' calamities?" It was the sort of language his father understood.

"What to do, Abu Khaled? Life is not easy. War has destroyed the economy. I am seeing fewer clients each day, and your daughters' expenses are so high. Sometimes I need to pay from my own pocket to feed them until you send more money. I didn't want to bother you. I wanted you to focus on your job in Dubai so you could keep sending money to feed your daughters."

Mazen clenched his fist, almost cracking the phone. The money he sent his father each month was enough to feed ten families in Syria, not only four daughters. "Yes Haj, I agree with you, but I don't want you to be under any stress because of my daughters. I am coming down to see what I can do to find the girl."

"Boy, you don't need to come," Haj Adel said. "You just focus on your job in Dubai, and I will handle the matter of Zakiya. Plus, it is so dangerous over here. If the rebels find out you came from Dubai, they will kidnap you and ask for ransom. Who has money nowadays to pay such a ransom? They ask for millions."

"Haj, don't worry," Mazen said, his voice barely audible, "I won't let you pay a single dirham for Zakiya or anyone else. Anyway, take care. See you soon." He hung up before his father had a chance to protest anymore.

Julie was beside him, her arm around his shoulders.

"I am so sorry," she said.

"It's ok, don't worry about it," Mazen said, forcing a smile. "Guess what I have for you?"

"Oh baby, you know I love you unconditionally," she said and hugged him tightly. "Please, let's just go back home."

"Don't be silly," Mazen said. "You don't know how many asses I had to kiss to reserve this place in the Royal Lounge. This place is completely unknown to most people on earth, and I did the impossible just for you, my love."

"But what about your daughter?"

"I will figure it out when I get to Syria," Mazen said as he pulled out the diamond ring. "Happy birthday Sweetheart."

Julie gasped, and her eyes glittered. Her happiness was priceless to him, so he had decided to postpone his proposal until he returned from Syria.

10

Mullah Abdullah

After Amani calmed down and told the mullah the news she had received over the phone. He called Haj Adel immediately "Salam Haj."

"Salam Mullah," Haj Adel said, his voice sounding weak, "Difficult times we are having these days, the war is merciless, our beloveds being killed, our mosques bombed, our possessions robbed, and now our children kidnapped."

"We belong only to Allah," the mullah said. "How do you know they kidnapped Zahra and Zakiyah?"

"One of the neighbors saw what happened and informed me." Haj Adel said.

"Who is that neighbor?" the mullah asked. "He might be able to help us find out who did it."

"I don't know who he is, he just called and said my granddaughters were kidnapped. And then hung up." Haj Adel said.

"Did his number appear on your telephone screen?" Mullah Abdullah asked.

"My phone is just a rotary telephone, it doesn't have a screen."

"Did he give you any description of the ones who did it? What did he see? Where did it happen exactly?"

"The only reason the neighbor would inform me about such a thing is to gloat over me." Haj Adel said,

"They envy me because I am a rich man."

The mullah squeezed the mobile phone so hard his knuckles were white. "We need to act as soon as possible before it's too late. Or are you just going to wait for the kidnapper to call and demand a ransom?"

Haj Adel said, "The last thing I need right now is someone demanding a ransom."

The mullah opened his mouth to respond, but he was speechless. What could he say to this senile old man who is still thinking only about his money, while his granddaughter has been kidnapped? He thought about what could happen to young females who are kidnapped and swallowed hard. "If ransom can solve the issue, it would be the simplest way, especially for someone blessed by Allah with such great fortune."

"What are you talking about?" Haj Adel snapped. "Do you know how much ransom those bastards are asking for one head? Tens of millions. Do you have this kind of money yourself? Myself, I am not ready to pay this much for a girl."

The mullah took a deep breath to calm down, "Haj, don't worry about my daughter, I will handle her ransom. I will come to you, so we can go to the authorities together."

"I am a busy man; I can't leave my business unattended. Since your daughter was with my granddaughter, you just go to the police station and report the incident. From here, I will call some of my powerful connections and persuade them to do something."

"We belong only to Allah," the mullah said, and without even ending the call, he threw the mobile phone at the opposite wall with all the strength he had left in his arm. The phone shattered, pieces bouncing and scattering across the floor.

The doctor had no objection to his discharge from the hospital, although he was still weak, and his head was still covered with blood-stained bandages. Maybe they needed his space in the hospital for people in more critical condition.

The taxi dropped him and Amani at Ibn Assaker street. From there he would go to the police station and Amani could walk home. Amani begged to be allowed to accompany him to the police station, especially since he was still weak and limping, but he refused because he didn't want her to go into the police station. He persuaded her it would be better for her to wait for him at home than outside the police station by herself.

Since the beginning of the war, the fifth territory police station and most government institutions have been surrounded by piles of sandbags and soldiers guarding the gates.

The mullah was limping even more by the time he reached the gate of the police station. He saw how the three Kalashnikov-carrying soldiers were scrutinizing his blood-soaked clothing and bandaged head.

The mullah said, "I am here to report..."

But a soldier interrupted, "Your ID."

The mullah handed over his ID. He thought his appearance would tell more than his words.

The soldier went inside, apparently to check online if the mullah was one of the people in the revolt at the beginning of the revolution against the government.

The mullah looked at the surrounding neighborhood while he waited. Gray five-story buildings, most of their windows covered by wooden shutters, in hopes of protecting the residents from a stray bullet. Sometimes desperate humans rely on illusion in their hopes for survival. As if a wooden shutter could stop a stray bullet.

The last time he'd come to this police station, it was to inquire about a fake death report related to a murder case he was working on. That time when he'd entered the police station, there was no one at the door to ask who he was or what he wanted.

The soldier brought the ID card back and asked the mullah, "What kind of incident are you reporting?"

The mullah said, "Kidnapping," then swallowed and couldn't get any more words out.

The soldier exhaled as if he'd seen this situation hundreds of times. He pointed at a table on the pavement, which held two huge ledgers, "You will write the details there," and turned away.

The mullah moved to the table and opened the first ledger to find each page crammed with details of missing people and their guardians.

The last page was only half full. He checked the dates and found that already today seven people had been reported missing; yesterday, twenty-seven. He glanced at the three soldiers, who were busy talking and smoking. He flipped the page back and counted from the beginning of the month until the thirteenth, today's date. Already, over two hundred people have been reported missing, and this is from only one location in this immense city. Only twenty-two males and the rest were all females. So, for every male, almost seven females were kidnapped or missing. The females' ages ranged in age from fourteen to twenty, while the males were all old men, apparently rich enough to afford ransom. The females were kidnapped for other purposes, of course.

His view of the page blurred as his eyes filled with tears. He wiped them with his sleeve and closed the ledger. Approaching the standing soldier, he said, "I would like to meet with general Zafer al-Abyad."

The soldier looked him up and down and said, "The general is not meeting anyone. If you have a situation, just record it in the report book, and we will call you in case we find the person dead or alive."

"This is not about reporting a missing person. Just tell him the mullah is asking to meet with him," the mullah said.

"I don't even know if he is here or not. His car always comes in by the back gate. If you know him personally, just call his mobile phone."

"Actually, he asked me to come in to meet with him." The mullah cursed himself for being forced to lie. "Just go tell him that Mullah Abdullah is here."

"If he wanted to meet with anyone, he would have included your name on the list of visitors," the soldier said, taking the list from his jacket pocket, "What is your full name?"

"Abdullah Al-Allab."

The soldier checked the list for a few seconds. "I don't see you on the list."

"Are you accusing me of lying?" The mullah snapped and turned abruptly, pretending to leave, expecting the soldier to call him back. When he didn't, the mullah stopped and turned to face the soldiers. "You will bear the consequences. I will inform the general you kept me from seeing him." He glared at the soldiers, waiting for a response, but they just looked at him in pity.

Embarrassed, the mullah limped away. Looking skyward, he whispered, "Oh Allah, help your poor servant." *Should I just go back home and wait?* He decided to pay a visit to Haj Adel and let him know his visit to the police station was fruitless.

The mullah raised his hand to remove his fez, then realized his fez was with Amani. She had taken it home because it was crumpled and stained with blood and dirt. He touched the bandage on his head, feeling wetness. He looked at his fingers. They were covered with blood and his hand was shaking. *Do I hate that senile old man that much, or maybe I'm just nervous?* He knew he shouldn't hold grudges against others. He should either empathize or sympathize, but not judge them, especially someone like Haj Adel. Allah would judge them in the hereafter. He knew he couldn't afford to lose his help right now; they must work together to find those poor girls.

The market with Haj Adel's shop was about a thirty-minute walk from the fifth territory police station. Most of the route was via Shagoor street, then turned onto the historical Medhat Basha road all the way to the Buzuriyah market.

A glance down at his bloody garment changed his mind. He decided to go home first, change into clean clothes, and put a clean fez on his head. Then he would go to see Haj Adel.

A white Peugeot 504 with black tinted glass stopped next to him. He glanced at it but kept limping. The car moved forward and turned slightly towards the mullah, forcing him to stop. The tinted window on the driver's side rolled down, revealing a man with sunglasses and a scruffy beard who inquired in a commanding voice,

"Mullah Abdullah?"

The mullah found himself staring at the pitch-black sunglasses of a man in a white Peugeot, a car most often used by secret intelligence agents. Sweat broke out on his back.

"Why were you requesting to see general Zafer al-Abyad?" he asked with a very heavy accent.

"Who are you?" the mullah asked with a shaky voice.

"I am no one. Just answer the question."

"The general is a friend of mine. I just needed to discuss a very important matter with him."

"He sent me to take you to him. Get in the car." It felt more like an order than a request.

The mullah swallowed hard, limped sheepishly to the rear door, and opened it. There was another man, also with sunglasses and a scruffy beard. He got in, and closed the door, saying "Peace be upon you,"

No reply. The last thing the mullah saw before the black canvas bag was dropped over his head was the driver's window rolling up. When the mullah tried to pull the bag off, a cold metal gun barrel was pressed against his neck. The man uttered a single word, "Don't," as he searched the mullah's pockets and took out his prayer beads, he asked, "Where is your mobile phone?"

"I don't have one," the mullah said.

"Are you kidding me? Are you still living in the dark ages? Where is it, take it out," the man said, and the barrel of the gun was pressed more forcefully.

The mullah swallowed and said, "I got angry when I found out my daughter had been kidnapped and I threw it against the wall. That was just before I came to meet with the general."

Only then did the car move forward.

11

Amani

Amani almost broke her key, trying to force the lock open. She slammed the heavy wood door behind her so hard the knocker rattled. She collapsed face down on the sofa in the liwan, using her arms as a pillow. She cried and sobbed, praying for Allah to bring her daughter home safely as soon as possible.

In a single day, her husband had been seriously injured, and her daughter kidnapped. *Aren't we a family of Allah? Isn't my husband a servant of Allah? How can such things happen to us? Why did they hit his mosque? Isn't it the house of Allah? How could they do such a thing? Oh, Allah, please, take me to you this instant or bring back my daughter to me.*

Her sobbing mixed with the chirping of the birds, who were jumping from branch to branch in the citrus aurantium. Two tiny birds landed on the back of the sofa. Their tweeting drew her attention, and she raised her head to watch them bobbing their heads and chirping. She couldn't help but smile at the delicate creatures. She stretched out her arm, and the birds flitted away to land on the fountain, still tweeting. She wished her life was as simple as the life of these birds. For them, this courtyard with its many potted plants was heaven. But for her, this same courtyard felt like a grave, without her husband and daughter beside her.

There was a loud knocking on the outside door. *Who can it be? The mullah has his keys.* The knocking continued. She swallowed hard and crept quietly to the door. She put her ear to the rough surface of the door and listened. Another loud knock startled her, and she blurted out, "Who is it?"

"It's me, Mom," Zahra said from the other side of the door.

It was the sweetest sound she had ever heard. She quickly unbolted and opened the door, then froze at the sight of the blood-stained scarf on her daughter's head. Pulling Zahra inside, she hugged her tightly, unable to control her sobbing. Finally, she pulled back and examined Zahra's head. "What happened?" Without waiting for a reply, she raised her hands and exclaimed, "Thank you, Allah."

"Where is Dad?" Zahra wanted to know.

Amani took Zahra by the arm, and they moved to the courtyard to sit on the sofa in the liwan.

"He went to the police station. We thought you were kidnapped." Amani picked up the phone receiver from the table next to her, but before dialing his mobile number, she remembered it was broken and in her handbag.

"But is he ok? Why didn't he come to pick us up from school?" Zahar asked.

"The mosque was hit by a mortar shell. But thanks be to Allah. Your father is fine."

Zahra's hand went to her mouth in alarm.

"I guess you went back to Zakiya's apartment when you didn't find us home?" Amani asked.

"They kidnapped Zakiya," Zahra said.

A gasp escaped Amani's lips. But then she lowered her

gaze to the ground, feeling guilty for being relieved that it wasn't her daughter who was kidnapped.

Zahra explained what had happened to them and how Ward was able to rescue only her.

Amani raised her head and said, "We need to help get Zakiya back..." she hesitated for a moment before continuing, "safe."

Zahra gave her Ward and George's phone number.

"I will ask your father to call and thank them for helping you." She smiled but couldn't help it as her eyes filled with tears again. "He will be so happy when he comes back and finds you safe."

Zahra went up to her room and when she came down, she was wearing her yellow T-shirt over brown stretch pants.

Amani brought the first aid kit to clean Zahra's wound but continued to raise her eyes now and then and repeat, "Thank you, Allah." Sitting on the sofa next to Zahra, she took out a new fold of gauze, poured iodine on it, and dabbed it on the wound over Zahra's eyebrow. Zahra bit her lip but didn't complain. She avoided looking into her mother's eyes. Amani said nothing, but she could tell something was bothering her daughter. Her skin was as pale as ivory. Her hair was soft and silky, the color of caramel flowing down over her yellow T-shirt.

"Did the two men," she wanted to say, touch you, "bother you in any way?"

"No," Zahra snapped, Amani thought the answer came faster than normal.

"Are you upset because they kidnapped Zakiya?" she asked, and instantly regretted it.

"Of course," Zahra said and blew out a breath. "She

is my best friend, and we are the only family she has besides her three sisters."

"I know, I am sorry," Amani said. "I am just so happy that you came back safe to me. To us. I promise we will do anything to bring Zakiya back home." She finished applying the bandage, then kissed the top of her daughter's head.

With no further comment, Zahra got up and went to her room.

12

Zahra

Without switching on the light, Zahra lay down on her pink bed, exhausted. Her head throbbed from the wound. She closed her eyes and took a few deep breaths to calm her anxiety. *What has happened to Zakiya? I will have nightmares until I know she is safe. Poor Zakiya. She must be in a living hell right now.* Zahra started crying, pressing her face into her pillow.

The room was dark when she awoke. *Evening, already!*

She slowly got up from the bed. Her head felt heavy. She touched the back of her hand to her forehead and decided she had a fever. She took three steps, paused to regain her balance, then slipped her feet into her fluffy slippers and went downstairs. Her mother was still sitting on the sofa in the liwan, her prayer beads in her hands and her eyes red from crying. Zahra forgot about her fever and hurried over and sat beside her, wrapping an arm around her shoulders. "What's wrong, Mama?"

"Your father," Amani said, as she stared off into the distance, "Why is he taking so long at the police station?"

"May Allah protect him," Zahra said. "Have you tried calling him?"

"When Haj Adel called and informed him you were kidnapped, your father was so angry he threw his mobile at the wall and smashed it."

"But why would Haj Adel tell Dad I was kidnapped?"

"What do you mean why?" Amani asked irritated, "Of course he must inform us."

"But Haj Adel knew I was not kidnapped," Zahra said, "Zakiya's sisters found out about the kidnapping from me, then they went to inform their grandfather."

"I don't know how to explain that old man," Amani said, "He even told your dad that his neighbor informed him about the kidnapping. Not Zakiya's sisters. And your dad still thinks you've been kidnapped."

"I have a fever," Zahra said.

"Oh dear," Amani said, as she hurried off to the kitchen to fetch a pill and a glass of water. "Mention the name of Allah before drinking it," she told Zahra.

"By the name of Allah, the most gracious, the most merciful," Zahra said, then tossed the pill in her mouth and washed it down with the water. Glancing at the clock on the wall, she said, "Do you want to go to the police station?"

"It is too dangerous for two women to leave the house at this time," Amani said. "We must leave him in the hands of Allah." After a quick look at Zahra's bandage, she said, "Let me change your bandage."

Zahra watched her mother's hands shaking as she tried to cut the gauze with the scissors. She was so nervous, "Let me cut them for you, and you just apply them," Zahra said, taking the scissors from her mother's hand. Amani said nothing, she was so distracted. By the time she finished, she'd spilled iodine in the first aid box twice. Her nervousness worried Zahra. *Is it possible something bad has happened to father?* The only time she'd seen her mother this nervous was when her father had been detained by the authorities on his way back from Dubai before the war.

The doorbell rang. Zahra and her mother looked at each other with puzzled frowns. Zahra understood her mother's confusion since her father had his own keys. While the war continued, it would be suicidal to go out after sunset. The doorbell rang again. Zahra got up to go, but her mother stretched out an arm. "No. I'll get it."

She watched as her mother went to the outside door at the end of the hallway. She switched on the outside light above the door and asked, "Who is it?"

Zahra couldn't make out the response but was surprised when her mother immediately switched the light off again.

"What are you doing here? Don't you know how dangerous it is to be out after dark?" her mother said to whoever was on the other side of the door, "My husband left earlier to go to the police station and hasn't come back yet. We are two women alone just now, so I can't open the door and let you in." She waved for Zahra to join her by the door.

"Zahra, this is the man who helped you today. He wants to be sure you are safe."

Zahra gasped, "George?"

"Yes, I am glad you are safe in your home now," George said from behind the door.

"Are you crazy to go out after dark?" Zahra said.

"Don't worry, we'll be fine. Ward is with me. He wants to say hi as well," Gorge said and laughed.

"Zana Ha aa u?" Ward said from behind the door.

"I am fine, thank you Ward. You are my hero."

"Thank you, both," Amani said. "I will ask my husband to visit you tomorrow to thank you personally. But now you must hurry back to your house. It's far too dangerous to be out at night. May Allah protect you both."

"Thank you, Madam," George said, "Good night, and please convey my greeting to your husband."

Zahra turned and hurried away, certain the heat in her cheeks had turned them red. She didn't want her mother to notice.

13

Mullah Abdullah

Mullah Abdullah tried to lean back in his seat, but there was no headrest. Even worse, there wasn't enough knee space to allow him to scoot lower and lay his head on the back seat. He was seated behind the driver, who must have extra-long legs since he had the seat pushed back as far back as it would go. Or maybe he simply wanted to torture anyone unlucky enough to end up in his car. He didn't care so much about the pain in his neck, but he couldn't ignore the throbbing in his head and the pain in his knees and hips. He forced himself to breathe more slowly and deeply as he recited his prayers, asking Allah to protect him and his family.

The advantage of being in this car was that there were no holdups at inspection points since the driver possessed passes usually carried by army officers. Consequently, they rarely stopped for anything. The mullah wondered if even a traffic light was sufficient reason for these two men to stop. When the car finally stopped, the man beside him pulled the cover from his head. The driver got out and opened the door on his side and pulled him out of the car by his arm. The mullah willingly followed them across an open parking lot surrounded by high gray walls with guard posts on top of each corner. The three of them entered a two-story building. The mullah got the impression this must be a top security facility.

These security branches had a sinister reputation. Many who entered were never seen again, while those lucky enough to come back out considered themselves reborn. During the war, these security branches had scooped up a lot of people. The government officials were too busy to find out if anyone was being held in error, and lots of innocents had simply been forgotten. *Oh, Allah, please help me.*

The man in the lead pushed a wooden door open to reveal a wide room with a broad expanse of carpeted floor. On the opposite wall hung an enormous portrait of Bashar al-Asad. A huge crystal chandelier hung from the center of the ceiling. Now the mullah was confused. This was way more luxurious than the typical interrogation facility. There was a door at each end, but they led him to a stairway in one corner and up to the second floor, then down an expensively carpeted corridor with doors on both sides. He was between the two men, one ahead and one behind him, as they led him all the way to the end of the corridor. The man in front opened a wooden door on the right and stood aside, motioned for him to enter, then closed the door behind him.

The room was dark, with only a funnel of light from a projector on a table in the middle of the room. Two chairs sat behind the table. Heavy dark curtains covered the entire left wall, probably hiding windows. Particles of dust swirled slowly in the light from the projector.

The door opened, and the mullah turned to face the newcomer, general Zafer al-Abyad.

"Salam Mullah." The general was wearing his uniform with all his medals mounted above the chest pockets.

"Salam general." The mullah exhaled, all the heaviness in his chest quickly evaporating.

The general clapped his hands twice, and the room burst into light.

The mullah's mouth dropped open.

The general gasped, "What the hell happened to you?" He took the mullah's hand and bade him sit on one of the chairs.

"They bombed the mosque today during afternoon prayers."

The general pulled out his mobile phone and called for a nurse to come and change the mullah's bandages, as blood had seeped out around the edges.

"I apologize for the way we pulled you in. When they informed me you were at the fifth territory police station asking to see me, I sent my men to fetch you immediately. If they were a little rough with you, it was probably because they thought you were guilty of something."

"Am I guilty of something?" the mullah asked, not even trying to hide his irritation.

"Not at all, but why were you asking to meet with me?"

"You asked your men to fetch me here to find out why I wanted to see you?"

"Partly." the general said, still standing. Then he took a seat on the chair next to the mullah, "Yes, I wanted to know why you asked for me, but there's another reason I wanted to see you."

"They kidnapped my daughter and one of her friends," the mullah said with a sigh.

"What makes you believe someone kidnapped them?" the general asked. "So many people nowadays are missing, either because they were shot by snipers or hit by a mortar shell. Still, their families think they were kidnapped just because they can't find their bodies."

Mullah Abdullah told the general what Haj Adel had told him. "I was hoping you could help me find my daughter," he concluded. "I mean the two girls."

"Certainly, I will do whatever I can to help find your daughters," the general said as he went to answer a knock at the door.

The general ushered the nurse into the room, and she immediately started changing the mullah's head bandage. While he waited, the general took a cigar from the inner pocket of his jacket and lit it with a matchstick. He puffed on it a few times until the tip glowed brightly, filling the air with the aromatic smoke.

When the nurse had finished and departed, the general said, "Mullah, this country needs more patriotic people like you to get us through critical times like these."

The pain in the mullah's head had eased a little.

The general asked, "What would you be willing to do to save this country from its enemies, mullah?"

"I would gladly sacrifice my life for my country. But I think the situation our country is in is hopeless."

The general didn't comment, he just puffed his cigar, causing the tip to glow brightly, as he blew out clouds of smoke.

"Damascus used to be one of the safest cities in the world. Women could go out anytime, day, or night, and no one would bother them," the mullah said. "For the sake of Allah, what has happened to our lovely country, general? Two girls walking home from school were kidnapped in broad daylight. To Allah we belong and to him we shall return."

The general put his cigar down in a ceramic ashtray on the table. He crossed his arms and looked at the mullah for a few seconds before saying, "I think Allah sent you to me today, because this country needs you."

The mullah was sure the general could sense his nervousness. *For heaven's sake, who wouldn't be nervous being brought here that way? To hell with trying to appear calm,* He said, "I want my daughter back, general, and I beg you to help me."

"You will help to bring your daughter back," the general said, "as well as the daughters of many other families."

"Me!?" the mullah asked. "How?"

"Have you seen the movie The Matrix?" the general asked.

The mullah's ears became hot. "General, I don't even have a television in my house."

"Oh man, is it against religious doctrine to have a TV nowadays?" the general asked.

"Everything that distracts from your purpose on this earth is against religious doctrine."

The general scratched his clean-shaven chin while staring at the mullah.

"You may think I am a backward man who doesn't even own a TV in these modern times. Well, I bought my daughter a laptop computer last year." Remembering his daughter caused a lump to rise in his throat. He looked down, and swallowed, "We used to watch the Huda religious channel on the internet every day after Assar prayer."

"I am sure you are always pure in thought and deed, mullah," the general said, "I am not sure if there are any other people quite like you left in this world. Anyway, forget about the movie and the red and blue pills. What I was trying to say is, if you want to help your daughter and many other daughters, you will agree to be part of a dangerous operation. However, if you say yes, you will not have the option to change your mind. So, I will give you one day to return to your home and talk it over with your wife. If you decide to be part of this top-secret operation, I will then fill you in on the details."

The mullah said, "General, are you joking? Of course, I'll be happy to take part in whatever operation you wish me to. She is my only daughter, and I will do whatever it takes to rescue her."

The general exhaled, "Mullah, these missions are extremely dangerous."

"I just told you. I volunteer."

"It's not about volunteering. If you agree to take part, you will sign a government contract. You will receive a basic salary for the rest of your life, and if you die during the operation, your family will be compensated as the family of a martyr."

The mullah nodded enthusiastically.

"Don't get too excited yet. Let me show you something first." He moved to the front of the room, pulled down a large screen, then came behind the table and pulled out a laptop. After pressing a few keys and a couple of clicks with the mouse, the projector started up with the whisper of a fan. The image wasn't too clear, but clear enough to show three headless bodies, a woman, and two boys. They had ropes around their chests and under their arms, which were tied behind their backs. Their severed heads were on the ground under their bodies, with their eyes open. Someone behind the camera was saying, "This will be the fate of all traitor agents of this infidel government." Then the camera turned to a seated man with a long beard. His purple eyes were swollen half shut from a beating. Blood seeped from the corners of his mouth, and his nose was bleeding. Behind him stood a man dressed in black, holding a sword in his hand. The man had pulled the tail end of his turban across his lower face, as if he was preparing for a sandstorm, leaving only his eyes exposed. He started talking when the camera was on him. He spoke classical Arabic, attempting to hide his original dialect. Still, it was obvious he was not from Syria, nor any middle eastern country. His accent indicated he was from North Africa. ".. this man is a traitor and a spy for the government. This was his family's fate and the fate of families of each one who thinks of spying on us, we are the knights of heaven, and warriors of God." He pointed the sword at the camera and said, "You should think very hard before sending someone to spy on us, because this will be his punishment." Grabbing hold of the man's hair, he jerked the head of the bearded man up, and with the edge of his sword, started to slit his neck as if he was slaughtering a sheep. Blood at first bubbled out of the cut, but then it became just dripping red lines on the stump of his neck. The masked man raised the head high with his left hand and the sword in his right, yelling, "Allah Akbar." Several voices from behind the camera repeated after him, "Allah Akbar."

The recording stopped with the severed head still filling the screen. The general turned to the mullah and said, "That was Sheikh Sadi Mabsot. He was our undercover agent inside their organization, which you will have to be part of if you say yes. However, you've now seen the punishment if they discover you work with the government."

The mullah's hands had gone cold. He wanted to speak, but his throat betrayed him. Only air passed his lips.

"I will give you one day to decide," the general said. He took out a small piece of paper and a pen from his inner pocket and wrote a number on it. "If you decide to be part of the solution, you just text 'yes' to this number. Be sure it is only that single word 'yes', nothing more. I will ask my assistant to order a taxi for you now. It is better not to be seen returning in one of our cars."

The mullah looked at the general's outstretched hand holding the piece of paper, but he didn't move. He was still seeing the head of Sadi, who had seen his wife and two sons decapitated before his eyes. *Is that really fair punishment for someone who betrays the soldiers of Allah to watch his family beheaded in front of him? And then to have his own head severed as well? What kind of judgment is that? Will this be my destiny if I do whatever the general asks me to do? Those monsters will do that to me if they discover me trying to serve my country, trying to prevent foul deeds such as kidnapping young girls in this country. Is that really betraying the knights of heaven, as the masked man claimed? Even if I am right and those monsters are wrong, do I have the courage to accept now, or will I be afraid my destiny will be the same as Sadi Mabsot? Maybe I should just tell the general no and go back home and pray that Zahra will be returned safely to me. But what if she doesn't come back? Will I be able to live with the guilt if I don't even try to rescue her? Well, to die trying is still better than to die waiting.* He pushed the general's hand away gently without taking the paper, and said, "I don't need twenty-four hours to decide. I want to take part in your operation."

"Are you sure?" the general asked, pointing at the ghastly image on the screen.

"Yes, I just need to go home and say goodbye to my wife. Is that possible?" the mullah asked.

"If my daughter was kidnapped, I don't think my wife would want me to waste another minute at home with her. She wouldn't blame me for not saying goodbye before heading out on a mission to find our child," the general said.

"You're right. Amani wouldn't be happy if I came home without Zahra. But I still need to at least call her and let her know I'm okay."

"Unfortunately, no," the general said as he avoided looking directly into the mullah's eyes, "If your final decision is to take part, you can't leave this building to go anywhere except to our training base. You can't even make a phone call."

"You're backing me into a corner. I can't go back home or even call my wife. It doesn't feel like I'm free to choose."

"Agreeing without hesitation shows your loyalty to your country and how determined you are to save your daughter. But you still have two other options besides agreeing now and starting your mission right away. You can say no and return to your daily life while your daughter remains with the bad guys. Only Allah knows what they might do to her. Or you can go home and decide there. I'll still give you twenty-four hours."

The mullah wondered for a moment if it would be better to go home now and spend the day with his wife to prepare her for his absence. *But in twenty-four hours, who knows what could happen to Zahra? What if they ...* He shook his head, trying to banish the image forming in his mind. *Amani would never forgive me if during those 24 hours something unspeakable happened to Zahra. She's a woman of strong faith and can be patient until I return with Zahra safe,* "No, I don't need to go home or make any phone calls."

"Are you sure?" the general asked, "Do you want 24 hours to decide?"

"Yes, I am sure," the mullah said.

The general stretched out a hand and shook the mullah's hand firmly. "Officially, Mullah Abdullah al-Allab no longer exists."

The mullah accompanied the general down one floor to a room with a long, oval conference table surrounded by plush leather chairs. Blood red velvet curtains covered one wall and a life-size portrait of Bashar al-Asad dominated the wall at the far end of the table. The room was as luxurious as the ministers' meeting room he'd often seen on the front pages of newspapers. *What is this place?*

The mouthwatering aroma of roast chicken assailed his nostrils. On the far side of the table was a stack of paper plates and platters of food, including chicken roasted in garlic sauce with pickles on the side, steamy Arabic bread, and two bottles of iced cola. The mullah remembered he'd eaten nothing since breakfast. As if his tummy heard his thoughts, it started to growl. He and the general seated themselves at the table and satisfied their hunger as they continued to talk.

When they'd finished gorging themselves on the tender but greasy chicken, they washed their hands and returned to the room upstairs. A glass pot of mint tea was waiting for them on the projector table. The mullah sipped his tea while the general smoked his cigar and explained the finer terms of the contract.

Contracts were made ready with colorful arrow-shaped stickers pointing at the spaces where the mullah needed to sign or initial.

The mullah had not expected a government contract to be so harsh, but it seemed their primary intent was to ensure he would not betray his country and switch to the opposite side. He could not reveal the details of his mission to anyone under any circumstances either before, during, or after accomplishing it. The contract spelled out in great detail the benefits his family would receive, whether he was alive or dead following the mission. Finally, it laid out the details of the training he would undergo.

The mullah asked the general a few questions amid clouds of cigar smoke and sips of aromatic black mint tea.

"I have to pray." He told the general, who was lighting a fresh cigar, "Where are the lavatories? I need to perform my ablutions."

"What prayer, Mullah?" the general asked, looking at his wristwatch. "It is past midnight already."

"Since after noon prayer I haven't prayed my obligatory prayers, I must perform them now."

The general called out, "Aamer," and a lanky young man, with a cleanly shaved head and face, and tanned skin, entered the room and stood at attention before the general, "Yes. Sir."

"Prepare a prayer mat for the mullah and show him to the lavatory to perform ablutions."

The mullah didn't delay any longer. He headed out the door with Aamer close behind him.

After he'd performed his ablutions at a marble sink in a luxurious bathroom on the first floor, Aamer led him to a nearby empty room with a rug in the middle of the floor, the prayer mat lay over the rug. The mullah asked Aamer, "Are you sure this is the direction of Mecca?"

Aamer avoided looking at the mullah, "I am not sure, I have never prayed in my life."

The mullah gasped, he wanted to advise this young man about the importance of prayer, but he changed his mind and asked, "which way is south?"

Aamer pointed to the south, and the mullah corrected the direction of the mat toward Mecca.

It hadn't been a full day yet without his family, but he missed them already. He tried hard to focus on his prayers, but more than once, he wondered what Amani was doing, or what had happened to Zahra. At the end of the prayer, he prostrated himself, pressing his forehead to the floor, and cried while begging Allah to protect his daughter from harm.

The general was waiting for him in the projector room on the second floor when he got back. Aamer closed the door behind the mullah and left them alone. The general stood up, stretched out his hand, and shook the mullah's hand. "May Allah accept your beneficences."

"May Allah accept the beneficences from both me and you," he replied. It is how Muslims greet each other after prayers.

"Let me brief you on your mission," the general said, pointing at a chair for the mullah to sit.

The mullah sat and listened to the husky voice of

the general explaining the details. The kind of details no normal human would wish to be involved with in a hundred years.

"You are aware how outsiders have secretly penetrated our society and recruited large numbers of agents to build a rift between our people. Many people in this country were naïve enough to believe it was a just revolution; however, not even a year passed before most of the naïve people realized a global conspiracy was being perpetrated against our beloved Syria. Many people changed their attitudes and refused to be involved with these people who called themself revolutionaries.

"These revolutionaries have been exposed as a gang of thugs who don't care about the country or the people. They have their own agenda controlled from outside our borders. Their main purpose is to destroy the government and take over the country, so they can steal our resources, just as they did in Iraq. Then a new group was born, also funded from overseas, but they operate under the name of the Free Army. This group mainly comprises dissidents from the Syrian Army and their followers. And that has affected us greatly."

"So, will I be one of them?" the mullah asked.

The general raised his right hand and said, "Wait, Mullah, let me finish first. You need to understand the situation completely."

The mullah nodded and motioned for him to go on.

"Our country has become the ideal environment for international criminal organizations to take advantage of a chaotic situation and use it as an opportunity to carry out their illegal activities. One of the most diabolical organizations set themselves up in this country recently. Like the others, it infiltrated the country under the guise of the revolution and recruited simple people by claiming theirs to be a noble mission. Their actual mission is to make their fortunes from human trafficking, sex slavery, the human organ trade, and the weapons trade. They recruited a team of professionals from around the world for these operations. They took advantage of the Arab Spring to become the most brutal organization in the world to make billions in Tunisia, Libya, Egypt, and now Syria. Mostly they use something called the dark web to communicate and run their operation secretly. We were able to infiltrate their dark web communications and plant our own agent, sheikh Sadi Mabsot, whose end you witnessed earlier.

"This organization's name changes depending on the time and location. In Syria, they called themselves the Sword of Truth.

"The Sword of Truth operates in two layers. The public layer consists of a group of fanatics pushing for the reinstatement of Sharia Law, convincing their followers that they will revive the Islamic Caliphate. The underground layer, however, is made up of criminals. The public group remains unaware of the underground faction, but the underground leaders are fully aware of the public group.

"The main purpose of this organization is to raise money. Their shrewdness allows them to exploit the public members to generate funds without their knowledge. The leaders of the public group are fanatical religious zealots who justify their acts of violence and theft by convincing their followers that they are the chosen people of God, and anyone outside the Sword of Truth is an infidel. They believe the Sword of Truth has the divine right to take their money, their honor, and even their blood when necessary."

"You want me to be a part of that?" the mullah asked, glancing at the closed door with a sinking feeling in his stomach.

"Yes, your mission is to become a member of the public faction in the Sword of Truth and set in motion the plan we have plotted out for you," the general said, blowing a cloud of smoke to the ceiling.

"How can I rescue my daughter if I become part of the Sword of Truth?"

"Mullah, in all probability, they are the ones who kidnapped your daughter. They kidnap the rich for ransom, women to sell as sex slaves, and healthy people to sell their organs. They smuggle guns and drugs into Syria and sell them on the black market. They steal natural resources and smuggle them out of the country, plus whatever new methods they can use to generate money."

"So, you're sure they are the ones who kidnapped my daughter?"

"I don't know," the general said, avoiding the mullah's gaze, "But up until now most of the kidnappings have been done by the Sword of Truth."

He swallowed and glanced at the door again.

Sensing the mullah's indecision, the general said, "Yes, I think they kidnapped your daughter and too many other daughters."

"What makes you sure you can insert me inside the Sword of Truth without the same result as Sadi Mabsot?" The mullah wiped beads of sweat from his forehead with his palm and wiped it on his dish dash over his thigh.

"This time we will avoid all the mistakes we made during the operation of Sadi Mabsot, and don't worry, you will not be working with the same people that Sadi worked with, they are dead already. We raided their camp and killed all of them. Your mission is completely different. More strategic and of much greater importance."

The general pressed a few keys on the laptop. The projector started with a clunk. The first image on the screen was a map of Syria divided into two different colors. Red for the northern and eastern parts, and blue for the southern and western parts. Within the red area, there were several triangles and squares sprinkled on the map.

"As you can see, the red territory is under the control of the terrorists. The squares are for a group calling themselves the Winning Wing, and the triangles are for the Sword of Truth. Relations between Sword of Truth and Winning Wing are amicable at present, but Sword of Truth is expanding their territory at the expense of Winning Wing. We don't expect the Winning Wing to last much longer, as Sword of Truth will soon take over completely."

The general drew deeply on his cigar, causing the tip to glow bright orange. When he blew out, his head disappeared in the thick smoke for a few seconds.

The mullah was still thinking about how he would rescue Zahra if he became part of the Sword of Truth when the general resumed.

"Our intelligence team tells us a new organization will soon appear on Syrian land coming across the Turkish border. This new organization recruits not only

Syrians but also people from all around the world. Wherever there is a fanatical son of a bitch, they recruit him, convincing him this land will be the promised land for the raising of the Islamic state once more."

"Any idea what the name of the organization is?" the mullah asked.

"They call themselves the Islamic State of Iraq and Syria–ISIS."

The general again pressed a few keys on the laptop, and a different map of Syria appeared on the board.

"The Sword of Truth's central administration is headquartered in Turkey," he said. "In Syria, their main operational base is in the city of Manbij, northeast of Aleppo. Ainal is the only remaining town in northern Syria that they haven't occupied, due to the presence of a Syrian military base there. This base has enough heavy weapons and missiles to destroy half of Syria's cities. The Sword of Truth couldn't capture it by force, but they used the lure of gold to bribe one of the highest-ranking officers stationed there. In exchange for millions of dollars deposited in an offshore account, the officer sold both the town and the base to them.

"A leader named Shaddad Abu Saif from the Sword of Truth will go to Ainal town to finalize the deal with the officer. Initially, his presence will be covert, but once their troops arrive to seize control of the town and the military base, he will be publicly announced as the prince."

"So, you want me to be one of the men around Shaddad Abu Saif?"

"No, you will be Shaddad Abu Saif himself," the general said.

14

Zakiya

The sunlight streaming through the cracks in the walls and the roof had disappeared a few hours ago, and the tin barn was now lit by a single bulb dangling from the ceiling. The sound of engines approaching made Zakiya think more new girls were being brought in. But the four men who entered were not carrying new girls. One of them threw down a sack, causing dirt and dust to fly into the air. He squatted and spilled the contents of the sack on the ground. Burial shrouds, obviously used recently, stained with brown spots of either dried blood or mud.

"All of you stand up," one of the men shouted.

The girls struggled to stand because of the ropes binding their feet. Zakiya managed to stand on her second attempt.

The four men used sharp knives to cut the ties on their hands and feet. Immediately, the girls used their freed hands to remove their gags.

"Listen up everyone," the same man shouted, gaining the girls' immediate attention. "We will be transporting you in the back of a truck, and the trip will take several hours. If the truck gets stopped and inspected en route, think twice before making any movement or even so much as a peep if you wish to remain alive." His accent was from somewhere in the northern part of the country, but Zakiya couldn't tell exactly where he was from.

"Where are you taking us?" one girl yelled.

One of the men slammed the butt of his rifle into her head, and she fell like a pile of jelly, blood pouring from an open wound on her forehead.

"Take off your clothes, even the underwear," the first man said.

The girls didn't move, so the man shouted again, "Either you take off your clothes or we'll do it for you" He grabbed one girl's sweater, pulling it off her shoulder and slashing with his knife. Blood spurted from a cut on her shoulder. The rest of the girls immediately started taking off their clothes.

The man threw a shroud in front of each girl and said, "Each of you step into a shroud."

One girl complained, the man nearest to her slapped her face, hard.

Zakiya took advantage of the movements of the girls. Picking up her shroud, she turned to keep the tin wall behind her. She didn't want any of the girls to see the ugly scars on her back. She took off her dirty and torn school clothes, stepped into the filthy shroud and pulled it up around her until only her head was still out.

Zakiya waited her turn as the men tied ropes around the legs and waists of the other girls over the shrouds, then gagged them with white gauze. Pulling the shrouds up to cover their heads, they bound the openings tightly, then threw the shrouded girls on the ground. One by one, each pair of men carried the shrouded bodies out and placed them in open coffins in front of the tin barn.

Zakiya smelled the stench of onion breath from the

man working on her ties. He covered her head and tied it, but before he could throw her to the ground, she dropped to the ground on her own to make the landing less painful.

They carried her out and lowered her into a tight space, then slammed the lid with a loud bang, causing it to become pitch black and quieter. Then someone nailed the cover shut as if she was already a dead person.

Inside, the box was blazing hot, causing her shroud to be soaked in sweat in no time. She was already having a hard time breathing, and her heart was hammering so fast it felt like it was trying to break through her ribs. *Oh Allah. Please help me.* The blackness spun faster and faster.

***

Zakiya found herself running on frozen ground, dodging around thick tree trunks, their tops concealed by fog. Wolves howled in pursuit of her, their breaths visible in the frosty air. Her feet were bright red from splashing in the icy water. Each step felt as if she was running on nails and razor blades. The pain in her chest grew with each breath. She kept running until the burning pain seared every cell in her legs. Finally, she fell face first but flipped over and scuttled backward on hands and feet like a crab without once taking her eyes off the approaching wolves. She covered her face with her hands as the wolves caught up and surrounded her. One of the wolves jumped on her chest, and she screamed as his sharp claws pierced her skin. Hot drops of saliva dripped on her hands, which were still trying to shield her face from the snarling, fetid mouth. With every fetid breath, a gag rose in her throat. She expected fangs to sink into her neck at any moment.

The ground vibrated. The wolves stopped what they were doing and howled at the sky. The ground vibrated again, and the wolf leaped from her chest, allowing her to breathe once more. The growling and snarling faded in the distance. The ground beneath her became dry and warm. The aroma of jasmine filled the air.

"Zakiya."

Zakiya peeked between her fingers. Her mom was standing there in front of her, wearing a white silk dress, her hair shining, and her eyes wet.

A warm feeling filled Zakiya's heart. Leaping to her feet, she ran and threw herself in her mother's arms, sobbing.

"They kidnapped me. I don't know what they're going to do with me. Life has been awful since you left us," Zakiya said. Her words came between sobs.

Her mother hugged her tightly and kissed the top of her head.

"Mama, take me with you."

"My dearest, be patient. Patience is the key to your relief. Surrender yourself to Allah and don't worry. Allah will protect you."

Zakiya awoke with a start as her coffin hit the ground, hard. She gasped as pain spread through her entire right side, from shoulder to ankle. Her heart beat furiously and her whole body shook from the extreme cold.

One of the men opened her shroud, and she inhaled deeply through her nose, the cold but refreshing air. The scent of Jasmine still lingered, causing her to smile despite all her pain and misery.

There were sixteen coffins. The men said two of the girls had frozen to death, but Zakiya suspected they were more likely to have suffocated or had heart attacks.

It was nighttime, but the sky was clear, and the full moon made the scene bright. They were in the foothills, at the head of a mountain pass. About 20 hobbled donkeys were grazing happily from a pile of hay. Spotting a pile of large empty crates nearby, Zakiya suddenly realized the men's intentions. These mountains must be between Kalamoon in Syria and Baalbek in Lebanon. The donkeys would be used to smuggle the girls into Lebanon in the crates. The smugglers would simply put each girl in a crate, then lash the crates on the back of the donkeys and let them go between the mountains, relying on their memory of the route to reach the other side where someone would be waiting to receive them and give them food and water. Then the donkeys would be sent back for another load. That way, if the authorities intercepted the donkeys, the smugglers would be in the clear since donkeys aren't able to confess under interrogation.

And they say donkeys are stupid.

15

Mullah Abdullah

The same two guards who'd brought the mullah to this mysterious place also transported him to the military airport. This time, they were much more polite and gentle with him. It was still dark outside, and the tinted car windows added to the gloom inside the car. The mullah thought about Amani. What would she do when she realized he wasn't coming back, unless Zahra was with him? Amani And Zahra were all he had in this life. They were like his two eyes, and he either had to have both eyes together or he'd lose them both.

They dropped the mullah at the foot of the loading ramp to a military airplane. As he reached the top, a man stretched out his hand, saying, "I am Asiad. I will be accompanying you to the camp." The mullah shook Asiad's hand and introduced himself.

The military plane had no windows, just a bare metal interior. The noise of the engines was like a giant rock grinder. The mullah pressed his hands over his ears. Asiad handed him a noise-canceling headset and a military uniform, asking him to change out of his religious garb.

Once the plane was in the air, the mullah changed clothes, a task which took him some time to accomplish because he was still so weak. Asiad informed him he was a linguistic expert and would be working with him on his speech. He explained that the mullah's vocabulary was much too refined compared to the vocabulary of the men from the cities to the north and east of Syria.

The flight wouldn't be long enough for the mullah to practice all the new vocabulary Asiad introduced him to, but there was time enough for Asiad to make an assessment and point out some of the weak points the mullah needed to work on. Asiad informed him that among the members of this organization there were experts who were able to identify government agents from their speech patterns alone. He warned him he must be especially careful during his Friday prayers and when he communicated with his subordinates.

The mullah found the long flight pure torture. By the end of the flight, his head was like a bomb ready to explode every time Asiad's voice erupted in his headset.

Once they'd landed and taxied off the runway, the mullah took off the noise-canceling headset and found it was smeared with blood that had seeped through his head bandage. When Asiad opened the plane door, the sky was a pale purple, the sun just starting to rise.

Two soldiers waited for them at the foot of metal stairs. Crossing the tarmac, the mullah's limp slowed him down so that Asiad and the two soldiers were forced to stop every few steps to wait for him to catch up. They crossed a wide stretch of arid ground to a row of shipping containers with doors and windows.

The two soldiers and Asiad led the mullah to a container that looked much like all the rest. One soldier opened the door. The second one said, "Please wait inside."

When they'd closed the door behind him, the mullah

found himself alone in a metal cube with only a table, a green rotary telephone in its center, and a single metal chair.

The metal chair groaned under his weight. The mullah shut his eyes and focused his thoughts on his family. *Amani will be concerned and feeling very much alone. How will she face the news of my disappearance? Will she be strong enough or will she collapse under the strain?* He stretched out his hand to lift the phone receiver to call her, but before he even touched it, its loud ringing startled him, and he almost toppled from the chair. *That would be enough to wake the dead.* The phone kept ringing, but he wasn't sure if he should answer. The ringing stopped for a few seconds, then started again. He picked the receiver up and put it to his ear.

"Yes, Mr. Abdullah, I want to talk to you," a man's voice erupted on the other end.

"Ok," he said, "May I know who you are?" *Why did I ask such a stupid question?* He rubbed his eyelids with the thumb and forefinger of his free hand.

"It is not important who I am. Just listen..."

The mullah interrupted him, "Why not talk to me face to face?"

"For safety reasons," the caller said. "Now, listen to me carefully, and don't interrupt me unless I ask for confirmation that you understand what I am saying."

"Ok,"

"First of all, this call is being recorded as a verbal contract between you and us. Do you agree?"

"Do I have the option to disagree?"

"Please answer only yes or no." The voice was much sharper now.

"Yes," the mullah answered.

"Am I talking to Abdullah al-Allab, born in 1968?"

"Yes,"

"Your mother is Salamiah Tahoon?"

"Yes."

"You will come in contact with a limited number of people during your training. This is to avoid putting too many people at risk in the event the terrorists discover you and torture you. Do you understand?"

"Yes." The mullah gulped.

"This camp is for people who chose to serve their country voluntarily. Just like you, none of the people being trained here come from military backgrounds. The same rules apply to them. You don't talk to anyone unless we introduce them to you as your trainers or members of your mission. Do you understand?"

"Yes." The mullah wiped his forehead with his sleeve.

"The less you know ahead of time, the better it will be for you and others. Don't ask anyone about their place of origin, their personal details, or background history. Do you understand?"

"Yes,"

"Unless you have special permission, you will not leave the camp during your training course, or you will be tried and convicted as a deserter. Do you understand?"

"Yes," *I understand, all right.*

"You will undergo an intensive training program, not only physical but also mental. You should know that there is always the possibility of death during your training course, and if you pass your training successfully, there is a strong possibility of being exposed, tortured, and killed by the terrorists. Do you understand?"

The mullah hesitated. *The general told me I don't have the option of backing out, so what's the point of saying yes or no now?*

The caller's raised voice pulled him back. "Do you understand?"

"Yes, yes," the mullah answered with a sigh.

The mullah shut his eyes and exhaled, "But..."

The caller interrupted, "Please just answer yes or no. The total number of people you will be introduced to during your training is eight. Seven of them are your trainers, and one will be your partner on your mission. Do you understand?"

"Yes,"

"If anyone from the group asks you for details of your mission, you will tell them nothing, or you could put your mission in jeopardy. You will report any such infraction immediately because we could be testing to see if you will report them, or they might be traitors. If you fail to report them, you too could be convicted as a conspirator with a traitor. Do you understand?"

"But how..."

The caller interrupted him again. "Please answer yes or no."

"Yes."

"You will address your trainers and partner as Comrade, and they will do the same. Whatever name you use after Comrade should not be their real name. Do you understand?"

"Yes."

"Thank you," the caller said, and the line went dead.

The mullah lowered the receiver and exhaled. He had so many questions.

The door opened and a very tanned man in a military uniform came in and stretched out his hand to the mullah. He wasn't taller than the mullah, but his arm muscles below his short sleeves were impressive.

"Comrade Raad, from special forces in the Syrian Army," he said while shaking the mullah's hand so hard it caused his head to bounce and made his neck hurt.

"Comrade Abd..." then he remembered he must not mention his real name.

Comrade Raad laughed when he noticed the mullah's confusion, and said, "If the terrorists capture and torture you, you will say anything they want you to say to escape their unthinkable torture methods. No point in stressing over minor details they don't care about. Just pray you die rather than get captured."

The mullah suddenly became lightheaded. He wanted to kneel or sit to hide his shaky legs. Raad laughed. Apparently, the mullah's reaction was nothing new to him, and he found it amusing.

"I will be your physical trainer and I will turn you into a lion, so don't worry. If you don't die during the training, you will be a beast, with the ability to smash a wall with one blow."

The mullah didn't know if he should be happy to hear that or deeply regret the situation he'd got himself into.

"Now, Comrade, follow me. I'll show you to your room. You have ten minutes before your training begins."

"I am thirsty," the mullah said, his voice coarse and weak.

"In your room you will find plenty of water," Raad said as he started off with the mullah close behind.

He was led to a field with rows of concrete cubes, with

only doors but no windows.

"The rooms are about three meters square, and as you can see, they are spaced about 12 meters apart. A surveillance camera on a post faces the sole entrance to each room." Comrade Raad said. The mullah wondered why he was telling him such details.

Inside the room assigned to him, the walls were bare concrete. The only window was in the center of the ceiling. There was a cot against the far wall, a long mirror on the wall next to a metal locker, and a table and chair in the middle. On the table sat a jug of water. The mullah grabbed the jug and gulped thirstily as water dribbled from the corners of his mouth and down his front.

He went to the door opposite the entrance door and opened it. It turned out to be the lavatory with a small basin and a squat toilet. The shower stall, a tight concrete enclosure, looked more like a prison cell than a place of relaxation. He washed his hands in the basin.

Raad called out from outside, "Comrade Shaddad Abu Saif."

The mullah jumped up to open the door and found Raad carrying a pile of clothes. He threw them at the mullah, who caught them gracefully, surprising even himself.

"From now on you will be known as Comrade Shaddad Abu Saif," Raad said. "You now have sixty seconds to change and get back out here," Raad said.

The mullah changed quickly and went out, as yet oblivious to the fact he was one step closer to hell.

16

Zahra

Zahra woke up to the sound of knocking on her bedroom door. She got up and opened the door. "Good morning, Mom."

"Please get dressed. You will skip school today. We must go ask about your father at the police station." Her mother had dark circles under her eyes.

Zahra wore her dark blue coat, white headscarf, and her black shoes. A glance at herself in the mirror showed a sensible, conservative girl. Downstairs in the courtyard, the fountain was silent. Most mornings her parents drank their morning coffee, soothed by the melodies of the splashing water.

It was a ten-minute walk to the police station, and Amani remained silent the whole way. When Amani spoke with the guard outside the station, it was like explaining a math problem to a butcher. They were refused entry to the station and left, having gained no knowledge of the whereabouts of the mullah.

Back at home, Amani went to her room and closed the door without a word.

Zahra sat in the Liwan and stared at her father's picture hanging on the wall. The telephone, on a small table in the corner between the two sofas, rang, causing her to jump. She snatched up the receiver. "Salam," she said without hearing the caller's voice.

"Hello Zahra," George said.

She gasped in surprise.

"Are you ok?" George asked.

"Yes … No … I mean yes, but how did you get this phone number?" Zahra said.

George laughed. "You dialed your number so many times from our house, I have it memorized."

"Oh, yes, that's true," Zahra said, "So why didn't you call last night instead of coming all the way to our house?"

"I was hoping to meet your parents last night," George said, "And also see you again."

Zahra put a hand to her cheek. It was hot to the touch. She pressed her lips firmly together to hide her smile when her mom opened the door of her room to see who was calling. She was wearing her prayer dress.

"I just called to see if your father was back yet?" George said.

"George is asking about Dad," Zahra told her mother while cupping a hand over the receiver. Then to George she said, "I went with Mom to the police station this morning, but they wouldn't allow us in, and the guard said he'd never seen my father."

George said, "Hopefully, he will come home safely."

"Hopefully," Zahra said.

"Please convey my greetings to your mother," he said, then whispered, "I'll call again tomorrow."

"Thank you," Zahra said. "I'll tell her."

She hung up the receiver and conveyed his greeting to her mother, who said nothing. She just went back to her room and closed the door.

The next day, Zahra walked to and from school alone for the first time. Even the smallest sound made her look right and left like a scared cat. On the main streets, she walked on the sidewalk, scrutinizing every passing person with suspicion. When she entered the narrow alleys of Shagoor, there was no sidewalk, causing cars to pass much closer to her. She would stop walking, and press her body against the wall, knees bent in readiness to run if a car stopped. Fortunately, no car or van stopped.

Zahra reached home without enough energy to even explain to her mom why she didn't have enough appetite to eat her lunch. She went up to her room and threw herself on the bed, waiting for her heart to stop pounding, and her nerves to calm down. She fell asleep.

When she woke up an hour later, she was soaked in sweat.

She went down to the courtyard, to find her mother sitting in the Liwan with her prayer beads between her fingers, uttering her supplications. Zahra took a seat beside her on the sofa.

"There is food in the kitchen. I cooked it, but I didn't have any appetite," her mom said. "Go put it on the table and let's eat together now."

"Ok," Zahra said, and she walked to the kitchen. Baked chicken and a sliced potato soaked in lemon juice and garlic, one of her father's favorites. She held back her tears. Carrying the chicken in one hand and the tabbouleh salad in the other, she went back to the liwan and placed them on the table in front of her mom. Then she made a second trip for the plates, utensils, and pita bread.

Zahra was famished, so she began devouring the juicy chicken and fresh tabbouleh. Meanwhile, Amani stared at the chicken thigh on her plate without touching it.

"George called again, asking about your father," Amani said.

Zahra didn't look up at her mother, pretending to struggle with cutting the chicken thigh.

"Where could he have gone?" Amani said. She dropped her spoon on the plate and covered her face with both hands, breaking into sobs.

Zahra moved to sit beside her mom, putting an arm around her shoulders, and hugging her. She didn't know what to say to calm her mother down, so she remained quiet.

Next day, after school, Zahra found her mom waiting for her outside the school gate, "Oh, Mom, did you come alone?"

"Yes, we have to go buy bread. Your father always bought it every day."

They walked together in silence until they reached the bakery on al-Ameen Street. As bread was a state-subsidized consumer item, the price hadn't changed since the beginning of the war, despite everything else jumping sky-high because of the decreasing value of the currency. For Zahra and Amani, who had never come here to buy bread before, the scene was eye-opening.

There were three small windows on one side of the building. One for males on the left, one for females on the right, and one for soldiers in the middle. The soldiers' window was the only one that could be reached directly from the street. The other two had what looked a bit like livestock chutes that zigzagged back and forth till they reached the window. The queue of men filled the chute completely and stretched several meters out into the street. At least the queue in the chute for females was much shorter.

Zahra and Amani entered the fenced cue. The sides were covered in wire mesh with metal panels on the top to provide some protection from the blazing sun.

"How long have you been waiting?" Amani asked the woman on her left through the fence in the next fold of the line.

"One hour. Is it your first time here?" the woman asked.

"Yes," Amani said, "But why does it take so long?"

"They open the male and female windows alternately. Each time they open, they serve only ten people, and only three bundles per customer. Only the soldiers' window stays open all the time."

"It could take us three hours to reach the window," Amani told Zahra.

Zahra didn't answer. The air was stifling in the lineup, and the ground was muddy underfoot. A few of the older women had brought an empty bucket, which they flipped upside down to sit on. Ten minutes passed in the unbearable heat and Amani and Zahra hadn't moved an inch. More women continued to arrive behind them.

"Let's go," Amani said, grabbing Zahra's hand and pulling her out of the lineup. It was like exiting a steam bath.

17

Zakiya

Zakiya opened her eyes. She was in a room three times the size of the room she shared with her sisters back home. She was lying on the floor, even though there was an enormous bed in the room. When she tried to sit up, she realized she was still wrapped in the dirty shroud. Her head throbbed with pain. Her throat was dry. She remembered nothing of the trip aboard the donkey. The last thing she remembered was an injection in her arm which rendered her unconscious for the duration.

The only light in the room came from behind a curtain. As she stood up, the shroud fell to the floor, leaving her standing naked in the middle of the room. Looking around, she found a cream-colored towel on the edge of the bed, so she wrapped it around her body, then walked to the window and moved the curtain slightly to one side.

She appeared to be on the second floor, with a view of a garden with a swimming pool surrounded by a high stone wall. Even from this height, she couldn't see what lay beyond the walls because of a line of tall sycamore trees. There were couches and tables around the swimming pool, but no one was around the pool or on the couches. The sky was a brilliant blue, without a cloud in sight.

She let the curtain fall back into place and turned back

to the room. She needed a few seconds for her eyes to adjust after the bright sunlight. The bed in the middle of the room was a four-poster with dark blue velvet curtains for privacy. Opposite the bed was a dresser with flowers carved into the wooden frame of the round mirror.

Zakiya approached the mirror and dropped the towel. She was so thin the bones of her shoulders looked as if they were trying to tear through the skin. Her chest was almost flat, and her sunken tummy exaggerated her hips' bones. Reluctantly, she turned around to get a view of her back.

Scars covered her back, from her shoulders down to her hips. The scars varied, some only faded, parallel white lines, others were long, thick gray marks, either raised above or carved into the skin. There was no longer any dry blood, but the scars remained from the last time she'd been physically abused two years earlier. Her back was a grim reminder of her painful past. Every time she took a bath in her apartment, she covered the mirror. Even a glimpse of her back would awaken memories and cause an anxiety attack. Had it not been for her belief in Allah, she would have committed suicide long ago. She picked up the towel and wrapped it around her body again.

Zakiya walked around the bed to the closet and slid open the door. A gasp escaped her throat when she beheld the contents. It was filled to brimming with all types of scandalous clothing and lingerie. She closed it quickly as if she had just had a glimpse of hell.

She glanced around the room in desperation. On the carpeted floor between the bed and window, there were two beanbag chairs and a low coffee table. Some sort of projector hung from the ceiling, but she couldn't see a screen.

The door to the room didn't have a knob, only a keyhole. It could be opened only from the outside.

It didn't take her long to realize what this room was for, and what was likely going to be expected from her from now on.

Zakiya entered the attached bathroom. It was her first time seeing a bathtub. She used the toilet and flushed. As she was washing her hands, she heard the door to the room open. She watched herself in the enormous mirror as she wrapped her body tightly with the towel, making sure her back was completely covered. Only then did she exit the bathroom.

A woman was standing in the middle of the room, chewing gum with her fists pressed to her hips. Her face was covered in heavy makeup, lipstick way too bright, and huge golden hooped earrings that brushed her shoulders with every head movement.

"I don't know what your name is, and I don't care," the woman said, snapping her gum. "From now on, you'll be called Lana, understood?"

Zakiya nodded.

"Lana," the woman said, her earrings clinking as she spoke. "I am Miss Mona, and I am in charge here. Do you understand?"

Zakiya nodded again. Mona was wearing tight jeans and a sleeveless top, which covered only the bare essentials, from the lower half of her huge breasts to just above her navel. Her skin was deeply tanned, which made Zakiya jealous.

"Where am I?" she asked.

"Lana, if you want to live happily in this house, don't

ask questions," Mona said, cracking her chewing gum between words, "Actually, it's better if you don't talk at all, especially since you have a Syrian accent. You must learn how to speak with a Lebanese accent."

Okay, so I'm in Lebanon.

"When you have a client, you will put a smile on your face, because, if I receive any complaints from your clients, I will put you in the cage for two days with no food or the use of a toilet. I bet you don't like to shit and eat in the same place, do you?"

Zakiya's eyes filled with tears, and she began to cry.

"Oh, your mother's dearest," Mona said, grabbing her by the shoulders and pushing her to sit on the bed, hard enough to make the mattress bounce. Mona sat beside her, facing her. Zakiya found the amount of mascara she was wearing intimidating.

"Let me be frank, Lana. You don't have any other option than to accept your new life circumstances, and it's really not that bad." Mona looked around her, waving with her right hand, "You have a nice place to live, and you'll have plenty of fun with a lot of hot guys. Some of them will tip you generously. Don't tell me you prefer the war-torn life in Syria?"

Mona's words brought more tears to her eyes.

Mona stood up and went to the closet, pulling out a red thong, a matching red bra, and a transparent black chiffon gown. She threw them on the bed and said, "Take a shower and put those on. Then wait for Nazih to come. He always tries out the new girls first."

Zakiya couldn't believe what she was hearing and threw herself face down on the bed and continued crying, now with loud sobs.

"Oh, your mother's dearest," Mona said, "You have

very little time. If Nazih doesn't like you, he will punish you severely. You can only hope he doesn't kill you."

Zakiya raised her head and looked at Mona, searching for any sign of a bluff, but Mona's face was dead serious. *My only refuge is Allah; I must beg Allah to release me from this dilemma.* She was still a virgin. She'd never had sex, kissed, or even touched a man before. She stood up and said, "I want to pray now."

Zakiya cringed at Mona's thunderous laughter.

"Oh, your mother's dearest," Mona spoke between gales of laughter. "You want to pray?" She looked around as if speaking to spectators. "Listen to her. A whore who wants to pray." She then looked at Zakiya and said, "You have only one hour before Nazih gets here. Don't worry, he won't hurt you; his sausage is tiny." She left the room, still laughing uproariously.

Zakiya's cheeks were hot, and she felt faint. She went into the bathroom, performed her ablutions, then, on the carpeted floor in the room, prayed and asked Allah to preserve her virginity until marriage.

***

Zakiya took a shower, then slowly put on the red thong and bra. She looked at her reflection in the mirror. The thong hung loosely, and the bra looked as if a boy was wearing it. She sighed and put the transparent black chiffon gown over her shoulders and sat on the carpet next to the bed. She hugged her knees and waited.

When the door opened, a clean-shaven man with an enormous belly came in. He wore sunglasses and his shirt was tucked into his denim pants. The scent of his cologne saturated the air in the room instantly. Zakiya jumped up and avoided looking him in the eyes.

"I am going to have a bath now," he said. "When I call

you, I want you to come right in." He started toward the bathroom, but then stopped, and said, "Drop the gown, and turn around slowly."

Zakiya was instantly paralyzed. She couldn't speak. It was her first time alone with a man who intended to have sex with her.

"Mona," he yelled.

The door opened and Mona entered, her earrings rattling. "Yes Nazih."

"Did you teach her what to do?" Nazih said.

"Of course I did," Mona said, looking directly at Zakiya. "She will do whatever you ask her to do." She winked.

"Drop the gown and turn around," Nazih said.

Zakiya didn't move or even raise her head.

"Your mother's dearest," Mona said while approaching Zakiya, "Don't be scared. Just drop the gown and turn around so Nazih can get a look at you."

Mona caught the gown and yanked it to the floor, then turned Zakiya's body around slowly. Both she and Nazih gasped in unison when they caught sight of her back. Both exclaimed, "What is that?"

Zakiya didn't speak or look at them.

"Bring my gun," Nazih yelled at Mona.

"What are you talking about? Relax a little, can't you?" Mona said.

"Don't you see her back?"

Mona stood in front of Zakiya, blocking his view of her. "Some men would be eager to have her."

"Have you gone mad," Nazih said, "Who would touch such a...?" He didn't say it, but he pointed his finger at Zakiya in disgust.

"There are too many dogs entering this house," Mona

97

said.

"I would sleep with a dog, but not with an ugly thing like this."

"I meant the clients, fool. Who asked you to touch her in the first place?"

Zakiya could only see Mona's back and hear her earrings rattling as she attempted to win the argument with Nazih, who continued to insist she must go.

"There will be no repeat of the Wima incident," Mona said. "Do you understand?"

"Mona, if you keep her, we will lose every client who sees her," Nazih said.

"Call the one who brought her and ask for a refund. Maybe they can move her to a cheaper place."

"They don't refund. Don't you remember what happened because of Wima?"

"It wasn't my fault," Mona yelled. "I am not a murderer. Wima was an accident. We were just lucky there was no investigation because no one even knew she was here. From now on, you ask for pictures of the girls before you purchase. So, they will be the ones to kill the ugly girls."

"What a predicament I've put myself in?" Nazih said, "I paid thousands for this monster."

Zakiya couldn't hold back her tears any longer. She covered her face with her hands and cried.

"Your mother's dearest," Mona said, turning to hug her. Zakiya buried her head in Mona's shoulder, continuing to cry.

"Get out," Mona shouted at Nazih. "You're the monster, not this delicate girl."

"Fuck!" Nazih yelled, storming out of the room.

Mona covered Zakiya's naked body with the bedcover,

her voice soft as she whispered in Zakiya's ear, "Your mother's dearest, we're just doing business here. Don't worry, I won't let him hurt you."

Zakiya cried out and hid behind Mona as Nazih suddenly rushed back into the room, aiming a gun at her.

"Are you crazy?" Mona screamed.

"Out of the way, bitch!" Nazih yelled, slapping Mona so hard that she fell to the floor.

Zakiya was sure Nazih was going to kill her. Mona lay on the floor next to the bed. Zakiya was grateful for Mona's attempt to protect her.

Nazih stood at the foot of the bed, his gun aimed at Zakiya's head. He flicked the safety off with a click.

Zakiya's hands and feet were ice cold. She wished he would just pull the trigger and end it.

"Relax, Nazih," Mona said calmly, getting to her feet and stepping between Zakiya and the gun.

It was extremely brave of Mona. Zakiya thought. *I never thought things like this really happened. I always thought it was only in movies.*

Mona reached out slowly toward the gun and said, "Put the gun down, and let me tell you what we can do with her."

"What?" Nazih grunted, lowering his gun.

What a coward. Zakiya thought. *He just needed an excuse to put the gun down.*

"Didn't we just discuss the high fees of the cleaning company and the two maids they send every day?" Mona asked, "Why don't we keep her? She could take over the cleaning duties in the villa."

Nazih didn't speak as he shifted his gaze back and forth between Mona and Zakiya.

"Just think about the benefits," Mona said.

"Are you stupid," Nazih said, "One girl makes in a week ten times what we are paying for cleaning in a month."

"I am not talking about only money," Mona said, her earrings rattling with every movement of her head. "Don't you remember what happened in the Rose Garden Villa? One of the cleaning maids tuned out to be an informer."

Zakiya wondered if Mona was telling the truth or had just made that up.

Nazih swallowed, "Ok, let's try her for a month. If the villa doesn't shine, I will kill her with my own hands." He spat on the floor and rushed out of the room.

Mona looked at Zakiya and said, "If you don't do your job well, I am the one who will kill you."

18

Mazen

Mazen scratched his chin through a three-day growth of beard. He hadn't shaved since the phone call with his father, Haj Adel. If his neighbors and friends in the narrow alley in old Damascus knew he put brilliantine in his black dyed hair before going to work, shaved his beard and mustache, and wore a necktie, they would consider him a punk. Well, what would those simple, uneducated people who never left Shagoor street understand about the luxurious lifestyle of a businessman like him?

At Beirut international airport, Mazen booked a car and driver to take him to Damascus. Since the war began in Syria, all the airlines had stopped landing at Damascus international airport.

When Mazen arrived at Shagoor street, he was barely conscious from sheer exhaustion. The trip from Beirut to Damascus used to take less than two hours before the war and cost only ten dollars per person. Now the same trip took six times longer because of the army inspection points along the way, and the fee was twenty times as much because the driver claimed he was forced to pay bribes at each inspection point to avoid delay. Without bribes, they would force him to park the car for several hours before allowing him to move again. Another reason for the astronomical fees was the dangers on the road. The driver claimed there were snipers along the way. Mazen didn't buy the second reason because no one would willingly drive on a road with snipers even if you filled his car with gold and silver. What good would the money be if you died while trying to earn it?

Mazen entered the dingy gate to the building. The floor was wet and muddy. The odor of rancid cooking oil was heavy in the air, and the noise of the water pumps whistling as they tried to pull up non-existent water was piercing to the ears. He avoided looking at the cracked wooden doors of the neighbors as he climbed the stairs to his apartment. Despite the time of day, the stairs were dim. The windows, which had once been left open, were now covered with boards to prevent anyone outside from taking a shot at someone climbing the stairs. It wasn't just a simple climb up the stairs; it was a heart-breaking revelation of the suffering endured by the people living in this building.

He couldn't believe he was now standing in front of his apartment door. The paint was peeling off, the small, engraved name plate was rusty, and the doorbell button was broken. The door to his apartment in Dubai was worth more than this entire apartment.

He raised his hand to knock, then dropped it, put his forehead against the door and closed his eyes. *Now I have to face the reality of how miserable my daughters' lives are in this dingy apartment, in this filthy building, in this dismal neighborhood. I must find Zakiya and get back to Dubai as soon as possible.*

He was afraid to face his daughters after the death of their mother. He hadn't even tried to make it up to them after her death. He just went on with his comfortable life in Dubai, pretending his daughters were happy with their lives.

He pressed the bridge of his nose between thumb and index finger, then exhaled, before knocking.

Seconds later, the door opened, and his three daughters were standing there looking at him.

He stepped inside, and all three of them hugged him.

The living room was empty except for a straw mat and two old sofas. He seated himself on the sofa facing the kitchen. The other sofa was between the door to his bedroom and the door to Khaled's bedroom, which was now empty because Khaled wasn't living there anymore. The girls' bedroom was on the other side of the hall. The walls were gray concrete blocks devoid of their original paint. The room was lit only by a single bulb hanging from the ceiling.

From where he sat, Mazen could see the so-called kitchen. It looked anything but healthy. The walls, once covered with porcelain tiles, were now naked except for a few tiles still stuck here and there to the cement. The cabinets were without doors, which in the past would have revealed multiple jars of olives and makdous when his wife Hadiya was still alive. Now only empty jars remained. Making makdous requires certain skills, and he doubted any of his four daughters had them. The kitchen badly needed a coat of paint, and the door to the toilet was rotting at the bottom and smelled musty.

Mazen wondered with misty eyes what had happened to the thousands of dollars he'd sent to his father every month. *Why is he not giving my daughters enough money to live a decent life?*

His three daughters, Farah, Marwa, and Ro'wa, sat on a straw mat on the floor, facing him.

"Oh, for your father's sake, get up and sit on the sofa with me," he said.

"We are comfortable here," Farah said, her voice sounding weak and strained.

"It's so long since we saw you last, we just want to look at you Papa," Ro'wa said with the sweetest smile a father could hope for from a daughter. Her words broke his heart.

The biggest dispute he'd had with their deceased mother was her insistence that their daughters should continue their higher education. In his mind, one advantage of the war was his daughters had been forced to quit their universities and stay at home. Only Farah had graduated with a journalism degree. Marwa was in her third year in dentistry, and Ro'wa in her second year of Arabic literature when mortar shells started falling on Damascus like winter rain, not distinguishing between government buildings or university buildings. That was when he had insisted they quit and stay at home. He believed women were born to be wives, serve their husbands, and bring up their children.

Mazen wanted to take Zakiya out of school as well, but the mullah convinced him she must at least finish high school. It was her second try. She hadn't passed the first time because of her mother passing away. He couldn't very well tell the mullah not to interfere in his daughters' affairs because, ever since his son Khaled had left, the mullah had taken care of his four daughters, for which Mazen compensated him, of course. The mullah had been his friend since childhood. The mullah had promised him he would look out for Zakiya's safety. Every day, he would drop off and pick up his own daughter, Zahra, and Zakiya at school. It wasn't even out of his way since the girls attended the same school.

Mazen hesitated for a few seconds before asking, "How were you able to inform your grandfather?"

The girls looked at each other, then Farah said, "We went to his shop."

"We wanted to tell the mullah first, but Zahra told us neither of her parents were home when she came to us. The poor little thing didn't even know at the time that her father's mosque had been hit by a mortar shell. We just panicked and rushed to grandfather's shop." Marwa said.

They had been warned never to leave the apartment unaccompanied in such dangerous times. The mullah was the correspondent between them and their grandfather, Haj Adel. Mazen sent money to their grandfather, and the grandfather, in turn, gave the mullah whatever money he needed for their daily needs.

"What if something had happened to you? Instead of one daughter kidnapped, I could have lost all four of you." He sighed. "And your grandfather's shop is in Medhat Basha street, where the retailers buy wholesale. Women walking in such a market were rare before the war, and now it is even more dangerous."

Ro'wa piped up, "I felt as if I was walking naked, and the men's eyes were devouring us." Her sisters shot her disapproving glances.

"I was walking with my hand in my handbag, clutching the gun, ready to use it in case anyone tried to take advantage of females walking alone," Farah added, "Plus, it was mid-afternoon. Broad daylight."

"You have a gun?" His eyes opened wide.

"Yes, after the war started, the mullah provided it and

taught us how to use it in case anyone tried to break into our apartment," Farah said.

"We knew very well our grandfather would be embarrassed if we barged right into the shop, so when we arrived, we just knocked on the glass from outside," Marwa said. "Of course, he didn't know we were there before we knocked because the windows are covered with old, yellowed newspaper."

"When grandfather came storming out of the shop, he looked all around him," Ro'wa said. She lowered her head and stared at the straw mat, and continued in a low voice, "He looked at us like he was ashamed of us."

"Yes, he was definitely ashamed of us," Farah snapped. "When he saw us, he shouted, 'Don't you know you should not leave your home?' With no greeting or even responding to our greeting."

Mazen was speechless.

"I remember tears streaming down my face," Farah said, "I wasn't sure if it was the news I had for him or his reaction that hurt more. I couldn't even speak, I was sobbing so hard. I just kept my eyes glued to the ground."

Mazen could see the pain in his daughters' eyes, especially Farah's.

Farah continued, "When I finally told him, 'They kidnapped Zakiya,' he asked, 'Isn't the mullah supposed to pick her up along with his own daughter every day? How could she be kidnapped, and his daughter wasn't?'

"I told him what happened with the two girls the way Zahra explained it to us. Then grandfather said, 'What do you expect me to do? Don't you know I'm a very busy man? I have three families on my shoulders plus you and your sisters. Your father lives happily in Dubai and leaves all his responsibilities on me.'"

"That was the last thing I expected him to say after learning his granddaughter had been kidnapped," Ro'wa said. "I wished Farah would just take the gun out and shoot him in the head."

"Ro'wa, stop it," Farah said.

Ro'wa looked at Farah, her eyes flashing with fire. "Because of his lying, Zahra has lost her father." She looked at her father, and said, "While we were still there, grandfather called the mullah, who was in the hospital at the time. He told him both girls had been kidnapped. So, the mullah went to the police station to ask about his daughter, and he hasn't been heard from since."

"Grandfather said, 'if he told the mullah both girls were kidnapped, the mullah would try harder to find the girls,'" Farah said. "'He himself was far too busy and couldn't spare the time.' Who knew the mullah would disappear trying to find the girls?"

"There is no power but from Allah," Mazen said. *Haj Adel did the right thing, telling the mullah both girls were kidnapped.*

"I told grandfather we must inform our father in Dubai. Could you please call him?" Farah said. "And he said, 'No, your father is a man with debts to pay. He has no time for such nonsense. Let him be. He's making money so you women can keep your bellies full. Now that I've informed the mullah, he will help to find Zakiya.'"

"When I told him that the mullah would know that Zahra was not kidnapped soon, he scolded me and told me not to interfere in men's work," Farah said. "I just nodded, and we walked back home."

"I had a hard time finding my way due to my tears," Ro'wa said, Farah forced a smile and slapped Ro'wa on the shoulder, saying, "You liar, you weren't crying. Marwa and I were the only ones crying."

"My heart was crying," Ro'wa said simply.

"From there we went directly to grandmother's house and called you because we weren't sure the mullah would still try to find Zakiya once he found out Zahra wasn't kidnapped," Farah said.

Despite his exhaustion, Mazen didn't go to bed. He spent the night listening to his daughters talk about their day-to-day existence. In a thousand years, he wouldn't have expected such things would happen in Damascus, or Syria, for that matter. The specter of death dwelt in the streets among the people, harvesting hundreds of souls daily. It turned out his daughter being kidnapped was not an unusual event in the daily life of Syrians since the war started.

19

Zahra

Zahra and Amani sat in the liwan together; Zahra doing her homework, and Amani reciting verses from the Holy Quran. The doorbell rang and Amani closed the Quran, kissed the cover, put it on the table, then dragged herself to the door.

She came back carrying two bundles of pita bread, "Zahra, have you been talking with George?"

"No, why?" If her mother had been any closer, she was sure she'd have heard her heart beating faster.

"George brought us some bread," Amani said, "I asked him how he knew we needed bread; he said a little bird told him."

"That's so kind of him," Zahra said, without smiling.

"Allah does good works through the hands of his servants," Amani said, "George is so nice and considerate, May Allah reward him."

"Mother..." Zahra started, but paused, debating with herself if it was wise to say what she wanted to.

Amani looked at Zahra, waiting.

"Why don't we ask George to do our grocery shopping and pay him for his time?" Zahra asked, waiting for her mother's blast.

"That's a good idea Zahra, please leave his number near the telephone. I'll call him tomorrow to ask him if he's willing to do that."

Zahra was speechless.

***

The next day, Zahra was happy to learn that George had agreed to help them for a small fee, and every day he would purchase the things Amani asked him to. When he brought the items; Zahra would pick them up from him, stealing a few precious seconds of conversation behind the door with him before he departed. Those stolen moments filled her days with sweet anticipation.

Amani had grown so pale, spending her days and nights waiting for the mullah, and if she noticed Zahra's excitement whenever George came over, she didn't show it. Or maybe she was too burdened with worry to notice.

One evening when a knock came to the door, Zahra's heart beat faster, but not for the same reason her mom's did. She ran to the door, very aware of her mother's eyes on her. "Who is it?" Zahra asked through the door.

"It's me, George," She inhaled deeply when she heard his voice.

"It's George," she called out to her mother to ease her mind.

She pulled her headscarf from the hanger on the wall and pulled it over her head, tucking her hair inside it, then opened the door. Seeing George's face, she swallowed hard. He had placed the plastic shopping bags in the hallway. His broad smile made her weak in the knees. Leaning her back against the wall, she smiled back at him.

"Where do you teach?" she asked. He had told her previously he was a schoolteacher.

"Assieh school, and you are studying in Shagoor high school, right?"

"Yes, I am," she said, dropping her eyes shyly.

"Ward sends his regards," he said, as he always did when they spoke. She didn't know for sure if Ward had really sent greetings or if George just used it to have something to say to her. Either way, she was happy.

They said their goodbyes and George left.

Zahra closed the door, then leaned her back against it. Closing her eyes, she smiled to herself.

20

Mazen

The next morning Mazen put on his dish dash and pressed his hair into place with wet hands. His beard was itching like crazy. He scratched at it a few times while sliding his feet into an old pair of slippers and left the apartment.

His mother's apartment was on the third floor of a four-story building on Ibn-Assaker Street. When his father married his second wife, he'd moved to his new apartment and never came back to visit his first wife, Sabah. Mazen knocked, and the maid opened the door for him.

His mother was sitting on the sofa with her prayer beads in her right hand, supplicating to Allah. This was her primary occupation all day long since she had become grossly overweight and suffered from severe pain in her knees. She used a walker to move from her bed to the sofa, or the bathroom. It had been several years since she last left her apartment. He doubted she even knew what year it was.

Mazen considered his mother the most important creature on earth, but as much as he loved her, he hated this apartment. All of his most painful memories centered around this very apartment. Back when he was married with three kids, they had lived in one room, his brother's family lived in one room, and his parents lived in one room. His first son, Jamal, fell from the balcony of this cursed apartment when he was just three years old, his life cut short in an instant. He never felt the same connection with his other children as he did with Jamal, and losing him destroyed him inside.

He bent to kiss her chubby right hand, then he kissed her forehead. Her hair was snow white. He could see in her eyes the pain of long years of suffering. There was no actual conversation between them, the same as when he called her from Dubai. Sabah would spend the entire call just asking Allah to grant him whatever he might wish for, unlimited fortune, and a long and healthy life. And that was how she spent the few minutes he spent with her this time.

The maid prepared a cup of tea for him, very weak and far too sweet, just the way Sabah liked it. He almost spit it out when he took his first sip.

His mother ended her litany of demands from Allah, and the apartment fell silent except for the sound of the maid running water in the kitchen sink. Mazen contemplated this fat old woman, who was counting down her final days. It was a pitiful sight.

The phone rang, and the maid rushed back from the kitchen to answer it. The maid was a hardworking woman in her fifties who had been helping his mother since the day his father left the apartment to live with his second wife. Upon hearing the caller's voice, the maid gasped.

Mazen looked up. "What is it?"

The maid looked directly at his mother as if he wasn't there and said, "Haj Adel has had a stroke. They've taken him to the hospital." She hung up the phone and went back to the kitchen, her apparent indifference sent a shiver down his spine.

His mother looked up and said, "Allah is great. He is my avenger."

Mazen was embarrassed. On the one hand, he couldn't scold his mother, but on the other hand, he didn't see his father's misfortune as vengeance. So, he just kissed his mother's hand once again and excused himself to go to his father's shop.

***

Haj Adel's shop was in the al-Buzuriyah market at the end of Medhat Basha street. Vendors there mostly traded in exotic herbs and spices, Arabic coffee, perfumes, and the Arabic abaya and cloaks. Mazen was well known for his business acumen and negotiation skills. He had been highly respected by everyone in the market except his father, Haj Adel. His father used to complain all the time that the shop wasn't busy enough for two partners, even though he never treated him as a partner. He treated him more like a regular employee, and that's why Mazen borrowed money and traveled to Dubai to start his own business.

Now in Dubai, he had his own cosmetics company with his girlfriend Julie as a partner. But even after he left for Dubai, his father never stopped nagging. He complained that the shop needed liquidity because it was not making as much profit as it did before Mazen left.

Before his wife Hadiya's death, Mazen had thought she was stealing his money and giving it to other members of her family. But his father kept asking for so much money even after Hadiya's death, and the situation he'd seen the night before in his apartment was proof that his family wasn't receiving all the money he'd sent for their upkeep. The money Mazen sent to his father was enough to buy a new shop as big as the one Haj Adel owned.

Mazen walked quickly through the market and if any of his old friends, the shop owners, greeted him, he simply told them his father had had a stroke, and he must hurry to catch up with the ambulance. Some of the shops' owners jogged along with him when they learned his father had had a stroke.

The parking spot for Haj Adel's 1980 gray Fiat was empty. The shop gates were open, but his father was not behind his exotic old desk.

No one was in the shop, not even the three or four porters his father usually kept around. Wholesalers usually employed strong men to prepare and load the heavy products into customers' pickup trucks.

Mazen stepped behind the desk only to find the money drawer open. *That's weird. It's empty.* The safe was on the left, its heavy door ajar. He pulled it open and looked inside, to find only a few black leather notebooks, but no money.

Three of the traders who had followed him were now looking at him questioningly. He didn't know what the explanation was for all of this. He picked up the receiver of the old rotary dial phone. Opening the telephone book, he found the number of Abu Sam, their neighbor, in the shop next door.

"Salam Abu Sam." Mazen said.

"Hi, who's this?"

"It's Abu Khaled. I'm next door in my father's shop." Mazen said. "Have you heard Haj Adel has had a stroke?"

"Oh, for heaven's sake," Abu Sam's voice seemed a bit shaky. "Am I dreaming? When did you get back, Abu

Khaled? Of course, I know about your father's stroke. I helped the medic put him on the stretcher with my own hands. Hold on, I am coming over to see you."

Mazen put the receiver back in its cradle, and the phone gave a short ding.

Abu Sam, with his huge belly and sweaty bald head, entered the shop and went straight to the side of the desk to kiss and hug Mazen. When he sat in the chair beside the desk, the sleeves of Mazen's dish dash were stained with Abu Sam's sweat.

"Where were you and where is your brother?" Abu Sam asked, his eyes reflecting concern.

"You know I was in Dubai," Mazen said, "And my brother is busy with his business."

"Your father is getting old, and not so spry lately." Abu Sam swallowed hard, looking right and left as if he was afraid of something.

"What is it Abu Sam?" Mazen asked, "Is there..." then Mazen changed his mind as it was obvious Abu Sam was hesitant to talk in front of the other three traders. "I am going to the hospital now to check on my father, would you like to accompany me?"

"No, I don't have anyone to stay in the shop. I will visit him after I close up for the day," Abu Sam said, "Please convey my best wishes to him." He avoided looking into Mazen's eyes when he said it.

Mazen was curious to know what was bothering Abu Sam, but he needed to hurry to the hospital. He got up to leave, and asked the other three traders who were standing still, "Would any of you like to join me?" The three made excuses and apologized, then left. Then he asked Abu Sam, "Do you know where my father's porters are? He usually has at least three."

"When the ambulance came, your father was alone, face down on the desk. No one else was around." Abu Sam again avoided looking at Mazen's eyes.

His father always left the padlock opened on the side of the table. He grabbed it and went out with Abu Sam right behind him. He closed the heavy wooden gates, inserted the padlock shackle through the slot in the metal bar, and locked the padlock onto the ring. Out of the corner of his eye, he could tell Sam was looking at his face. When he turned back, he asked, "Is there anything you want to share with me?"

"Yes," Abu Sam said, "But now you must hurry to check on your father, we will talk later."

The trip to the hospital took over three hours, as the taxi was forced to stop in long queues at every checkpoint. As the cars crept ahead, the sun beat down mercilessly. Mazen's underarms were stained with sweat, his beard itchier than ever. When the taxi finally pulled up to the man at the inspection point, or the boy, he looked too young to be a man. He wore army attire, complete with a bulletproof vest and several belts filled with ammo and grenades. When Mazen took out his ID, the young man took it and handed it to another man, who disappeared into the guard shack with it.

The taxi driver, a lanky old man, switched off the engine while they waited for their IDs to come back. They had been more than an hour in this queue alone. Mazen had been counting and up to this point, the driver had stopped and started the engine thirty-seven times.

"How long have you been a taxi driver?" Mazen asked.

"Only a year." The driver's face was expressionless, only his eyes betrayed the depths of his pain and disappointment. His lips were parched and dry, his face badly sunburned, "I am from the suburbs of Aleppo, where I owned a textile factory. I had a mansion on the outskirts of Aleppo and an apartment in the city. Last year, armed rebels raided my factory and stole all the machinery and burned the building, then a gun was aimed at my head, and my family and I were forced to leave with only the clothes we were wearing. If I had protested, they would have killed me. We moved to an apartment in the city, but a few months later a mortar shell hit it and killed my wife and two kids, so I couldn't stay in that apartment any longer. I sold it for a quarter of what it was worth. With the money, I bought this taxi and came to Damascus to work."

"Man, that's tough," Mazen said, almost suffocating from the heat.

"What brought you to this country at a shitty time like this?" the driver asked.

"What?" Mazen shifted positions, trying to catch any small breeze. "How do you know I don't live here?"

"From your looks," the driver said while staring at his face, "The suffering of war leaves distinctive marks on the faces of the Syrian citizens. Your face doesn't have these marks. Your face looks like you spent the day at the spa, your hands so soft, your eyes so compassionate. I can see from the redness under your beard that you're used to shaving every day, but when you arrived in Syria, you thought a beard would help you blend in."

The armed guard returned Mazen's ID and waved to the driver to leave.

The car shuddered to life when the driver turned the key, then moved ahead with a jerk as the driver stomped the accelerator.

Mazen was reluctant to tell the driver he lived in Dubai. He might be a crook and try to kidnap him. "I live in Lebanon," he said while pretending to look out the window, "I just got here yesterday."

The driver's laugh was high but short, "Try again, man." The traffic was so bad, they were only traveling 10 km per hour. "Syrians in Lebanon are suffering just as much as we are suffering here."

"I think age is an important element that defines how we look," Mazen said. "For instance, you appear to be older than my father, who is in the hospital where I am going now to visit."

The driver sighed, "How old is your father?"

"In his eighties."

"Your father could be my father," the driver said, "I am only forty-two years old."

Mazen thought to himself, *that's crazy*. As if the driver had read his thoughts, he took out his ID and handed it to Mazen. Sure enough, the driver was born in 1971, which made him forty-two.

The driver stretched out his hand for his ID and said, "Anyway, I didn't ask you where you came from, and I don't want to know. I asked you what brought you here with such bad timing. Nowadays, most people are thinking of leaving the country."

Mazen just looked at the driver, trying to decide what he should tell him. *Maybe he can help in some way, especially since he is working on the streets every day*, "My daughter disappeared, we believe she was kidnapped."

The driver's face transformed. Mazen had never seen anyone look so terrified by a single sentence. It was as if the driver's own daughter had been kidnapped. His hands gripped the steering wheel so hard, his knuckles turned white.

"Someone you know who was kidnapped?" Mazen asked.

"My niece," the driver said, "She was kidnapped from Aleppo. My sister's husband is an officer in the army. When the kidnappers found out the father was in the army, they sent her head to him in a trash bag."

"How do you know that was the reason?" Mazen asked, trying very hard not to appear skeptical while praying that his daughter's destiny would not be like the driver's niece.

"There was a letter in the bag with the head, telling him he was an infidel and they explained in the letter how many times they raped his daughter and how they had tortured her, and how she died during the torture. Then they cut off her head."

Mazen couldn't find words to say. He opened his mouth, closed it, opened it again, then decided to remain silent. By the time they arrived at the hospital, his underwear was soaked in sweat. Mazen wasn't sure if it was from the heat or from the horror he felt over the possible fate awaiting his kidnapped daughter.

A security guard at the hospital gate took his ID and asked him to wait.

The crowd outside the hospital was overwhelming. Hundreds of people were waiting like him. From their attire, it appeared many of them were not originally from Damascus. Most of them were farmers from rural areas. Some of them were sitting on their luggage, which was mostly bundles of clothing. Some used it as a pillow and slept on the pavement. Like the taxi driver, these people's faces were a picture of human suffering. The sun was baking their heads.

A taxi sped up to the front of the hospital emergency gate, almost running over three of the waiting men. At the last second, they jumped out of the way. The rear passenger side door opened, and a man got out and began to pull on a blanket, with a body on it, or at least what was left of a body. Both legs were amputated at the knees, the white ends of the bones were exposed. The arms were there, but not connected to the body. They were laid over the man's chest. The face looked like it had been peeled, leaving only blood-red flesh.

Mazen couldn't believe what he was looking at. He looked at the people around him, who were showing no signs of surprise. Some glanced, then looked away as if such scenes were commonplace. Mazen's stomach started cramping as another fellow exited the car, and the two men carried the blanket and its contents quickly to the emergency entrance.

When Mazen's name was called, he rushed through the emergency gate into the triage area where there were eight beds bearing the bodies of unfortunate people who either had raw flesh exposed, or missing limbs like the one who had just been delivered in the taxi. He quickly scanned the eight beds, but his father was not on any of them. Mazen's legs became weak, and his head was swimming. He took a deep breath, trying to control his panic.

"Who are you here to see?" a male voice pulled him back to his senses. A short, fat, bald doctor stood in front of him, his once-white coat splattered with blood. Mazen understood immediately this doctor was going through hell and he didn't have a second to spare for polite conversation.

"I am looking for Haj Adel Mis'ed," Mazen said. "He is

my father. But I don't see him anywhere."

The name caused the doctor to raise his eyes from the report he was reading and look directly at Mazen. "We just put him in the ICU after we gave him a CT scan. Your father's brain is bleeding."

"Oh, merciful Allah," Mazen said, "Is it because of the stroke?"

"What stroke? Your father either fell on his head or was hit on the head, which caused internal bleeding. I am not sure if he's going to make it."

Mazen swallowed.

The doctor pushed a paper toward Mazen and said, "Please sign here, and here. And please leave a contact number where we can update you about his situation."

Mazen took out a pen from his inner pocket and signed. He handed the report back to the doctor, his eyes full of tears.

"Please don't come to the hospital anymore unless we call you to come for him." the doctor said, and he left to attend to a woman who was crying next to a bed bearing a body bandaged from head to toe, Mazen assumed it was her son.

***

The following morning, Mazen went back to the market, to his father's shop. He didn't want to be stopped and questioned on the way, so he deliberately went earlier than the other shop owners.

Before going to bed the night before, he'd called Nora, the third wife of Haj Adel, who currently lived with him. He asked her if Haj Adel usually drove himself to the shop in the mornings. She confided in him that Haj Adel had recently been suffering from Alzheimer's and had stopped driving a few months ago. Now, one of his porters drove him and then took the car home each night. Haj Adel hadn't had a problem with that.

When Mazen arrived at the shop, he didn't find any of the porters waiting. He looked around at the other shops. All the porters were waiting for the owners to come and open their shops. Some were sitting on the ground, some were just leaning against the wall, either smoking or chatting. *This is weird.* He looked across at Abu Sam's shop. It was still closed, but three porters stood there talking. He walked over to them, "Salam," Mazen said. They were too young to have been working years ago when he was still working with his father. "I am Mazen, the son of Haj Adel."

"We are deeply sorry to hear what happened to Haj Adel," the one in the middle said. He didn't sound very sincere, but Mazen didn't care. He knew most porters don't like their masters, or any masters for that matter.

"Do you know who has been working with Haj Adel nowadays?" Mazen asked the boy in the middle.

The three boys looked at each other before the same one answered, "Yes, Abdul, Rawad, and Sameer. They are from Khraibeh."

"But aren't they supposed to be here by now?" Mazen asked and immediately thought better of it, *how on earth would these boys know the reason for the actions of my father's employees?* "Never mind. Don't worry about it. They're probably just late. Tell me, where are you from?"

"I am from Utaibah," the middle boy said.

"I am from Nashabiah," the one on the right said.

"I am from Nashabiah as well," the third answered.

"Are you friends with..." Mazen said, trying to remember the names of the porters. But when he couldn't recall the names, he said, "...the boys from Khraibeh?"

The three boys instantly and in unison replied, "No."

"But you know them from your daily activities in the market, don't you?" Mazen asked.

"No," the boy in the middle said.

***

Mazen went back to his father's shop and opened the gates under the pitying glances of the other porters. It was unusual for a shop owner to open his own shop. He was glad he'd come early so the neighboring shop owners wouldn't see him in this humiliating situation.

The smells in the shop always made him nostalgic. It wasn't only the cleaning detergents and hand soap smell; it was a mixture of cleaning products, the dusty smell of the rice sacks, the boxes of cookies, and chocolate, the cooking oil, and ghee, plus the smell of the ancient wood shelving covered with layers of ground in dirt.

He switched on the light and the ceiling fan, which first quivered, then slowly started to turn, making rhythmic clicks with each revolution. He slipped in behind the exotic desk his father had been using for over forty years. The seat and backrest of the swivel chair, both originally covered with black leather, were worn through and only the gray padding was left. He opened the wooden cash drawer. It was supposed to be filled with money, that is how it had been when he used to work with his father, but now it was empty.

Taking the telephone book off the top of the safe, he opened to the page where his father usually wrote the names and contact details of his porters. He found a long list of names along with start and finish working dates. The last three names had only start dates. Abdul, Rawad, and Sameer.

Lifting the telephone receiver, he slowly dialed the first number on the rotary dial. Abdul's number was not in service, Rawad's was a wrong number, and Sameer's was also not in service. *So, there is no way to communicate with these three porters.* He pulled open the heavy door of the safe and his heart sank as he looked inside. The money tray wasn't there, only two leather ledgers, a few invoices and receipts, and some contracts. He opened the small box built into the top corner of the safe, but there was no money, only two used receipt books and a few other documents. He took out the two leather ledgers and pushed the safe door shut. These were the books his father used to record his daily transactions from the beginning of this year. He got so engrossed in reading his father's financial details; he lost track of time. When he finally looked at his watch, two hours had passed already, and not a single customer had come in. That was weird, this was usually the busiest time of the day. It was even weirder than the porters not showing up. He picked up the phone and called Abu Sam.

"Salam brother," Mazen said.

"I am coming to you," Abu Sam said without even replying to the greeting.

Abu Sam arrived, and the first thing Mazen said was, "I don't understand why our porters haven't come."

"They won't come."

"What?" Mazen said, thinking he hadn't heard correctly.

"Your father didn't have porters working for him, he had a gang stealing from him. Your father's mental health was not at its best recently, and those three dogs took advantage of that."

"I tried to call the three of them, but I couldn't reach any of them."

"Your father's ego wouldn't allow him to call an employee and ask why he didn't show up to work. I doubt if he ever tried to call any of them."

"What makes you say they won't come anymore?" Mazen asked.

"Do you remember Nabil the Blond? He used to be a very good customer of your father's shop, back when you used to work here. But since last year when your father started to forget things and make mistakes in calculating prices, Nabil as well as many of your father's other customers changed their habits and started to come to me. Anyway, to make a long story short, Nabil was placing an order in my shop and when he finished, he told me he was going to stop at Haj Adel's shop to order the olive oil your father always buys from Horan. Only a minute after he left my shop, he came running back and told me your father was unconscious, with his head down on his desk and no one was in the shop."

"Maybe they were in the market delivering orders," Mazen said, trying to convince himself more than Abu Sam.

"The ambulance took more than an hour to get here. During that time, not one of your porters showed up. If they were busy in the market doing errands for your father, they would have been back long before the ambulance arrived. Also, you came after the ambulance left and they still hadn't showed up."

Mazen rubbed his face with both hands, then said, "So they left him unconscious and ran away." He sighed,

"In the hospital, the doctor said, Haj Adel has internal bleeding due to a severe blow to the skull."

Abu Sam gasped.

"Do you think those porters murdered my father?" Mazen asked himself as much as Abu Sam.

"I am sure they were stealing from your father," Abu Sam said, "But murdering him?"

"What made you sure they were stealing from him?"

"Recently, your father sent one of his porters to borrow money from me several days in a row. Then, after a few days, I sent my boy to ask for the money back. Your father was surprised and said he didn't borrow anything from me. So, I brought him the receipts written and signed by him. He took the receipts and opened the ledgers, but he couldn't find any record of the borrowed money. However, Haj Adel paid me all the money, as per the receipts I gave him. Ever since that day, I've had my suspicions."

"So, you think he was borrowing the money and forgetting about it?" Mazen asked.

"That was my first thought, but when I met the pickle vendor Abu Karam, and the nut vendor Abu Fustuq, they both said Haj Adel had recently borrowed money from them. I asked them to show me the receipts and when we looked at them, we noticed all the handwriting was identical. The only difference was the name of the person it was borrowed from and the dates. Even the amount was always same, five thousand. After our meeting, Abu Karam went and asked Haj Adel about the money. Haj Adel was surprised he didn't have any record on his ledgers. However, because Abu Karam presented the official receipt, your father paid the amount back in full. Ever since then, we knew the dogs working for your father were forging the receipts with your father's signature and asking for money from the people around."

"Have you tried telling all this to my brother?" Mazen asked, "He could have come and investigated, I believe he could have opened my father's eyes to what was going on around him."

"Of course, I met with your brother," Abu Sam said, "I am not sure if he did anything, but the situation with your father didn't change."

Abu Sam stood up, "Please excuse me, I have to attend to my clients." He moved toward the door but before leaving he said, "My advice is to conduct an inventory, you might find more details you need to know about."

After Abu Sam left, Mazen sat staring at the dusty shelves in front of him. The rhythmic clicking of the ceiling fan lulled him into a kind of trance, so when the telephone rang, it startled him. He raised the receiver to his ear and listened without speaking.

"Mr. Mazen Mis'ed?" a female voice asked.

"Yes," Mazen said and knew what's coming next.

"I am Rashida from the City hospital. I regret to inform you that your father passed away an hour ago. Due to the crowding situation, the hospital can help you by delivering the body to the graveyard directly, but we do that only to the Bab al-Sagheer graveyard, if that's where you want to bury him."

"Yes, that's where we bury our family members," Mazen said. He couldn't help it, tears came to his eyes, but he managed not to make a sound.

"At the graveyard, they have all the services available. They will perform the death prayer and the washing and shrouding of the body. The delivery vehicle will leave here in one hour."

Mazen didn't wait for the nurse to finish speaking, he just hung up the phone and rested his forehead on his arms on the desk, finally letting his sobs escape. He cried freely, like he'd never done before. His crying drained all the tension that had built up inside him since he'd arrived in the country. Only been a few days since he'd left his paradise in Dubai, and he felt the tension of an entire lifetime on his shoulders. He wondered how the people who live here all the time managed to relieve their anger and frustrations. Maybe that's the reason people had started killing each other in this part of the world.

He raised his head, wiped his tears with his sleeve, and got up to go to the graveyard.

He took a taxi, prepared for the torment of waiting through all the inspection points along the way. Added to that was the unbearable heat of the sun. It was as if the sun had made a deal to make Syrians' lives more hellish than it already was because of the war. He stared out the car window as he thought about how miserable his father's circumstances must have become. The whole time Mazen had been in the shop, no one entered. No customers, no neighbors, no porters, not even a debt collector. Was it possible his father had spent his final days in solitude like that? Or maybe today it was because people knew his father wasn't there, so they thought the shop was closed.

He was determined to find out in the coming days.

21

Mullah Abdullah

The mullah stood staring at his reflection in the long mirror, wearing nothing but his shorts. After the first week in the camp, he'd removed all the bandages. Now two weeks had passed, and because of the intensive physical training, he'd lost eight kilograms. His cheeks were saggy and two new lines had appeared, one on each side of his nose running down to the corners of his mouth. He puffed out his cheeks, and the two lines disappeared, then he blew out the air, and they reappeared. The transformation was incredible. Mullah Abdullah no longer existed, and, in his place, Shaddad Abu Saif was born.

He bent closer to the mirror, examining his teeth, trying to distinguish which one contained the advanced communication device that had been implanted in his tooth.

Comrade Ali from Lebanon, an expert in communication technologies had told him, "Every word you speak will be transmitted to the operations room, where those who are monitoring will take action immediately in the case of an emergency. So, you won't need to worry, since you will have the support of the special forces, twenty-four-seven." That put the mullah's mind at ease somewhat. He was just glad they had knocked him out for the procedure. He had never been fond of dentists.

He wore a small earphone in his right ear to receive instructions. He found it uncomfortable for the first few days, especially when his head was still bandaged. Every time a voice erupted from it, his brain vibrated, and he would quickly remove it, but then he would put it back quickly so as not to miss any orders being given to him.

Comrade Fazl from Der al-Zour, an expert in Arab genealogy, taught him about the Arab tribes that existed in the region and made him recite his new family lineage over and over so people he came in contact with wouldn't become suspicious. Comrade Fazl taught him that Shaddad Abu Saif was originally from the tribe of Bani Dabab in the south of Iraq, and his lineage went all the way back to Shimer Bin Ziljoushan, the killer of Imam Hussain bin Ali, the grandson of the prophet Mohammad, in the battle of Karbala, thirteen hundred years ago. Every bit of that man's life disgusted the mullah. It was because of men like Shaddad Abu Saif that his daughter, Zahra, was in danger now.

Before sunup, the mullah left his room, jogging to start off his physical training with Comrade Raad. The enormous camp was in the middle of nowhere, surrounded in all four directions by vast areas of barren ground. The chilly morning air stung his bare chest and shoulders, but in a few minutes, his body was covered in sweat, and his muscles radiated heat.

When he reached the training field, the other trainees were already standing attentively waiting for Comrade Raad to give the signal for them to start the running session. Every morning, they started with a ten-kilometer run. The mullah was very curious about the other trainees because they all appeared to be a lot like him, older and not very fit. After his first day of intensive training, he realized he wouldn't have the time or the energy to interact with any of them, except comrade Abu Moos, his mission partner.

When comrade Fazl briefed them, he told them that after this training program, the mullah and Comrade Abu Moos would become fanatics whose hearts were full of hatred, bearing grudges against anyone who didn't agree with them because they believed they were the chosen people of God.

Comrade Raad from the special forces in the Syrian Army gave the start sign and all of them darted off like gazelles.

The mullah ran with his shoulders thrown back and his chest thrust forward, as if embracing whatever life threw at him. Each day, the running became easier for him. The first few days after only a few hundred meters, it had felt like knives stabbing his lungs, burning sensations in his legs, and either a parched mouth or a dizzy head and excessive saliva in his mouth. Now he simply focused on his breathing and ignored the flailing of his legs and the length of his strides. If he thought about his legs, his feet would falter, and his body be thrown headfirst to the rough ground like a kicked pebble.

After the running session, with no water to drink or recovery time, they started crossing the battlefield. The field was rife with coils of barbed wire, infested with murky swamps and deep trenches, and bristling with deadly sharpened stakes. They crossed it, crawling on hands and knees. For the first few days, his elbows and knees took a terrible beating, and he often prayed for an end to the unbearable pain. Eventually, he learned to simulate the movements of a lizard, so the friction between his skin and the rough ground decreased to almost zero. This time, the damage to his knees and elbows was far less severe.

Next, they did an exercise that required them to move a large inflatable boat down a hill as a team. Six trainees carried the boat while the other four were lying in it, so the weight of the boat with the four bodies exceeded four hundred kilos. Five of the carriers were blindfolded and had to follow the instructions called out by the sixth member from the front of the boat. They had to deliver the heavy boat to the opposite side of a hill, maneuvering around trees, avoiding mud pits, and dodging sharp rocks. Comrade Raad told them this training would sharpen their leadership skills and improve the teamwork of the blindfolded men. Overall, it was intended to refine their listening skills, since on the battlefield they might not be able to see what's going on, but still follow directions from someone who was in a position to see.

When they'd completed the exercise, they dispersed for their midday break. The mullah went back to his room and threw himself on the dry straw mat on his cot. Every atom of his body screamed from exhaustion. He had two hours to pray, eat lunch, and rest before going out again to resume training.

He and Comrade Abu Moos had classes on the history of the strategic war during Islam's golden era, with comrade Wisam, a professor from Aleppo, plus a session about the tactical thinking of the leaders of al-Qaeda.

By that time, daylight would be fading, allowing the

glittering stars to once again ornament the inky black sky.

Then the mullah attended a session at the indoor gun range with Comrade Hamad, a weapons expert and army officer from Dar'a, who taught them the weapons they would be required to use and how to dismantle them and clean them.

After that, in the explosives lab, Comrade Ghulam, an expert from Afghanistan who spoke surprisingly good Arabic, taught them the various types of handmade explosives and how to dismantle them when possible.

During his daily training, the mullah felt at times like he was suffocating, having a heart attack, experiencing shortness of breath, and unable to feel his fingers. He couldn't swallow anything, not even water, despite his severe thirst. When he went back to lie down on his cot, he suffered from insomnia despite his exhaustion, because anxiety took over.

He would stare at the sky through the skylight above his bed and think about how many ways he had learned so far to kill himself quickly and easily. However, it wasn't the contract with the government that stopped him from ending his life, but thoughts of his daughter Zahra. The only reason he had agreed to be part of this mission was to rescue her from the hands of murderers.

He closed his eyes and pictured Zahra's face. A smile crept across his lips, and a tear leaked from the corner of his eye as he whispered, "By Allah, I won't give up until I've rescued you or died trying."

Comrade Raad was witness to many of these emotional conflicts and used them as a reason to push the mullah to the max. If his arms gave out and couldn't pull his heavy body over the bar, Raad would shout,

"Come on. You're here to rescue Zahra." That would ignite a fire in the mullah's muscles and allow him to pull himself up, not only once more, but three or four times more. He used it to keep him climbing the steep steps, which felt like a mountain. He used it to keep him running despite the searing pain in his lungs and legs. It even kept him fighting back, even when his face was covered with blood from the punches of comrade Raad during boxing training.

"For the sake of Zahra," was the magical sentence that kept him going and transformed him into an unbeatable weapon.

22

Mazen

The next morning Mazen went to his father's shop to take inventory. Like the day before, he saw his neighbors' porters, but not his father's. The shop held the same unique mixture of smells. He switched on the lights and sat behind the desk. *The lady in Dubai who cleans my office has a better desk than this.* The shelves around him were stacked with cartons of cookies, chocolate, and candies. He realized he didn't know their prices. What if a customer came in to buy? *That won't be a problem, I can just call Abu Sam and ask him for help pricing things.*

His father did everything "old school". No computer to keep track of inventory or sales. He just wrote everything down in his leather-bound ledgers. The most advanced electronic device he owned was a calculator. That calculator had once been white but now so old and covered with grime, the only clean spaces on it were the keys. They were so worn some of the numbers were hard to read.

Mazen got out the ledgers and started to take inventory.

"Salam Alaikum - peace be upon you," said a man as he entered the shop wearing a black jacket, sunglasses, and a thick black, medium-length beard.

"Salam, brother," Mazen said, "Please do me the honor

of taking a seat."

"Thank you," the man said, "Where is Haj Adel?"

Mazen looked at the man for a few seconds, trying to decide what he should answer him. If he was a customer, it wouldn't be a problem, he could handle him. "Unfortunately, he's not in today. I am his son Mazen. Let me know what you need, and I will be happy to get it ready for you."

"Today was our appointment to go and register the land in my name," the man said.

"Excuse me," Mazen said, "What land?"

"I bought some land from your father," the man said. "Last Tuesday I paid him in full, and today we were supposed to go to the land registration bureau and register it in my name."

Mazen's ears heard the words, but his brain was not comprehending. "You paid in full last Tuesday?" That was the day his father had been hit on the head. "Were you here alone with Haj Adel?"

Mazen assumed the man was looking at him from behind the sunglasses before he calmly took a paper from his pocket, opened it, and gave it to Mazen. "This is the receipt he gave me."

Mazen took it and looked it over. It was a receipt for twenty-five million Syrian pounds, equal to approximately five hundred thousand American dollars. His father's description on the receipt showed it was payment in full for a piece of land in an area called Kuswa. The land size and location were listed in addition to the record number for the registration bureau. Mazen read the man's name, Kamal.

"Mr. Kamal, I don't mean to doubt you, but were you alone with Haj Adel when you paid him?"

"Three of his employees were standing here," Kamal said and pointed to the space beside the rows of soft drinks boxes.

That's what Mazen had been afraid of.

"Is Haj Adel, ok?" Kamal asked, "It is not my first time buying from him, last year he sold me land in Ghouta. Your father is an honorable person."

"Haj Adel has passed away," Mazen said. "That's why I asked you if you were alone with him. On Tuesday, we found him unconscious at his desk. He was alone and his porters were nowhere to be found. There was no cash in the safe or in any of the drawers. It seems most likely that Haj Adel was murdered for the money you gave him. It's easy to imagine who might have murdered him for that much of money."

Kamal gasped and took off his sunglasses. "We belong to Allah and to Him we shall return." Then he looked at Mazen and said, "I am so sorry to hear this. Have you reported this to the authorities? Have the police caught them?"

"The porters have not shown up since then," Mazen said. "I haven't reported them, because I have only now realized they must have murdered him. Before you came in, I had only suspected they could have hurt him, but now with this much money disappearing, I am sure they are the ones who took it. They appear to be the only witnesses to what occurred Tuesday morning, but if they are innocent, why have they disappeared?"

"Where are they from? Someone should try to find them?" Kamal said.

"I will go to the police station later today and report them," Mazen said.

"Do you know where they are from?" Kamal asked

again.

"From Khraibeh."

"Oh man," Kamal squeezed his eyes shut.

"What?"

"Khraibeh is not under army control, it is in the hands of an organization called the Sword of Truth. It's possible they are not coming back because they are not able to. Since the Sword of Truth took over that area, it is nearly impossible for people to go in or out."

"So maybe they didn't steal the money," Mazen said, "Maybe they are just not able to leave the Khraibeh. But they still have Haj Adel's car."

"Anything is possible, but Khraibeh has been under Sword of Truth's control for more than a week now. If the porters were aligned against the Sword of Truth, they wouldn't have a chance to leave at all, supposing they would even be allowed to live."

"You mean they could only leave the Khraibeh if they're allied with the terrorists?"

"Yes," Kamal said.

"But how could they pass the army inspection points if they are on the side of the terrorists?" Mazen asked.

"Unless they've had a confrontation with the army previously, they won't have any record as terrorists. Also, they were the only ones here in the shop when Haj Adel took my money. So, if they didn't take the money, at least they might have answers about who else came into the shop after I left and what happened to Haj Adel."

"Brother Kamal," Mazen was curious how this man knew about the Sword of Truth, "What do you do?"

"I own a construction company."

"But how do you know so much about the Khraibeh?"

"My older brother is an officer in the army," Kamal said. "I have some real estate in the Khraibeh, and my brother warned me to be careful and not go near it right now. If they know my brother is an officer in the army, they will kidnap me or kill me."

"So how do the porters leave and go back to Khraibeh, then?" Mazen was talking to himself more than to Kamal. "I'm pretty sure they are the ones who stole the money and killed Haj Adel."

"What details do you have about those porters?" Kamal asked.

"I am not sure," Mazen said, "Let me check if there are any IDs, or employee information in the safe." Mazen spent a few minutes looking through the papers in the safe, then looked at Kamal. "I have only their names. I already know the phone numbers I have for them are false since I tried to call them on Tuesday."

"You don't even know what they look like. How do you expect to report them to the police? Their names are not enough," Kamal said.

"What if I gave the police the details of Haj Adel's car?" Mazen asked.

"Since the beginning of the war, hundreds of cars have been stolen daily. I'm not sure reporting a stolen car would provide any beneficial information. We could give it a try," Kamal said, as he took out his mobile phone. He called his brother, and explained the situation to him, giving him the plate number of the car. As he hung up the phone he said, "My brother says you should try to find out more details about these porters from other porters in the market. They all seem to know each other. With a little more information, my brother will try to help more."

"Do you mind if we do it together?" Mazen asked, "Now."

Kamal looked at his watch and said, "I am sorry, I really have to go."

Mazen sighed, "I totally understand."

"I don't think legally anyone can register the land under my name until you complete the inheritance inventory transactions," Kamal said and stood up to go.

"Would you like to wait for that to be done, or would you rather have your money back?" Mazen asked.

"How soon can you give back the money?"

"Honestly, today is only my third day in the shop, and I know nothing about Haj Adel's financial situation yet. I must ask his wife if he has any cash at home. My father never put his money in the bank."

Mazen noticed Kamal's confused expression, "My father has three wives, he lives ... was living with the third."

"Ok, just let me know when I should come to collect the money." Kamal took out a business card and handed it to him. "Please call me when the money is ready, and if you learn more about the porters, let me know."

"By the way, if I'm unable to find any cash of my father's, I could just transfer the amount to you from Dubai," Mazen said, "I live and work in Dubai."

"That would be great as well," Kamal said, as he put on his sunglasses and stepped out of the shop.

Mazen called Abu Sam, told him what he had just learned, and asked for his help in finding more information about his father's porters through his own. A few minutes later, Abu Sam came over with one of his porters.

"I am so sorry for how things turned out," Abu Sam

HUSSIN ALKHEDER

said, "This is Omar from Utaibah." He sat down next to Mazen and Omar stood in front of them, his hands clasped with fingers intertwined, in front of him, like a guilty student standing in front of his teacher.

"Yes, I met him yesterday morning and asked him about our boys," Mazen said.

"Tell Mr. Mazen what you know," Abu Sam instructed.

"I don't know anything," Omar said, looking at the ground.

Mazen looked at Abu Sam, who looked like he was thinking the same thing. Omar was too scared to talk.

"Son, we think those men stole a large amount of money," Mazen said, "If you know anything about them and you hide it, you could be considered an accomplice."

Omar remained silent and didn't even raise his head to look at Mazen.

"Omar," Abu Sam said in a soft voice, "Look at me."

Omar raised his head slightly and looked at Abu Sam.

"No one on earth will dare to harm you as long as you work for me. Don't worry about that. If you know anything, just say it."

Omar went back to staring at the floor, and said, "You don't know how bad those families from Khraibeh are."

Mazen's throat went dry, "What families? Haj Adel had only three boys. They were working for him as porters, no more, no less."

"They lied, or at least they did not inform Haj Adel that they are all cousins," Omar said.

"What?" both Mazen and Abu Sam said. The unbreakable, unwritten law among the traders in the market was they would never hire two porters from the same family. This was in case the trader had a problem with an employee and was forced to fire him, it wouldn't turn into a revenge situation between the other family's members and the trader.

Mazen took out his father's address book and opened it to the page listing porters. "Haj Adel has recorded them here, each with a different family name, Abdul Thakafi, Rawad Khalil, and Sameer Zatoon. So, which of these three families do they belong to?"

"These are all three fake family names," Omar said, "Those three are all from a family called Ghosn."

Mazen stared at Omar's face, trying to detect a hint of a lie, but Omar's eyes reflected only honesty. His skin was tanned from working under the sun. He was wearing worn-out jeans and a gray T-shirt, both dirty from the dust on the boxes in Abu Sam's shop. Of course, these were the clothes he wore during the workday. When he'd seen him the previous morning, Omar was wearing inexpensive clothes, but they were spotless, unlike now. "So, no one even tried to inform Haj Adel that these three were from one family?" Mazen asked.

"I didn't know that they faked their family's name, but I knew it was a rare thing for any shop to accept two porters from the same family," Omar said. He looked from Mazen to Abu Sam before continuing hesitantly, "Everyone is afraid to face Haj Adel's porters."

"You mean any porter of his, or only those three cousins?" Mazen asked.

"The cousins," Omar said. "They are from a family with a long history of vandalism and murder."

Mazen wondered how Omar knew the history of the family; maybe he was exaggerating.

"Of course they didn't start out all working together," Abu Sam said, looking at Mazen, "Can you find out which one started working here first and with whom he worked? Maybe we can find porters who worked with them previously."

"It says here in the book that the first cousin to work for Haj Adel was Rawad, eighteen months ago," Mazen said, glancing at the date in the address book. "At that time, Haj Adel had two other porters, Yusof, and Fahed. Then Fahed stopped working here six months after Rawad arrived. There is no reason written here other than he didn't show up anymore, so of course Rawad and Yusof wouldn't be enough, Haj Adel must have hired a third porter to replace Fahed and that was Abdul."

Mazen looked at Omar before continuing, "Only a week after Abdul's arrival, Yusof stopped showing up for work, and Sameer was hired as Yusof's replacement."

"Omar, do you know where Yusof works nowadays?" Abu Sam asked.

Omar shook his head.

"We won't let him know you are the one who told us how to find him," Mazen said.

Omar looked at Abu Sam.

"I promise, he won't know that you are the one who told Mr. Mazen." Abu Sam said.

"He works at the shoeshine workshop in the alley behind the candy market," Omar said.

Mazen wrote a note on a yellow sticky note.

Omar continued. "Sameer, Rawad, and Abdul always talked about Haj Adel with the other porters in a very bad way. They claimed that Haj Adel never gave them their salaries on time and always deducted too much from their pay. They always referred to him as that senile old man." Omar said. Then, as if he felt guilty for saying such a thing, he continued, "But of course, no one believed them because of their reputation. Many of the porters working in other shops had worked with Haj Adel previously and knew he was never late paying wages."

Mazen remembered Abu Sam's story about the written receipts from Haj Adel without records in his ledgers. He asked, "Do you know where Fahed works right now?"

"He was found dead behind his house. He was also from Khraibeh, and every porter in this market knows who killed him and why," Omar said.

As soon as Abu Sam and Omar left, Mazen closed the shop and headed out to find Yusof.

Similar to the Medhat Basha market, the candy market was covered with a curved ornamental tin roof. Sunlight penetrated the hundreds of holes in the roof, caused by the bullets fired during the revolution against the French occupation of Damascus. These markets, with their rusty roofs, were the best witness to the ferocity of the battle between the two sides.

The market was dim; the air saturated with the scent of rose water, one of the key ingredients of the sugar-coated almonds most of the shops sold. They were called *Mulabbas* and were commonly distributed at weddings and during the ceremony celebrating the birthday of the prophet Mohammad.

Mazen enjoyed the traditional appearance and exotic atmosphere of the market. He was thinking about how he could convince Yusof to talk if he could find him in the first place. The alley behind the candy market had a small gate on the right between a couple of shops.

He stepped into the alley, leaving the relatively dark market for the glaring sunlight. He squinted against the brightness until his eyes adjusted. The alley was very rough with dirty greenish water filling many of the holes in the ground. As Mazen proceeded along the alley, he was forced to jump over the pools of dirty water. There were a few workshops along the alley. He first passed a carpenter shop and then noticed a few boxes of shoe polish stacked next to a black iron gate. One side of the gate was open, revealing a hallway stacked with the same boxes. Mazen didn't need to ask if that was the right place. A blond-haired boy was stacking boxes on the ground. He wore overalls that had once been gray, now almost completely covered in black shoe polish. His sleeves were rolled up and his arms and hands were covered in black. The boy straightened up and looked at Mazen.

"Hello, Yusof." Mazen wasn't sure if this boy was Yusof, but he decided not to give him a chance to deny it, in case it was him.

Mazen expected the boy to ask who he was and what he wanted, but the boy simply stared at him with a shrewd expression.

"Are you related to Haj Adel?" the boy asked.

Mazen exhaled, feeling a lightness in his chest. *It is Yusof.*

"I am his son Mazen,"

"How is Haj Adel?"

Mazen stared at Yusof, trying to catch any hint of deception.

"I am here to talk to you about him," Mazen said, "If you haven't had your lunch, we can have lunch together and talk. It's on me."

"I had my lunch already," Yusof said, "And I can't leave the workshop now, anyway. My boss would deduct from my pay."

"I can come back after you finish work," Mazen suggested. He didn't want the boy to think he was desperate, which, in reality, he was.

"The last bus to Utaibah leaves at 8 and I finish at 7:30. I really need to rush to catch the bus at the garage, otherwise I will end up sleeping in the street."

"Yusof," someone called from the workshop behind a black iron door.

Yusof's confidence disappeared. "That's my boss," he whispered and hurried back inside.

Mazen stood there in the middle of the shop, surrounded by stacks of shoe polish boxes, the air saturated with the smell of the polish. *God knows what kind of crap they mix to make these cheap products.* He realized he could talk with Yusof in a much easier way. He went inside and knocked on the iron door.

A fat man in a shirt and jeans answered, "You are welcome." His large belly strained the buttons of his shirt. A jangle of keys hung from his belt. His bald head gleamed.

"Salam Boss," Mazen said. "I am Mazen Mis'ed, the son of Haj Adel. Do you know Haj Adel?"

"Yes, of course," the man said, "He used to order from us every week, but the last few months he hasn't ordered anything. I don't know why."

"Could you just send his usual order to his shop?" Mazen said.

"Yes, of course," the man said, "Yusof," he yelled.

Yusof came out and looked at his boss, ignoring Mazen.

"You will take ten boxes to Haj Adel's shop as soon as you finish the delivery to Mahmoud's shoe factory." Then he looked at Mazen, "Brother, in one hour, the order will be in Haj Adel's shop."

Mazen thanked him and went back to the shop to wait for Yusof.

When Yusof arrived, pulling the cart with the ten boxes, he left the cart outside and entered the shop.

Mazen hurried outside and helped Yusof carry the boxes in from the cart. Yusof protested that he could carry the boxes inside by himself, but Mazen wanted to break the ice between them.

After the boxes were inside, Yusof gave Mazen the invoice to sign. "Where are your boys?" he asked, looking toward the room at the end of the shop where the boys would usually hang out.

Mazen put the invoice on the desk and said, "Please have a seat."

Yusof opened his mouth in shock as if Mazen had asked him to take off his clothes and stand naked in the middle of the room.

"It's ok," Yusof said, "I don't need to sit, I'm ok standing."

Mazen thought quickly, should he push him to sit? Usually, porters would refuse to sit out of respect for the shop owners. He decided not to push it.

"Is Haj Adel, ok?" Yusof asked. "He never takes a day off." He paused as if he was weighing whether he should say what he was going to say, and then he added, "At least when I used to work here." He looked down at the ground.

Mazen needed to answer quickly and decided to be totally honest with Yusof. "Haj Adel passed away yesterday."

Yusof looked up at Mazen, "What?" He stood there fidgeting in his spot and glancing at the back of the shop as if a monster might come out of the boys' room and eat him. Finally, he said, "I am sorry to hear that sir." He pointed at the invoice and said, "Can you please sign it so I can go?"

Mazen ignored the invoice and said, "I think our porters killed Haj Adel."

Yusof looked into his eyes for a few seconds, which felt like an hour to Mazen. "I am sure they did," Yusof said.

"They stole a large sum of money as well," Mazen said. "We want to catch them, but unfortunately, Haj Adel didn't have any real identification for any of them. Even the phone numbers they gave were false. I'm hoping you can help me track them down."

"Boss, it is not a problem to find them," Yusof said. "The Ghosn family is very well known in Khraibeh, but going to Khraibeh is a death sentence. I don't think you will leave Khraibeh alive if you go after them."

Mazen swallowed. "May I know why you stopped working here?"

"Because of them," Yusof said.

"You mean Abdul, Rawad, and Sameer," Mazen asked.

"I worked only with Rawad and Fahed," Yusof said, "But after Rawad killed Fahed, he brought Abdul to work here. I couldn't stay with Abdul and Rawad more than a week or I would be killed like Fahed."

Mazen asked, "Do you know why Rawad killed Fahed?"

"While I was working with them, I suspected they were stealing from Haj Adel. But one day, Haj Adel received a large amount of money from overseas. I think it was ten thousand dollars. On his way home, two masked men attacked him and took the bag of money. I have no doubt that Fahed and Rawad were the two men who did it. Then we heard Fahed had fought Rawad over a share of the money, and Rawad killed Fahed."

"But there is no evidence to prove they were the men who robbed Haj Adel," Mazen said.

"After Fahed didn't show up here in the shop, Rawad told Haj Adel that Fahed ran away because he was the one who robbed him with the help of his family. Haj Adel didn't know that Rawad and Fahed were from the same family."

"What?" Mazen said, "Fahed is also from the same family?"

"Fahed was the one who brought Rawad in," Yosuf said. "I tried my best not to let them know that I knew they were from same family. That worked until Abdul started working here and Rawad no longer bothered to hide the fact he was stealing from the shop. They asked me many times to steal with them and take a share, but I refused, so they made me leave."

"What sort of things did they do?" Mazen asked.

"You can't imagine the things they used to do, but the worst was changing Haj Adel's medicine."

"What medicine?"

"I don't know what the disease is called. It's when old people forget things that happened only a few minutes earlier." Yusof said. "Haj Adel used to send one of us to buy his medicine from the pharmacy, Rawad always swapped the medicine for ordinary headache pills."

"But how did that help them?" Mazen asked.

"When Haj Adel couldn't remember if he gave Rawad

the money to pay any of the neighbors, Rawad simply took the money, then came back and told Haj Adel that the neighbor was asking for his money. Haj Adel had already forgotten he gave Rawad the money a while ago and would give him more. That happened every day with a few different shops, but they would change the name of the shop every time. Also, they used to tell Haj Adel that there was a traffic fine owing on his car and the police had come and asked for money to remove the fine and spare Haj Adel the hassle of going to the police station to pay the fine. So, Haj Adel would give them the money to pay the policeman. They would repeat the same lie every day. Also, they used to take petrol from the tank of Haj Adel's car and sell it, then ask for more money to fill the tank. That too would happen every day. Also, they would carry Haj Adel's bag for him if he went home on foot, and while he was not looking, one of them would pull cash from the bag. I only saw them do that once, because I did my best to avoid being near them."

Mazen's head was growing hotter, and he could feel the pulsing of a vein in his forehead. "Those sons of bitches."

"Can you sign the invoice for me, please?" Yusof asked.

"Yes sure," Mazen signed and stamped the invoice, but before he handed it to Yusof, he asked, "Do you know how I can find them?"

"I told you, if you just go to Khraibeh and ask about the Ghosn family, you will find them. They are one of the worst families on earth." Yusof said. "Sometimes one must strike the oppressors with even stronger oppressors."

"Do you know who would be best to ask?" Mazen asked.

"There is a fellow named Khanjar who works as a freelance porter and always stands at the head of Dakkaken street nearby. He is from a family in Khraibeh called the Fas. The Fas are mortal enemies of the Ghosn family."

Mazen wrote the name on a small piece of paper and handed the invoice to Yusof as he asked one more question, "May I ask, why did you leave when they asked to leave? Why didn't you report them?"

"I didn't leave when they asked me to," Yusof said, "and I paid dearly for it. The next day, they tied me up in the storeroom and hit me with an iron rod, breaking my left leg. They threatened me if I told anyone what happened, they would kill my whole family."

When Yusof had gone, Mazen closed the shop and went to Dakkaken street, only a five-minute walk from his father's shop through Medhat Basha market. A few freelance porters were standing beside their carts, waiting for any truck driver or shop owner to ask for their service. Most of them wore Turkish shalwar, which was traditional attire for most porters, partly because it was easier for them to work with such loose-fitting pants, and their T-shirts were worn out and dirty.

"Salam guys," Mazen said, not talking to any one porter in particular, "Is Khanjar with you today?"

An old man sitting on his cart who was rolling a handmade cigarette said, "No one of us filled your eyes. You're not interested in any of us, you are asking only for Khanjar?"

"All of you are more than enough if I need someone

for a job," Mazen said, "I just need to finalize my last job with him. You know, settle up his pay." Some of the porters glanced up at Mazen but didn't comment.

One of the younger porters said, "Khanjar hasn't come to the market since Khraibeh was liberated. You will find him in Khraibeh, if he is still alive."

"Does he have a mobile phone?" Mazen asked.

The porters laughed as if Mazen had cracked a big joke. A couple of them were repeating what Mazen had said. "Mobile phone," and laughing.

"In your dreams, someone like Khanjar would have a mobile phone," the old man said and spat a gob of yellow saliva on the ground. "Where do you think you are? In Dubai?" They all laughed again.

Mazen held back his anger and asked, "Does anyone know his home phone number, then?"

None of the porters answered, or even bothered to look at Mazen again. Like a nagging child being ignored by his parents. Mazen gave up and left.

He went back to the shop and put the two leather ledgers in a plastic bag. He was just getting up to switch off the lights and close the shop when a young man entered the shop. He wore a Turkish shalwar and an open shirt showing his chest muscles and Palestinian keffiyeh wrapped around his head like a turban.

"Salam, boss," the young man said.

"Salam brother," Mazen said. He was still standing, with his hand stretched towards the light switches.

"You asked about Khanjar, a while ago," the young man said, glancing outside the shop as if he was afraid someone would hear him.

Mazen relaxed and sat back with his arms crossed. "Yes, I need to find him. Do you know how I can reach him?"

"He is my cousin," the young man said.

Mazen waited for more, but the young man remained silent. "How are you able to leave the Khraibeh, but he is not?"

"I don't live in the Khraibeh, my wife is from Utaibah. We live in a room in her father's house." The young man said. "If you tell me why you need Khanjar, I can try to reach him and let him know?"

Mazen was thinking it made no difference whether he talked to Khanjar or his cousin. All he wanted was to find the three porters. With his arms still crossed, he asked, "How long have you worked in this market?"

"For five years."

"Do you know my father, Haj Adel?"

"Everyone in the market knew your father," the young man said with a smile that exposed teeth that had never been touched by a toothbrush.

"So, you know the porters who worked here as well?"

"Abdul, Rawad, and Sameer." He spat on the ground and said, "Everyone knows those dogs."

Mazen's heart beat faster. He unfolded his arms and said, "What's your name, brother?"

"Rabe'."

"Please have a seat Rabe'," Mazen said, "What else can you tell me about those three dogs?"

Rabe' didn't sit, so Mazen chose not to push him.

"So, you want Khanjar for that matter?" Rabe' asked.

"Yes, I was told Khanjar could lead me to them."

"Khanjar's father was an officer in the army. He was killed by the Ghosn family. The Ghosn family had a big part in liberating Khraibeh from the Syrian army. They belong to an organization called the Sword of Truth, which considers the taking of other people's money, possessions, and even human life as permissible for its followers. Your father's porters bragged in front of the other porters in the market how much money they'd extracted from your father. They used that money to buy weapons to help free Khraibeh from the army's control. Far too many porters from Khraibeh found the actions of these three men inspiring and extracted money from their bosses in similar ways, sometimes using violence, like those three dogs did to your father."

"What violence?" Mazen asked. His heart was jumping in his chest, his hands shaking. He didn't realize he was grinding his teeth together until he felt the pain in his jaw.

"They sent a masked man inside the shop with a Kalashnikov. He held it to Haj Adel's head until he gave them all the cash he had." Rabe' said, "Since the war started, such incidents have happened a lot."

"Can you help me find those dogs? Or at least ask Khanjar to help me?" Mazen asked.

"I can't go to Khraibeh myself, but I will talk with Khanjar tonight. He has no phone in his house, but my father has a phone at his farm in Khraibeh. I will call him and ask him to ask Khanjar to call me back from there."

Mazen promised Rabe' a gift for helping him and Rabe' promised to let him know the details by Saturday morning.

23

Zahra

Zahra exited the school gate, backpack slung over her shoulder. There, just outside, stood a figure she recognized. He leaned against a wall, a leather bag at his feet. Zahra closed her eyes for a few seconds and again stole another glance. He was still there, waiting. A giddy feeling, light as air, filled her. Why had no one ever told her life could feel this wonderful? She held back a smile as butterflies did flip-flops in her stomach.

"Hi, Zahra," George said.

He had the sweetest smile she'd ever seen. She smiled back at him.

"I just thought it would be better if we walked home together. Yesterday, I heard terrible stories about more girls being kidnapped on their way home from school."

She nodded and started walking as he fell in beside her. She didn't care if he was being genuine or just making an excuse to walk with her, she wanted to scream and tell him, 'Yes of course I feel safer walking with you.'

"Aren't you going to say anything?" George asked, suppressing a smile.

"What should I say?" Zahra asked. Her throat was dry, her voice sounded like the first words after waking up from a long sleep.

"Any news about your father?" he asked.

She didn't speak, just shook her head no.

"By the way, Ward sends you his greetings."

I know, you say that every day.

"Are you ok?" George asked.

"Yes, I'm just a bit shy," Zahra whispered. Her cheeks were in flames.

George turned his head away for a moment.

Is he smiling?

When they reached the alley to her house, she stopped. "I'm not going home just yet; I am going to visit Zakiya's sisters."

"Who's that?" George asked.

"Zakiya? She's the other girl who was with me when Ward rescued me."

"Was that the apartment Ward and I dropped you at the first day we met?"

"Yes, exactly."

"Ok, let me walk you there."

She smiled and started walking. It was only a few minutes' walk, but the happiest few minutes in her day, walking beside him.

They reached the gate of the building and George stretched out his arm to shake her hand.

Zahra smiled, "I can't."

George blushed and pulled his hand back, "Bye then, see you later."

"Bye," Zahra said and entered the building, controlling the urge to bounce up the stairs.

Marwa opened the door wearing a long, dark blue dress. Zahra entered, kissed Marwa's cheeks, and put her bag on the sofa.

Ro'wa came out of the girls' bedroom wearing shorts and a T-shirt and kissed her on the cheeks.

"What a nice surprise?" Ro'wa said.

"What did you have for lunch?" Zahra asked.

"Farah cooked some Mujaddara before she left," Marwa said, "Are you hungry?"

"Yes, but my mom will be waiting for me. Where did Farah go?"

"To visit our grandmother," Marwa said.

Zahra sighed, "I have so much to talk about. My mom used to be a great listener, but since my father has been gone, she barely says a word all day."

"A woman without her man is like a tree without roots, any breeze will shake her," Ro'wa said.

Marwa rolled her eyes, "Enough of your poetic philosophy. Our father was always away, and our mom was like a mountain in the middle of a tornado."

"I am just trying to be supportive here," Ro'wa said.

Marwa started to say something, but Zahra interrupted, "Do you believe in love?"

"Someone is in love," Marwa said, looking at Ro'wa and they both laughed.

Zahra's face flushed hot, and she looked down.

Both Marwa and Ro'wa sat on the floor in front of her.

"Tell us about it," Marwa said.

"I really don't know if it's real or I'm just imagining it," Zahra said, still not raising her eyes.

"Yes, I believe in love," Marwa said and sighed, "Love is the sweetest feeling if it is mutual, and most bitter if it's one-sided."

"You should be careful," Ro'wa said, "Men these days will say I love you just to fulfill their own desires."

"Don't scare her," Marwa told Ro'wa. Then, turning to Zahra, she said, "Tell us everything; where did you meet, how did you meet, what are you feeling?"

Zahra's hands were ice cold. "I don't know, I have to go."

Marwa's and Ro'wa's laughter echoed in the corners of the room. They stood up and Marwa put her hand on Zahra's shoulder. "You know we are like your sisters. When you feel ready to talk, we will be good listeners, you'll see."

Zahra smiled and said, "Thank you."

***

Every day, George waited for her outside the school gate and walked her all the way home. He was the first male she had ever walked alone with, besides her father. But walking with George was not just the mere movement of feet to reach a destination while distracted by trivial daily thoughts. It was a complete physical and mental experience for her. As if George was a radiator, her body would get so hot. Her brain would play tricks on her, making her answer his questions faster or slower than usual. Sometimes causing her to make embarrassing slips of the tongue that sent flames to her cheeks. Ignoring the skeptical looks from passersby, she absorbed every single word from George's mouth, as if they were the elixir her life depended on.

Zahra didn't dare breathe a word about it to her mom.

24

Mazen

Next morning Mazen skipped going to the shop and instead headed to the apartment of his father's third wife.

Nora lived in an eighteen-story apartment tower facing the airport roundabout, not very far from where his mother lived. It was just a short walk from the shop to both apartments.

Nora opened the door to Mazen and ushered him into the living room. She was less than half his age, and all three of his sisters were older than her as well. Her face was withered despite her young age, maybe because of the sorrow she felt from losing her husband. She was wearing black from head to toe.

The TV was on the Qur'an channel, and the intonations of the reciter filled the apartment. The room was dazzling due to a large picture window in the front room, showcasing the exotic architecture of old Damascus.

Nora brought tea and put it in front of him, then took a seat to one side of him, out of his direct line of sight, out of modesty. This was Mazen's first time visiting Nora. She reached for the remote and muted the TV, then sat in silence. He thought she was waiting for him to speak. He felt rather awkward.

"It is an enormous loss for all of us," Mazen said.

"Yes, it is," Nora said, "It is so nice of you to come to console me."

Mazen turned to look at her. *Is she being genuine, or is she mocking me?* She looked at him, her eyes full of tears, "You are the only one of Haj Adel's family who remembered he has a wife that deserves to be consoled."

Mazen pressed the bridge of his nose between his thumb and forefinger, squeezing his eyes tightly closed. *What if she realizes I'm not here to console her? God help me.* "I apologize on their behalf. My mother sent me to convey her condolences," he lied, "As you know, she has problems with her knees and can't climb stairs, otherwise she would have come herself."

"That's so nice of her," Nora said while wiping her tears with a tissue, "After the mourning ceremony, I will go to visit her and thank her myself."

Oh no, please don't do that. "She will be so happy to see you," he said while staring out the window. "You have such an enormous skyline here."

"Every evening Haj Adel enjoyed the view while drinking his herb tea."

"Yes, I can see why he enjoyed it," Mazen said, still looking out of the window. The brown roof of Umayyad Mosque with its three minarets and single dome stood out magnificently among the other rooftops of old Damascus houses, most of which had been converted to either very expensive traditional hotels or restaurants.

"I think it was a shock for you," Nora said, "It was so nice of you to come back to the country on such short notice. I think you are an obedient son to Haj Adel."

"Of course, I would leave everything and come back for such an occasion," Mazen said, "But my father was not the reason I came back from Dubai. My daughter

Zakiya was kidnapped a few days ago, that's why I came. I arrived Monday, one day before Haj Adel was taken to the hospital."

Nora gasped.

"Didn't Haj Adel inform you about Zakiya?" Mazen asked.

"No." She started to cry, hiding her face with her hands. "It has been months since Haj Adel has told me anything." Using the same tissue, she blew her nose before continuing, "His Alzheimer's medicine was not helping at all. He was forgetting more and more every day."

"Why didn't you reach out and let us know?" Mazen asked.

"Haj Adel insisted I must not tell you or your brother, so you would not force him to stay at home and not go to his shop anymore."

"There is no power but from Allah," Mazen said.

"What happened to Zakiya? Have you found her?"

Mazen was not pleased by the change of topic, but he answered with pain in his heart when he remembered Zakiya, "Not yet. The death of Haj Adel was so sudden, it completely distracted me. Has anyone told you how he died?"

"Your brother told me over the phone, it was a stroke," Nora said.

"Unfortunately, that's not true," Mazen said. Nora got up and moved to sit in the chair opposite him. With a look of horror on her face, she asked, "What are you talking about?"

"Haj Adel was murdered."

Nora gasped and covered her mouth with both hands.

"All fingers point to his porters," Mazen said, then told

her what he'd learned so far.

"Tuesday morning, Haj Adel received a huge amount of cash; payment for a parcel of land he sold recently," Mazen said. "By any chance, did you receive any money on Tuesday morning?"

"No," Nora said. "Not only that, but recently Haj Adel stopped bringing cash back from the shop with him. Every time I asked him about it, he would say the situation was bad and there was no turnover from the shop."

"That means the porters stole the money," Mazen said, then hesitantly, in a lower voice, he said, "And they killed him."

"Oh, merciful Allah."

"So how are you managing living expenses if Haj Adel was not bringing cash home?"

"During the last year, since he got Alzheimer's, I noticed the only time he brought cash home was when he received your money from Dubai after work hours. He would bring the cash home in the evening and take it to the shop the next morning. Then the cash would disappear. More than once, I asked him why all the cash was vanishing from the shop. He said it was because of the enormous debts owed to the merchants. I had many doubts, but it didn't occur to me that someone might be stealing from him."

"So may I ask when was the last time he brought cash home with him?"

"Six months ago, he received ten thousand dollars from you, and I made up a story about having an operation at the hospital and I needed money. I took the cash and have been using that money for daily expenses."

"Is it possible for me to take a look at his domestic ledger?" Mazen asked. "I want to understand where all the money I sent him disappeared."

"Yes, of course," Nora said, getting up and leaving the room.

Mazen opened the ledger he'd brought with him to the page listing his payments to his father. At the head of the page was written Our Son Mazen Mis'ed. It was the payments for 2012 and most of 2013, only the last payment of seven thousand dollars he had sent two weeks before his flight to Syria was not registered in the book. That meant the porters had found a way to steal the money before Haj Adel even had a chance to record it. The month before that, he had sent Haj Adel nine thousand dollars, and the month before that, ten thousand, and the month before that, nine thousand. That was four months from the current year, now at the end of April. *Where did all of those payments go without spending them on his family?* He added up the money he'd sent during 2012, a total of one hundred and six thousand dollars. It should have been enough for his daughters to live a very luxurious life.

Nora appeared with a small notebook and gave it to Mazen. He opened to the page titled 'Our Son Mazen.' The last time Haj Adel had brought cash to this apartment was in November 2012. Ten thousand dollars Mazen had transferred to him. The amount was recorded in his handwriting as used for an operation for Nora. The entry before that was seven thousand dollars in August. Mazen showed Nora the entry and asked her. "This seven thousand, did he take that with him the next morning?"

"Yes, and that evening he came home with only two

hundred Syrian pounds in his pocket."

Mazen took out his mobile phone and logged into his bank account to check the exact date Haj Adel received the seven thousand in August. It was the twelfth. He opened the shop ledger of the daily transactions for twelve of August. There was no payment registered on that date, but it was registered on the thirteenth of August. That would be the next day when Haj Adel took the money with him to the shop. On the same day, the only big payment Haj Adel made was to the company that was fertilizing his land, for the amount of one thousand dollars. Mazen checked the date of the payment for September. He had sent nine thousand dollars on the fifth of September. Haj Adel recorded the payment on the same day. Mazen went back day by day from the fifth of September to the thirteenth of August to check what significant payments Haj Adel had made that might cause the seven thousand dollars to disappear.

The second large payment was to the company that sprayed insecticides on the trees at his farm in Ghouta, the amount of one thousand dollars. Other than that, the daily expenses were recorded from the thirteenth of August to the fifth of September for the four families. His daughter's apartment and Haj Adel's three apartments came to two thousand dollars. His daughters got the smallest share. From the seven thousand, Haj Adel spent only four thousand, which left three thousand missing.

Mazen knew he was not calculating accurately because the amount in the account of Haj Adel should be much more than the seven thousand dollars he received from Dubai, if the shop was making a profit.

If the only money coming into the shop was seven thousand dollars, then there were three thousand missing.

Mazen took no notice of the time. Using the calculator on his mobile phone and writing notes in the notebook Nora brought to him, he calculated that, out of the one hundred and six thousand dollars he'd sent to Haj Adel during 2012, only thirty-five thousand was recorded as spent money and the rest had mysteriously evaporated. In addition to that, during 2012, Haj Adel had sold six of his landholdings for a total exceeding three hundred thousand dollars. So, in 2012 alone, Haj Adel should have had a financial surplus of about three hundred and fifty thousand dollars. When the battery of his mobile phone died, Mazen raised his head and noticed the sun was setting, and Nora had switched the lights on. He asked her, "Do you know if Haj Adel kept money any place other than the safe here?"

"I don't think he would remember if he did that. He used to have his porters pick him up from our gate, so he wouldn't lose his way going to work. They would drop him back home after work."

"In 2012, Haj Adel sold six parcels of land. Do you know why?"

"He didn't even tell me he sold them." She avoided his eyes. He sensed how hurt she was.

"Do you know if he bought any new land during this year or last year?"

She stood up and said, "Let me bring you the case with his real-estate properties, so you can check for yourself." She left the living room and soon came back carrying a black briefcase. She put it on the tea table in front of Mazen.

Mazen opened the case and checked all the documents. Haj Adel had added no new land or apartments to his real-estate holdings in the last five years. Mazen closed the case and left it on the table. He said, "After the mourning ceremony, we will need these documents to complete the inheritance determination transactions."

"You can take them with you now if you like," Nora said.

"No, the lawyer will come to collect it when he needs it," Mazen said as he stood up to go.

"You didn't drink your tea," Nora said.

"I am sorry." He picked up the cold teacup and drained it in one shot. Putting the cup on the table, he walked out of the room with Nora following him. Before leaving, he turned to her and said, "From the records, at least three hundred thousand dollars are missing from 2012."

He left her standing with her hand over her mouth in dismay.

25

Zakiya

Zakiya opened her eyes, stretched her arms, and groaned. As she got up, she hit her head on the low ceiling of the space under the basement stair where she slept. She rubbed her head ruefully. How many more times would she have to hit her head before she remembered where she was? She hit the button to turn off the alarm. The clock showed 5 am. The last client should be gone by now.

Her sleeping space was only big enough to fit a single mattress, but Zakiya didn't mind. She was just so grateful to have this private space only for her. She slid the deadbolt and pushed open the wooden door. She switched on the single bulb hanging from the grimy ceiling. A weak orange light illuminated the basement enough to reveal its use as a storage area for the supplies needed to maintain a huge house such as this.

Zakiya went to a faucet in the corner. She filled a basin with water and took a sponge bath. When she'd finished, she poured the water carefully down the drain under the faucet, then wiped up the water around it.

A few bundles of used clothes lay at the far end of the basement. The girls had stopped using them, and now they were just waiting to be recycled or given away. She searched through them and chose a loose dress and a headscarf.

Then she unrolled her prayer rug and performed her dawn prayers.

Following prayers, Zakiya ascended to the second floor, where the ladies attended to their clients in any of the twelve service rooms. Each room had an attached bathroom and modest furnishings. None of them were as luxurious as the room she'd woken up in on her first day. That room was the VIP suite reserved for special guests. She went through room by room, picking up trash, collecting empty plates, glasses, and leftover food, then swept and wet mopped the floor. Finally, she gathered up the bed sheets, blankets, and pillowcases and took them to the laundry room.

Two weeks had passed, and she still had met none of the service ladies. The rooms were always empty by the time Zakiya started her morning routine. The girls were always exhausted from their night's efforts, and walked like zombies to their common bedroom, which was like a hospital ward with twenty beds, eighteen of which were occupied.

It took her two hours to finish the twelve service rooms, but that wasn't the end of the cleaning process. Once the laundry was done, she would clean them all again and put the clean bedding back on the beds before evening, when the clients would start to come in again.

She went down to the kitchen on the ground floor, where she washed the dishes and pots and pans, mopped the floor, then cleaned the common bathrooms. She swept and wet-mopped the living room floor before a glance at the clock told her it was eleven, time to wake up Mona.

Zakiya went back to the kitchen, prepared Turkish coffee, and poured it into a tiny porcelain cup. Placing the cup on a spotless golden tray, she carried it carefully to Mona's room and knocked on the door.

"Your mother's dearest," Mona answered from the inside.

As Zakiya entered, she was hit by the stench of stale cigarette smoke. "Good morning, Miss Mona." She set the coffee on a night table beside the bed.

Still beneath the bedcovers, Mona reached under the pillow, pulled out a cigarette packet, extracted a cigarette, and lit it. "Empty the ashtray," she said without even looking at her.

Zakiya picked up the overflowing ashtray and emptied it into the trash can.

"What's the menu for lunch today?" Zakiya asked while standing at the open door.

"Let me enjoy my coffee first. I'll see you in the kitchen in a bit."

Zakiya went to the basement to perform her ablutions and pray the noon prayer. Then she picked up the notepad she used every day to record whatever supplies Mona needed to order. Then she went up to Mona's room, put the list on the night table, fetched the empty cup and took it to the kitchen, where both Mona and Nazih stood talking and smoking.

Nazih continued talking to Mona as if Zakiya wasn't there.

"What would you like me to cook today?" Zakiya asked as she stood at the sink washing the cup and pot.

"You freak," Nazih snapped, "Can't you see Mona and I are talking?"

"Relax, Nazih," Mona said, "We need to start cooking unless you don't want to eat on time."

Nazih glared at Zakiya and stormed out.

"Your mother's dearest," Mona blew out a cloud of smoke, "Today we'll have tabbouleh, hummus, baba ghanoush, mushroom soup, upside down eggplant, raw kibbeh, and a tray of baked chicken."

"Ok, Miss Mona," Zakiya said, waiting for further instructions. She was still learning how to cook.

"Write this down. Soak ten cups of fine bulgur and wash the tomatoes and parsley and chop them finely for the tabbouleh. Roast half of the eggplant in the oven for the baba ghanoush and slice the other half and fry the slices for the upside-down eggplant. Slice the potato and cut up the chicken breasts for the chicken on a tray. Soak fifteen cups of basmati rice. And don't forget to peel and crush five cloves of garlic and mix them into a cup of fresh lemon juice."

Zakiya wrote it all down, then started immediately to work through the list. When everything was ready, she called Mona to start the cooking while she assisted. Soon the fresh aroma of lemon juice and olive oil mixed with the mouthwatering smell of grilled chicken filled the kitchen. Before long, the food was ready and only needed to be carried to the dining table.

Zakiya prepared Turkish coffee for the girls and Mona took the coffee up to wake the girls up. While Mona was upstairs with the girls, Zakiya prepared the table for the girl's lunch. She glanced at the table, filled with steaming dishes enough for twenty people, inhaled the delicious aromas, and smiled. She went to the kitchen and waited for Mona to come back and inform her she could go up to clean the girls' room.

From the kitchen, Zakiya could hear the hurried footsteps of the girls on the stairs mixed with their gay laughter and cheerful voices. She was grateful not to be in any of those girls' shoes. She vowed she would kill herself if she was ever forced to have sex with a stranger.

Mona came into the kitchen, "Okay, go clean up." Then she left to have lunch with Nazih and the girls.

Zakiya went up to the sleeping hall, changed the bed sheets and covers, collected up the dirty ones along with the used towels and loaded them into the washing machines in the laundry room next to the kitchen. She went back to empty the trash cans, and sweep and mop the floor, then she went back to the basement, prayed Assar prayers, and waited for Mona to call her up to clear the table.

Once she'd cleared the table, she had her own lunch in the kitchen alone, then switched the laundry from the washers to the dryers.

It was six o'clock by the time she'd finished washing the plates and pots and wiped down the marble counter in the kitchen. Following that, she got the clean bed sheets and covers out of the dryers, folded them, and went up to the service rooms to put them in the bedding closet.

It was eight in the evening by the time she'd finished with the last of her chores.

Zakiya always followed Nazih and Mona's instructions exactly, otherwise she would face the cruelty of the punishment room, which was the only room she never opened or cleaned in this two-floor villa. Only Nazih had the key for it. After her long, tiring day, Zakiya went down to the basement, took a sponge bath, prayed the rest of her daily prayers, then climbed into her bed. She would follow the same routine the next day and every day.

"Oh Allah, when will you take me out of this place," she begged, as she cried herself to sleep.

26

Mazen

The desire for revenge raged within Mazen like an all-consuming fire. The oppression his father had experienced at the hands of those three dogs was unforgivable. They had taken advantage of his vulnerability and justified it by calling themselves revolutionaries.

Zakiya was still missing, and still he had done nothing to find her. But what could he do? He still had no clue where to start. The circumstances of his father's death had shocked him to his core and broken his heart. All night Mazen tossed and turned in his bed, as sleep evaded him. His level of anxiety was overwhelming. Depression sat like a weight on his heart. He told himself he must find those three dogs and kill them with his own hands. As the sounds of the *Azan* erupted from the minarets of the nearest mosque, he got up, performed his ablutions, and prayed the dawn prayer.

As the first rays of the sun crept over the city, Mazen took his laptop and went to his father's shop. It was still early; no porters were there waiting for their bosses yet. Mazen was the first to enter the market and open his father's shop. It was not a new practice for him. In Dubai, he often went to his office early, enjoying the quiet of the morning, as he drank his coffee, and read the morning newspaper.

He connected the laptop to his mobile phone's hotspot to check his emails and catch up with his work in Dubai. He wasn't really worried since his girlfriend, Julie, was more than competent to take care of everything. He smiled to himself. He would make her his wife when he returned to Dubai once he'd solved the issue of his missing daughter and his father's murder. The cosmetics business was booming in the Gulf countries. So many spas and clinics; the demand was always high. He supplied laser devices used to cure a long list of skin problems. His company also supplied an American brand of hyaluronic acid fillers that plastic surgeons used to treat wrinkles or fill the saggy bits of faces and bodies to make them firmer or slightly larger.

Someone entered the shop and greeted him, "Salam, boss."

Mazen raised his head to find Rabe' standing in front of him. "Good morning, Rabe'."

"What morning? It is already afternoon," Rabe' joked, his smile exposing his damaged teeth.

"Oh, I didn't realize the time," Mazen said looking at the time on his laptop screen, "Were you able to reach Khanjar?"

"Yes. Tonight, you can meet him at my place in Utaibah. We'll leave together after I finish work. I usually catch the last van to Utaibah at eight in the evening. I'll meet you at the garage at ten minutes before eight."

Mazen's mouth was open, he didn't know what to say. He hadn't expected to be going to Utaibah to meet Khanjar, "So if we are taking the last van to Utaibah, how will I get back to the city?"

"Khanjar can only meet with you after midnight, so

even if you leave earlier you will have to wait until midnight to see him. You can spend the night at my place and in the morning, you can come back in the first van into the city with the first batch of porters coming to work."

"Ok, I appreciate your help," Mazen said, "See you this evening then."

After Rabe' left, Mazen called Kamal to let him know he was going to Utaibah that night to meet with someone who could help him find the three porters. Kamal promised to inform his brother.

Mazen then closed the shop and went back to his apartment to take a nap. The lack of sleep was catching up with him.

***

The van was full, and the journey to Utaibah took two hours because of the intermittent stops at inspection points, plus dropping and picking up passengers along the way. It wasn't the first time Mazen had traveled the pitch-black roads of Ghouta at night. Before the war, all that could be heard outside the vehicle was the symphony of nature, its instruments, the insects and animals in the various trees and fields. Nowadays, the dominant noises were rifle shots and bursts of machine gun fire in the distance. The discussions inside the van were even more horrific than the distant sound of flying bullets. Talk about the horrors being perpetrated by the Sword of Truth as they occupied more and more towns and villages in the area.

The van finally came to a stop in the square in front of the Utaibah garage. A single lamppost did a poor job of lighting up the area. The area was surrounded by an impenetrable blackness. Mazen got out with Rabe' and followed him down a dried mud path. Mazen could only see Rabe's faint silhouette, as if he was floating in a black cloud. The scent of sunbaked earth hung heavy in the air, as a chorus of katydids and crickets filled the night. A tiny orange glimmer, getting closer with each step, turned out to be the lightbulb over the door of Rabe's parents' house. Outside was a square porch, where an old man and an old woman sat leaning against the wall with their legs stretched out in front of them. With them were two other men and three women. Rabe' greeted them and introduced Mazen. He introduced the old man and woman as his parents-in-law. The two men were his brothers-in-law. Two of the women were their wives, and the youngest woman was Rabe's wife. Her pretty face shone like a full moon on a dark night.

They were sitting on a straw mat on the ground. Rabe' asked Mazen if he wanted a chair to sit on, but he politely declined. He thought it would be awkward if he was the only one sitting on a chair. He just pulled up the hem of his dish dash slightly and sat down across from them. The three women got up to prepare dinner.

The men were discussing some of their neighbors' issues and Mazen sat quietly listening to them without much interest in the content of their discussion.

The dinner was Mujadara, a common dish comprising black lentils and bulgur, which has all the nutritional elements the human body needs but at the cheapest cost. As a side dish, they had yogurt with grated cucumber, along with fresh-cut onion and green olives. The Mujadara was served on a large plate in the middle, and everyone used their spoons to eat from the same plate. Mazen was hungry, and the aroma of the food was enticing. He didn't care if they all ate from the same plate or even used one spoon. He ate greedily, filling his stomach with the oily Mujadara, washing it down with spoonfuls of yogurt and cucumber. He didn't hesitate to grab pieces of the freshly cut onions and crush them between his teeth to feel the spicy juice seeping under his tongue and the sharp smell penetrating his nasal passages.

After dinner Mazen patted his tummy and said, "Thanks to Allah for this blessing," Then looking at the old man and woman, he said, "Thank you for this lovely food, may Allah sustain these blessings upon you."

"You are more than welcome," the old man said in a deep voice.

The women took away the plates and brought a large pot of tea and some cups. They poured out the strong tea and passed out cups to everyone. Mazen took his and sipped. As the bittersweet brew passed over his tongue, he closed his eyes and savored the moment. A cool breeze touched his face like a silky feather, as if nature sensed his pleasure.

It was almost midnight when the whole family finally vacated the porch and went off to sleep. Only Rabe' stayed awake with Mazen. They hadn't waited long when a masked man appeared on the porch like a phantom in a nightmare. Mazen thought the masked man intended to attack him, but then the man untied the end of his turban, exposing his face. "Salam brothers."

Both stood up and Rabe' hugged the newcomer while patting him on the back. Then with his hand still on the man's shoulder, he turned to Mazen and said, "My cousin Khanjar."

Mazen stretched out his arm and shook Khanjar's

hand, surprised by his powerful grip. Khanjar was the same height as Mazen. His body size was not impressive, but his eyes radiated danger. The weak orange light was not enough to reveal the actual color of his clothes, but Mazen assumed they were black. He wore a Turkish shalwar and a jacket with many pockets, like the ones hunters wore in some of the movies he'd seen.

They sat down together on the porch, and Khanjar's voice was like a hissing snake. "Rabe' tells me you are looking for the boys who worked for Haj Adel. I think you are a relative of Haj Adel, are you not?"

"I am his son," Mazen said.

"I can tell. You have the same warm eyes as your father. How is he?" Khanjar asked.

"He's dead. Those boys killed him and stole a huge amount of money from him."

"Killing is not unusual for them. They have killed plenty of people, including my father," Khanjar said, "The Ghosn's are a mercenary family. Since the beginning of the revolution, they have become super rich by every evil deed that could enter the human mind. Everything from kidnapping to sex slavery, robbing rich people, killing, and organ trading. You name it."

Mazen's heart thumped harder in his chest, and a shiver went through him. He felt short of breath, and his mouth filled with saliva. He swallowed hard to avoid drooling and took a couple of deep breaths. The two men stared at him.

"Are you ok, brother?" Rabe' asked, concern obvious on his face.

Mazen raised his right hand, palm facing them to assure them he was ok. His left hand went to his chest as he closed his eyes and took several deep breaths, blowing them out slowly. He took a few minutes to calm himself.

Khanjar asked, "Do you have a heart problem?"

"Not at all, it's just that my daughter was kidnapped a week ago, and I don't know how to find her."

"Sorry to hear that," Rabe' said, as he avoided looking straight into Mazen's eyes, "Thousands of young women have disappeared since the war began."

"What is the fate of such women?" Mazen asked.

"Jihad al-Nikah," Rabe' said.

"No," Khanjar said "They don't kidnap women for Jihad al-Nikah. They smuggle the kidnapped women into Lebanon, Jordan, or Turkey and sell them as sex slaves."

Another shiver went through Mazen. "What are the chances of any of those women being rescued?"

Both Rabe' and Khanjar remained silent, avoiding Mazen's gaze.

"So why do you want to find those men?" Khanjar asked.

Mazen looked at Khanjar as if he was talking Turkish, "Are you serious? If someone killed your father and stole his money, wouldn't you want revenge?"

"They killed my father and yes, I want revenge, but they are powerful and extremely dangerous. They have joined the Sword of Truth. The stated purpose of this organization is the fight for freedom, which would be noble, but their real purpose is to make money, and that suits the Ghosn family very well."

"I want revenge for my father," Mazen said.

"But you are only one person, and they are a very large organization," Khanjar said.

"That's why I asked to see you, and I am ready to pay whatever it costs to find these boys and..." Mazen paused, then said, "...and kill them."

Khanjar said, "If you think you will have any chance against them, you are mistaken. You don't have the resources to fight them. The Syrian army knows them very well and even they won't go against them yet. You are certainly not smarter or stronger than the Syrian army."

"So, are you telling me you agreed to see me just to tell me I can't do anything?" Mazen folded his arms.

Khanjar took out a small metal box, opened it, and began rolling a cigarette. While he was licking the edges of the paper and wrapping it around the tobacco, he looked at Mazen intently.

"If they are the ones kidnapping people, do you think I will have any chance of finding my daughter?"

"There is only one way to get what you want from those wicked people," Khanjar said as he lit his cigarette with a match.

"What is that?"

"Money." Khanjar blew out a cloud of smoke. The smoke rose slowly in the dim light of the bulb, making Mazen feel as if he was sitting in on a witchcraft ritual.

"So, I should pay them money to get my father's money back?" Mazen asked, the corner of his mouth twisted sarcastically.

"I don't think you can get your money back," Khanjar said, "But If they are the ones who kidnapped your daughter or if they know who kidnapped her, they might bring her back if you paid them a ransom."

Mazen's hopes were raised a little. Was it possible he could find his daughter? Was negotiating with his father's killers the only way to free his daughter? "Would it be possible for you to arrange for me to meet with them?"

"If anyone from that family sees me, they will shoot me immediately," Khanjar said.

"What about someone from the Sword of Truth?" Mazen asked.

"They are members of the Sword of Truth," Khanjar said.

"Can you tell me the real reason you agreed to see me?"

"The same reason you came here. For revenge."

Mazen looked at Rabe' and asked, "Didn't he just say I have no chance against them?"

Rabe' didn't comment, he just looked at Khanjar as if waiting for an answer.

"Unlike you, I have a plan," Khanjar said.

"Is there a role for me in your plan, and what do you see as the outcome of your plan?"

"Purely revenge only," Khanjar said as he watched the smoke rising from his lips. "All I need is a car bomb, and I will blow up their entire stockpile of weapons."

"How much would that cost?" Mazen asked.

"Only one hundred thousand dollars," Khanjar said.

"So, if I could get you that much, you would blow up their warehouse? But I don't see how that will get my father's money back or rescue my daughter."

Mazen stared at the mosquitoes dancing around the bulb. Khanjar and Rabe' just looked at him.

"I can give you the money for revenge on one condition," Mazen said.

"What is that?"

"If you arrange for me to have a meeting with them as

a human trafficker."

"That would be very dangerous," Khanjar said, "and there is no guarantee they are the ones who kidnapped your daughter. They won't let you go free if they don't have your daughter. They will only take your money and you will be lucky if they don't kill you."

Mazen didn't know if he was driven by heroism or stupidity. Maybe if he was able to get inside the lion's den, he could find a way to kill his father's killers or, at the very least, die trying.

"If you want to carry out your plan to blow up their weapons warehouse, you must arrange for me to meet with them and not worry about my safety," Mazen said.

***

Next morning Mazen headed back to the city in the first van, leaving Utaibah. Unlike the night before, he was now able to see the destruction on both sides of the road. Before the war, when he used to drive out to his father's farm, the road passed through a virtual tunnel formed by the intertwined branches of trees and bushes on both sides, so thick one could barely glimpse the farms behind them. Now it was a long depressing road, with burned tree trunks on both sides exposing a blasted expanse of soil only good for burying the hundreds of martyrs of the war.

Khanjar had agreed to arrange a meeting for him with someone from the Sword of Truth. He'd told Mazen to call him when he had the money put together.

When Mazen entered the apartment, his three daughters gathered around him like butterflies around a sweet, scented flower.

Farah, the eldest, prepared breakfast and they devoured it while he told them what he'd learned about

Haj Adel's porters and his meeting with Khanjar the night before.

"Now I have a problem," Mazen said, "How can I transfer such a huge amount of money to Syria? The entire country is under extreme sanctions."

"How did you transfer money to grandfather?" Marwa asked. She wore a maroon dress, a perfect match for her fair skin and curly honey-colored hair.

"I never transferred more than ten thousand dollars at one time to Haj Adel. I just deposited Emirates dirham at a money transfer company in Dubai, and Haj Adel would receive the amount in Syrian currency based on the exchange rate of the central bank. It was all very costly and slow, but completely legal. I didn't want to cause any problems for Haj Adel with the authorities here."

"So now you need to change the money to American dollars instead of Syrian pounds?" Ro'wa asked. She was wearing denim pants and a green sweater. Her skin, like Marwa's, was fair, but her hair was straight and black. Of the four girls, she looked the most like her mother, Hadiya. That's why she was the least favored daughter to him, but he never revealed that to anyone except his girlfriend Julie.

"Yes, but the maximum that can be transferred monthly is ten thousand dollars."

"Why don't you ask Uncle Bassem? We heard recently he converted his fortune to dollars and buried it all in a cave." Farah said, the three girls giggled. She wore yellow pajamas, and unlike her other sisters, her complexion was slightly darker. He smiled not because of her joke but because he was remembering the reason he named his first daughter Farah. Farah means happiness. He thought if he named her happiness, his life would be less miserable. But he was mistaken.

"You know, my brother Bassem never showed up at the shop, or the hospital, or even the graveyard after your grandfather passed away. I know relations between them were not ideal, but I didn't know it was to the point of not speaking to each other at all. I think if Bassem had interfered earlier when Haj Adel's neighbors spoke to him, the…" Mazen paused, he didn't want his daughters to think badly of their uncle.

"Uncle Bassem hasn't left his apartment for more than a year," Farah said, "His family says he has been ill and can't even move. But we know the truth. When the war started, many rich people disappeared and their families received calls from kidnappers asking for huge ransoms. The sad thing is, most of the time, those rich men were returned to their families as mutilated carcasses or never returned at all, in some cases."

Mazen swallowed.

"His wife told us he received threats. They put a five hundred-thousand-dollar price on his head even without kidnapping him," Marwa said.

"He didn't need to receive threats to be cautious. Many of the rich men in the neighborhood were kidnapped," Ro'wa said.

Mazen touched his throat.

"What about before the war? Did your uncle Bassem visit you even after your brother Khaled left?" Mazen asked.

"He has never visited us," Farah said.

"The only ones who cared about us, especially after mom passed away, were Mullah Abdullah and his wife Amani," Marwa said.

"The mullah used to be my closest friend in our school days," Mazen said, "We share some fantastic memories. But after he studied Islamic Sharia at university, our relationship grew cold."

"His daughter Zahra told us the mullah once told her a very funny story about your reading teacher in your school days, who was a wet talker," Marwa said. The three giggled.

His cheeks got hot, and he wondered if his daughters noticed his embarrassment because they went from giggles to laughter. "It was in the seventh grade. I used to sit in the front row, and that teacher was reading to us out loud when suddenly a big droplet of spital flew from his mouth and landed on my face. The teacher merely wiped my cheek with his hand and continued the reading as if nothing had happened. He had terrible halitosis, and the smell of his saliva just about killed me until the class was over and I could go and wash my face."

His daughters were enjoying the story.

"The mullah was the only real friend I had throughout my school days."

"It's really sad how he just disappeared," Ro'wa said.

"He's one in a million." Mazen said, "But now, I have to find someone to take care of you, especially after losing your grandfather."

The smiles disappeared from his daughter's faces as they looked at each other.

"Why don't you come back and stay here with us?" Ro'wa asked.

"Ro'wa!" Marwa and Farah said in unison.

"Well? We need someone to look after us, don't we? Uncle Bassem has never cared about us. With

Grandfather passing away so suddenly and Mullah Abdullah disappearing like thousands of others, we're left with no one. If our father doesn't take care of his daughters, who will?" Ro'wa said with a shaky voice while giving her sisters a pleading look.

"Enough, Ro'wa," Farah snapped as she turned to Mazen, "Don't listen to her. We know you're busy in Dubai, and we appreciate everything you do for us."

Ro'wa started to cry, and Marwa put an arm around her shoulders, saying, "Don't cry, Ro'wa. Allah never let us down before, and Allah won't let us down now." Marwa shot Farah an accusing look.

Mazen thought about how his father had forced him to marry Hadiya. He hadn't had the audacity to voice his objection, but he had never loved her. He'd never felt happiness until the day he left to live in Dubai and met Julie. Mazen looked at his three daughters. He really didn't want to come back and live with them because every time he looked at them, it would remind him of Hadiya. This was not his life anymore. His life was with Julie, and he wanted to spend the rest of his life with her. His daughters were used to their life here, and surely the war would not last forever. When the war ended, they would marry and become their husbands' responsibilities.

"I am more useful to you in Dubai than if I stay here. Don't worry, I will make sure you have enough money to live decently. And I will pray for the three ... the four of you to get married and live happy lives."

"We don't want money, we want you to be with us," Ro'wa said.

"Ro'wa, please stop it," Farah said in a soft voice.

Ro'wa stood up and ran to their bedroom, slamming

the door behind her. Farah and Marwa avoided looking at him.

"I am going to go see Bassem, he might help me," Mazen said to break the awkward silence, as he stood to leave.

"Dad, please don't say anything to him about what we told you," Farah said in a low voice.

He didn't reply, just nodded to them and went out the door. His brother's apartment was only fifteen minutes' walk. His wife opened the door, and her wide smile revealed a toothless mouth. After a few words of greeting, she led him to his brother's bedroom. The room smelled of saliva, and body odor.

Bassem was overweight, the rocking chair barely visible beneath him. When he saw Mazen, he smiled, but only with his lips. His fat saggy cheeks didn't move.

"Please forgive my manners, for not standing to greet you," Bassem said, his voice raspy, his extra wide dish dash stretched to its limit, barely containing his bulk.

"Don't worry," Mazen said. He couldn't see a place to sit, so he moved to sit on the edge of the bed. "How are you, brother?"

"I am not good, brother. This sickness is destroying me," His breathing was labored. "I can't walk any distance," he wheezed. "I can't climb stairs. I've stopped going to my business," Bassem started coughing, his face turning purple. Mazen stood up and glanced at the closed door. Then he came nearer him and asked, "Are you ok?" But his words were drowned out by Bassem's violent coughing. Again, Mazen glanced at the closed door.

"Don't worry, I won't die, at least not yet." Bassem's wide chest shook as he made alarming noises in his throat, clearing mucus from his airway, which he spat in a bucket beside his rocking chair.

Mazen sighed, "Thanks be to Allah."

"How is your business?" Bassem asked, "I am sorry I couldn't come to help you with Haj Adel's burial, but Allah is the greatest. I am glad you came back at the right time."

Mazen informed Bassem about Zakiya and the matter of the money.

"Oh brother, I wish I had that much to help you," Bassem said.

"I don't want money from you," Mazen said, "I just need a way to transfer the hundred thousand dollars from Dubai as soon as possible."

"That's not a problem, pass me the phone please," Bassem pointed to the table at the side of the bed. Mazen stood and brought the cordless phone to him.

Bassem dialed a number and waited for a response, holding the receiver to his ear, "Hello. How are you.... I need one hundred kilos of pistachios.... No......." He covered the receiver with his hand and whispered to Mazen, "From where?"

Mazen whispered back, "Dubai."

Bassem uncovered the receiver and continued, "Dubai ... How much? ... How long ... uhuh ... uhuh ... uhuh ... ok, thank you." and he hung up.

"To receive one hundred thousand dollars here will cost you a hundred and twenty-five thousand dollars," Bassem said.

Mazen opened his mouth, then closed it and swallowed hard. "Ok. To whom do I transfer the money in Dubai, or is it some other country?"

"You want cash delivered here, you give cash to a

guy in Dubai," Bassem said, "You don't need to know to whom, you just give me two numbers, one for the person who will provide the money in Dubai, and one for the person who will receive it here."

"Do you trust this man?" Mazen asked.

"You don't need to worry about him, you know me," Bassem said, and winked.

"But you said you don't have that much. What if the man takes the money in Dubai and doesn't deliver it here?" Mazen asked.

"Don't you worry. You will get your money all right," Bassem said and coughed. Again, he cleared his throat loudly and spat in the bucket.

Mazen gave him Julie's number in Dubai and told him to give the man his father's shop number to receive the money. Then he left Bassem's apartment. Once outside, he drew a deep breath and exhaled slowly.

Mazen went to his father's shop and called Julie in Dubai to prepare the cash and wait for a call from the courier. It wasn't the first time they had contacted each other since he arrived in Syria – they texted daily, like teenage lovers – but it was the first time they had spoken on the phone. Her voice was like cold water pouring over his heart, refreshing and soothing. The elation he felt was exactly what he needed after all the gloom surrounding him. He explained everything to her, from the situation with his daughters to what had happened with his father. Julie was a perfect listener, and that was one of the many things he loved about her, along with countless other qualities.

Ten minutes after they hung up, he received a text from her, letting him know she had already received the call, and the courier would be there to collect the money the next day.

Mazen then composed a long email to his lawyer in Dubai, including the phone numbers of his mother, brother, and the mullah's house. He instructed the lawyer to reach out to his daughters if anything unexpected happened to him during his mission. If he was kidnapped, the lawyer would transfer the money to his daughters to pay his ransom. Of course, his lawyer was a woman – he wouldn't let a man contact his daughters.

The next day, while he was in the shop, Julie called, and he answered his mobile phone like a child grabbing candy before anyone else could.

"Hi love," Mazen said softly.

"Hi Sugar," Julie said, "The currier came and collected one hundred and twenty-five thousand dollars in cash."

"Thank you, I'll let you know when I receive it," Mazen said.

"The lawyer called and told me about your concerns," Julie said. "I am worried. There's no good news coming from your side, and what you told me yesterday made me even more anxious."

"I'm sorry love, I didn't mention it yesterday. I just didn't want you to worry," Mazen said, "I promise I'll finish what I came here to do, and then I'll come back to be with you forever."

"I'm praying for your safety," Julie said. She then briefed him on some business matters at the office, and before ending the call, added, "Don't worry. If anything happens to you over there, I'll move mountains to bring you back."

27

Mullah Abdullah

The mullah wore a loose white linen shalwar, which barely covered his calves, leaving his shins and ankles exposed. Over that he wore a long white linen shirt which covered him down to his knees, and a brown vest. He positioned his turban on his head, with its free end dangling down the left side, which he then threw over his right shoulder, so that it crossed under his chin and around his neck. Comrade Ghulam from Afghanistan had informed him that this attire, including the Perahan Tunban, was the traditional Taliban Pashtun dress. He slipped his feet into his sandals and inserted the tiny earphone into his right ear.

He stared at his reflection in the mirror and didn't recognize the man looking back at him. After eight weeks of shirtless training in the sun, his skin was a ruddy brown. Flabby fat had been replaced with firm muscles in his belly and chest. His white beard was now the color of rusty metal after he'd dyed it with henna. He looked exactly like the men from Afghanistan he used to see on the news. Now he was one of them.

As he left his room, the wind was blowing so forcefully it took all his strength to close the door. The wind roared in his ears like a shrieking ghost, and the flags flapped frantically, threatening to tear at any moment. He tilted his head to prevent the flying sand from entering his eyes, and leaning against the wind, he crossed the parched ground to the main building, which was a cluster of shipping containers converted into the classrooms they used for training. A white land cruiser was parked outside the main building. Today was the last day of training for him and his partner, Abu Moos. They were about to be briefed for their first mission.

The mullah entered the windowless meeting room to find an army officer standing in front of the whiteboard. Abu Moos and three other men he'd never met before were sitting on metal folding chairs. They were all dressed in clothes and turbans just like his, all with the ends slung under their chins. Their beards were also long and tinted with henna. The mullah felt as though he had traveled back in time a thousand years.

"Peace be upon you," the mullah said.

Everyone stood up and replied, "Peace be upon you, Your Highness."

The mullah turned to see if some royal personage had entered the room behind him, but there was no one there. He realized they were greeting him. Comrade Ghulam had informed him that Sword of Truth members always addressed their high-ranking leaders as 'your highness,' as they considered them to be princes.

The officer approached and greeted him with a snappy salute, then shook his hand. "I am Lieutenant Hazem, Your Highness," he said, then with a sweeping gesture of his hand toward the rest of the men still standing, he said, "This is your team." Hazem's orangey brown hair was cut short, army style. His wrinkled face was deeply tanned and clean-shaven.

"Understood," the mullah said. When he had taken

his seat, the rest of the men sat down. Hazem went to the whiteboard, picked up a marker and wrote at the top, "Your Highness Shaddad Abu Saif."

"Remember now, you are, Your Highness Shaddad Abu Saif," Hazem said.

The mullah raised his head as if he had just awakened from a dream.

Hazem proceeded. "These men will accompany you on the first phase of the operation. They are among the government's best agents who have been planted within the rank and file of the Sword of Truth organization for more than a year now. They are men you can rely on."

"Ok," the mullah said.

Hazem unrolled a paper map and secured it to the whiteboard with magnets, then started his explanation.

Hazem turned to the mullah, "By now, you know your assignment is to take the place of Shaddad Abu Saif who's being sent by The Sword of Truth to Ainal town to complete a deal with the officer in charge of the Syrian military base there to occupy both Ainal town and the military base. I will now brief you on the method by which you will replace him and his assistant."

Hazem took a packet of cigarettes from his shirt pocket, pulled one out with his lips, and lit it. His cheeks hollowed as he held a match to the end, then blew out a puff of smoke before continuing. "The real Shaddad Abu Saif and Abu Moos will attend a meeting with their top leaders in Zondar village in Turkey, which is along the Turkish border with Syria. They will cross the Syrian border at the Ain Dewar checkpoint. From there they will travel by road to Ainal. The convoy of Shaddad Abu

Saif and Abu Moos will comprise six cars, all of them white Land Cruisers, like the one you saw outside. One for Shaddad Abu Saif and Abu Moos plus two guards; the other five will have only one man in each."

"At Ain Dewar checkpoint, your team will take the place of the five guards in the cars following the car of Shaddad Abu Saif and Abu Moos. Then, before they arrive at Ainal, we will attack the convoy, causing the real Shaddad Abu Saif and Abu Moos to radio Ainal for backup. By the time the backup arrives, the real Shaddad Abu Saif and Abu Moos will be dead and replaced by you. For anyone who has never met Shaddad Abu Saif and Abu Moos, you will be accepted without question. Then they will accompany your convoy to Ainal, and you will begin your duties there." Hazem paused and looked at the men who were staring back at him as if he'd just finished disarming a nuclear warhead.

The mullah glanced at his team, expecting the four of them to flood Hazem with questions, but no one showed any sign of curiosity. He shifted his gaze to Hazem and asked, "How will we replace the guards?"

"We will take the five men into custody at the border. You will drive their cars and accompany the car of Shaddad Abu Saif and Abu Moos all the way to five kilometers outside of Ainal town. That's when the army will attack, causing Shaddad Abu Saif to call for support."

"How will we be able to replace the five guards without Shaddad Abu Saif and Abu Moos noticing that the five men accompanying them are different?" the mullah asked again.

"The border point at that time will be under the

control of the special forces of the third wing of the army, so there will be no room for error." He dropped his cigarette butt and crushed it with the heel of his boot. "Shaddad Abu Saif and his men will be held in separate glass-walled interrogation rooms equipped with cameras and special voice recorders. While they are being questioned, a technician will program devices to mimic the voice tones of the five men driving the five cars accompanying Shaddad Abu Saif and Abu Moos. That way, when you take their places, your voices will sound the same over the two-way radio."

"What about ..."

"Hold on, one moment, your highness," Hazem interrupted the mullah. "Throughout the interrogation, Shaddad Abu Saif and Abu Moos will be able to see their men the whole time through the glass walls. They will not be out of sight for a moment. Once we release them, they will meet and converse outside, and naturally Shaddad Abu Saif will want to know what questions the interrogators asked his men. But that will be the last time Shaddad Abu Saif and Abu Moos see the original drivers before you take their place."

Hazem lit another cigarette, exhaling a long plume of smoke.

The mullah seized the chance to ask, "Wouldn't a better time to replace the guards be during the interrogation, how will we replace them after they leave the interrogation rooms?"

"We will use a distraction technique with Shaddad Abu Saif during the interrogation," Hazem said. "Our officer will ask for a bribe to allow his vehicles to pass through customs with minimal inspection while also permitting their personal weapons, especially since their weapons are made in Israel, and that is a big no-no. Shaddad Abu Saif will inevitably agree and pay the bribe. Of course, the officer will emphasize to Shaddad Abu Saif the need for complete discretion to ensure no one suspects a bribe was involved. Shaddad Abu Saif will explain all this to his men when they meet after the questioning."

"The first car to enter the inspection hangar will be Shaddad Abu Saif's. The soldiers will pretend to search it, overlooking any weapons. After Shaddad Abu Saif's car passes inspection and leaves the hangar, each of the remaining five cars will enter the hangar in turn. The drivers will be taken into custody, stripped of their clothing, and you will take their places after putting on their clothes. Then you'll drive the vehicles out." Hazem dropped his cigarette butt, not bothering to crush it with his boot this time.

"What if Shaddad Abu Saif doesn't drive away but instead waits for the other cars after passing the inspection? Won't he notice his drivers have been changed?" The mullah asked.

"At the Ain Dewar checkpoint, the inspection hangar is the last stop, and when the cars leave the inspection hangar, they won't be allowed to stop before the exit. It is unlikely Shaddad Abu Saif will stop and wait for others outside the checkpoint, because in their protocols they don't stop or leave their cars on traveled roads. Shaddad Abu Saif and Abu Moos and the two guards in their car will not know that the other drivers were changed, and if they try to communicate by radio, the voice-altering machines will change your voices." Hazem said.

"What if they don't cross the border through the Ain

Dewar checkpoint?" the mullah asked.

"Sword of Truth agents always move through official channels. They are managed by organizations like Mossad and the CIA, they know how things work in this country. They never take the mountain roads. However, our intelligence agents among them will inform us in case they change their route."

"Why go through all this hassle? Why not just arrest the corrupt officer at the army base in Ainal to prevent the deal from happening in the first place?" the mullah asked.

"First, your mission is not to prevent the deal from going through. The exact opposite. We want you to negotiate with the officer through the final stages. Second, we don't know who the officer is. We only know through intercepting their communications that someone will complete the deal with the Sword of Truth."

"Then if you don't know who the officer is, how will I know who he is after killing Shaddad Abu Saif and Abu Moos?" the mullah asked.

"That's why we are not killing Shaddad Abu Saif and Abu Moos until we attack them outside of Ainal and force Shaddad Abu Saif to call for help. Remember, he is working in disguise in the beginning, so his communication will be only with the officer who is completing the deal. When he calls for support, the only person he will call will be the officer. Then, when the officer sends his troops and rescues you, the real Shaddad Abu Saif and Abu Moos will already be dead, and you will be in their place."

"But the forces won't see the bodies of Shaddad Abu Said and Abu Moos?" the mullah asked.

"The officer at the army base doesn't know what Shaddad Abu Saif or Abu Moos look like or even who the people are that the Sword of Truth is sending to meet him. So, when our army kills the real Shaddad Abu Saif and Abu Moos, and the two guards in their car, and you take their place in their car. The four dead bodies will be put in the other cars behind the steering wheels as if they were killed in the attack."

"Won't the officer be suspicious when Shaddad Abu Saif calls him about the attack on the convoy and think he's been exposed?" the mullah asked.

"Our army will attack under cover, as if they are just another rebel group. Their vehicles will be normal trucks, and they'll be in civilian clothes. There will be nothing to show they are part of the official army."

"When we reach Ainal and I meet with the officer, how will I be in touch with the Sword of Truth leaders to know what they will offer to the officer?" the mullah asked.

"The laptop and mobile phone of Shaddad of Abu Saif will be in your possession. Our technicians will extract all the information and will tell you what to do next," Hazem said.

"What if Shaddad Abu Saif doesn't call the corrupt officer? What if he calls his leaders in Turkey, and they are the ones who call the officer?" the mullah asked.

Hazem folded his arms, a sly grin twisting the corner of his mouth, "It doesn't matter who calls the officer. The moment he dispatches the rescue force for Shaddad Abu Saif's convoy, his cover will be blown. So, if you don't have the chance to complete the mission by replacing the real Shaddad Abu Saif and negotiating the deal with the officer, we can still extract that information through interrogation once we know who he is. But that would mean your mission didn't succeed as planned."

"But what about the Sword of Truth if we do succeed? Don't you think they will discover that I am not the real Shaddad Abu Saif," the mullah asked with crossed arms.

"We have thought through all these details. You are not alone in this mission, there is a huge team working to pull it together. As you were taught in your training, not everything you see and hear is reality. At times we may appear to be weak and losing the battle, while in reality, we are working to win in ways neither Mossad nor the CIA have even thought of," Hazem said.

***

The smoothness of the Land cruiser astonished the mullah. It was as if he was riding on a cloud. So powerful, yet so responsive. Comrade Abu Moos was beside him in the passenger seat, and the other three men were in the back.

Finally, after several hours of driving, the blue signboard 'Welcome to Ain Dewar' came into view. The mullah relaxed his foot on the fuel pedal, slowing the Land cruiser to prepare for the exit.

"After the entrance ramp, turn right. Enter the hangar, and wait for further instructions," the voice in his ear said. The mullah did as directed.

Over the entrance to the hangar, a sign read: Vehicle Maintenance. The car bumped slightly upon entering and the mullah drove forward, stopping the car at the far end of the hangar.

This vehicle was certainly much higher off the ground compared to the old cars he was used to riding in Damascus. He almost had to jump down to reach the ground. When he closed the door, it made a satisfying muted click. His team did the same and circled him.

A young soldier entered the hangar carrying two plastic bags; one filled with sandwiches and the other contained white bottles.

"Falafel and yogurt," the soldier said, handing each man his share.

The mullah was enjoying the warmth of the mashed falafel with tahini when the voice erupted in his ear again. "The subjects will arrive in about forty-five minutes. Stay alert."

The mullah finished his sandwich and crumpled the paper wrapper as he drained the last of his yogurt. He threw the paper and the plastic bottle in the plastic bag they'd come in. Then the voice in the mullah's ear told him the convoy was approaching and what he must do next. He spoke to the men around him. "Comrades, our target will arrive in a few minutes, so be prepared. Wait for my signal to move over to the search hangar."

More than an hour passed before the voice erupted in his ear again, "We have a complication." The voice went on to explain the change in plans to the mullah.

The mullah looked at comrade Abu Moos and the other three men, all of them wearing Perahan Tunbans. Their rust-colored, hennaed beards, bushy and wide like dustpans. Their turbans looked like eagles' nests on their heads. "The plan has changed," the mullah said to the men, looking at him.

"The Sword of Truth drivers must stay with us in the cars," the mullah said.

The men looked at one another with wide eyes and open mouths.

"The GPS chips are planted in the drivers' bodies, not

in the cars, so we need the drivers to be inside the cars as long as the real Shaddad Abu Saif and Abu Moos are alive."

"How are we supposed to be in the cars while they are in them?" Abu Moos asked.

"They won't be any trouble, since they'll be dead," the mullah said. He couldn't believe what he was saying. It was like the movies he and Zahra watched together. A sharp sting pierced his heart as he remembered his daughter, igniting a fire in his soul.

***

"They just wanted to humiliate us. Sons of adultery," a voice erupted from the radio of the car the mullah was driving in place of Abu Mus'ab whose body was stuffed in a body bag and lying on the floor between the front and the back seats. It was late evening by the time the six cars left Ain Dewar and were speeding down the ink-black road to Ainal. Abu Mus'ab's Uzi and the handgun provided by the officer in Ain Dewar lay on the seat beside the mullah.

"Allah won't allow anyone to humiliate his righteous servants," said another voice, farther from the microphone. *Ah, that must be Shaddad Abu Saif and Abu Moos in the lead car,* the mullah decided. *They're sharing their frustrations with the other drivers. Too bad they can't hear them anymore.*

"There is no power but from Allah," the first voice said, "Thirteen hours have passed since we entered Ain Dewar. It's obvious they just wanted to humiliate us?"

"Don't worry, brother Abu Moos, the days of this criminal regime are numbered." *I was right, that must be Shaddad Abu Saif.*

"Yes, your highness, that's the hope."

"Our top leaders are negotiating the possibility of uniting with the Winning Wing in the south so we will be more powerful, then we will come from north and south of Syria, like crocodile jaws ready to crush the government," Shaddad Abu Saif said.

Did they forget the radio is on or are they talking over the radio purposely to let all the drivers hear them?

"I think the Winning Wing leaders only care about money and power," Abu Moos added.

"Our leaders in Turkey are optimists, the newly assigned caliph will throw all his strength into uniting all the oppositions so that as one Islamic state we will vanquish this criminal regime. Once more, we will rise as a powerful Islamic state over this blessed land and return the glories of the Umayyad states. Once more we will spread the real Islam to all parts of the earth, starting from here," Shaddad Abu Saif said.

"Your Highness, what about the other newly born Islamic state, the one arising from the west of Iraq? Do you think they will agree to be a part of our state as well?"

"They must obey the Sword of Truth, otherwise, they will taste the sharpness of our swords. In the history of the Umayyad states too many tiny new states tried to rise up, but they were smashed down, like Abdullah bin al-Zubair who tried to take over the city of the prophet Mohammad in Saudi Arabia, but the army of Yazid bin Mu'awiyah destroyed him."

Quite a pep talk for his men. In the time of Yazid bin Mu'awiyah, there were no Saudi. The army of Yazid attacked the city of the prophet and killed most of the prophet's companions, then he went to Mecca and battered the Kaaba with catapults, using fireballs until they burned it down. Now this man wishes to return the glories of that state. Oh man, my days will be long and tedious If I have to imitate this fanatic.

"You just wait, brother Abu Moos, you will witness how the Islamic Caliphate will rise from the ashes and perform miracles. We will crush our enemies like bugs. We will behead every traitor among us after crucifying his family in front of his eyes." Shaddad Abu Saif was certainly laying it on thick for his men.

The mullah was sweating despite the coolness of the night. His heart was beating like a drum against his ribs. He concentrated on the conversation between Shaddad Abu Saif and Abu Moos in their car until he could no longer see the car ahead of him, only the ones behind him in his rear-view mirror. He stomped the fuel pedal, and the car tore up the road in pursuit of the lead car, which seemed to have been swallowed by the night. A few minutes later, all the cars were together again. The mullah's heart was beating faster now in anticipation of the ambush to happen soon.

The next hour passed without a word from Shaddad Abu Saif or Abu Moos.

The cars swam in a sea of darkness, the road straight and empty. The mullah switched on the cruise control so he could relieve the stress in his leg. He flexed his back and shoulders, taking deep, slow breaths. *Is it possible that Shaddad Abu Saif and Abu Moos suspect something? Why are they not talking?*

The sounds of distant gunfire alerted the mullah. He looked in the rearview mirror to see trucks approaching from behind at breakneck speed. He turned off the cruise and stomped the fuel pedal. The engine roared, and the car shot ahead like a rocket. He expected to hear instructions over the radio from Shaddad Abu Saif, but he didn't comment or reply to any of the other drivers who were asking what they should do.

Ahead, the headlights of more trucks coming from the other direction. Intermittent muzzle flashes from the trucks coincided with the sound of automatic gunfire. The car behind the mullah veered sharply to the right and rolled over several times. The mullah hoped the driver's death would be quick and painless.

What is going on, why have they killed one of our own men? Aren't they supposed to kill only the four men in the lead car?

The next car behind the mullah left the road in a rain of bullets, blood spattering the glass as the car skidded to a halt. The mullah's heart was beating hard, his forehead wet, ears burning, throat dry, and his fingers icy cold. *What's going on? Why are they killing my men?* Shaddad Abu Saif's land cruiser was barely visible on the road ahead. *Why haven't they stopped it?*

A truck sped up right beside his car. Not a military truck. Just like Hazem had said, they were using camouflaged civilian trucks. Next to the driver, a masked man with an Uzi was waving for the mullah to pull over.

The trucks ahead of them were blocking the road. Several masked men with Uzis aimed at him were screaming something. The window glass shattered behind him to his left. He dropped his head and stomped the brake, forcing the car into a skid as he gripped the steering wheel. He didn't raise his head even after the car came to a stop.

A masked man wrenched the door open, jerking him out as if he was his mother's killer. The mullah fell forward, the hot asphalt scraping his palms. Before he could raise himself up, the masked man kicked him in the belly, throwing him over onto his back. A boot smashed into his face until his eyes were covered in blood and he blacked out.

28

Mazen

Mazen's nerves were frazzled. More than a week had passed and still no one had come to his shop with the money.

He called his brother Bassem to tell him he hadn't received the money yet. Bassem asked him to be patient because moving money between countries is extremely dangerous, especially during wartime.

Then a couple of days later, a man in military uniform and sunglasses came into the shop, dropped a black plastic trash bag on the desk, and left without a word.

When Mazen opened the bag, the sight of many bundles of hundred-dollar notes caused a wave of relief to wash over him. He counted it to make sure it was all there, then he called Rabe's father-in-law and asked him to convey the message to Khanjar that he was ready.

Next day, at six in the evening, Rabe' showed up at the shop. "Ok, let's go,"

Mazen was disoriented. "Go where?"

"To my house. Khanjar will come and pick you up from there."

Mazen got up and closed the ledger to put it in the safe. His hands were shaking so much, he dropped the ledger. He picked it up, fumbled it into the safe, and closed and locked the door. He picked up the backpack with the money in it and said, "Okay, let's go."

They remained silent throughout the entire trip, as Mazen spent the time thinking of what to do about his daughters. He eventually decided to let them move in and live with their grandmother. It wasn't right for them to be living alone in that apartment. He decided not to tell them until he'd finished the business with the porters and found Zakiya.

In Utaibah Mazen found Khanjar on the porch waiting for them, He said to Rabie, "Can you please give him a Palestinian keffiyeh so he can hide his face?"

Rabe' went into the house, came out with a keffiyeh, and handed it to Mazen. Mazen wrapped it around his head and covered his face with the end, only leaving an opening for his eyes.

Khanjar stepped off the porch, and Mazen followed him. As they moved from the light into the inky night, he was as blind as if he was at the bottom of a well. He stopped for a minute until his eyes became accustomed to the blackness, then he hurried to catch up with Khanjar. As they walked across a field, the soil beneath his feet was soft and spongy. Khanjar didn't speak, but from time to time he would stop, put a hand on Mazen's arm, and listen intently. Mazen didn't know how Khanjar was able to hear anything from under the keffiyeh wrapped around his head. They kept walking and stopping for at least an hour until they came to a huge tractor.

"We will cross the fields until we reach the Khraibeh," Khanjar said.

"On this?" Mazen asked. He had never ridden on a farm tractor before.

"Yes, it is the only vehicle that can go through the fields without getting stuck," Khanjar said,

The tractor, with only a single driver's seat nestled between its two massive back tires, offered no room for an extra passenger. The only option Mazen had was to stand on the sidestep the driver used to climb up, clinging to the mirror on the side of the bonnet so he wouldn't fly off with each bounce of the tractor over the rough ground. The journey was exhausting for Mazen, and soon his legs were trembling from the effort of keeping his balance against the violent movements of the tractor. His fingers became numb from his death grip on the side mirror. He knew if he fell under the huge tractor tire, he would be crushed like an eggshell.

The breeze was chilly and made Mazen's eyes water. The tractor's headlight cast a weak beam into the inky blackness of the moonless night. Khanjar often had to swerve abruptly to avoid a rock or a hole, each swerve sent searing pain through Mazen's arms. He longed to stretch them to relieve the throbbing pain, but he was afraid of losing balance and ending up under the giant tire. He didn't dare turn his head to look at Khanjar. He continued to stare out as if observing the ghostly fields would keep him safe. Mazen thought *what a waste for such vast fields not to be growing any crops.* Unfortunately, the war had completely paralyzed both the land and the farmers.

He wanted to ask Khanjar to slow down, but he was sure his voice wouldn't leave even his throat, he was so terrified. He remembered the stories of the Jinn, his grandmother used to tell him and his brother Bassem. These barren fields without trees or crops were the perfect dwelling place for Jinn. They lived in the barren fields, the desert, or the mountains. Would a Jinn appearing in front of them now be more terrifying than a group of terrorists aiming their rifles at their heads? He shuddered. Either option would be scary enough to make him shit himself.

Mazen thought they were completely exposed because of the tractor's headlight, but even if they drove without lights, the monstrous roaring of the engine would give them away anyway and they could easily be hunted and shot by even a blind shooter.

What was I thinking, agreeing to come with Khanjar and put myself in such mortal danger? My father is dead now, and finding the porters will not bring him back. But how could I ever live peacefully if I don't seek revenge? They say revenge only kills the person seeking it. Is it revenge or anger? What will I gain from putting myself in such a situation? What happened to my father was because of his massive ego. If he had just reached out to me, I could have prevented it. He is the one to blame, and now I've acted irresponsibly because of him. I should never have left Dubai in the first place. Zakiya might be dead by now, and there's no way I can bring her back. I should ask Khanjar to stop now and take me back. But what about the hundred thousand dollars? Better to lose the money than lose my life.

Mazen turned his head and started to yell to Khanjar, but the silhouette of figures running and shooting at the tractor caused the muscles of his legs to go soft as a marshmallow. Bullets rained around them, causing sparks when they hit the metal hood of the engine. Then a bullet struck Khanjar in the head. The burst of blood – was it brain? – was the last thing Mazen saw before he lost his grip and was ejected from his tenuous perch, just as the tractor came to a sudden stop.

Mazen didn't see the ground coming at him, but the

searing pain in his head when he landed headfirst was unbearable. He rolled a few times like a thrown stone. His body came to a stop at an awkward angle and lay motionless, his eyes wide open and staring at nothing.

29

Mullah Abdullah

The mullah opened his eyes and blinked a few times, but all he could see was blackness. Not mere darkness, but inky, impenetrable blackness. "Hello," he called out. A sharp pain pierced his throat. His voice was husky, as if he'd been crying and yelling for a long time. What was wrong with his eyes? Maybe he'd lost his sight. Nothing scared him as much as losing his sight. To him, sight was the most valuable gift Allah granted to humans, and now he'd lost it. *Oh Allah, what I have done to be punished in this way?* He immediately regretted the thought and started repeating, "Oh Allah, take until you are satisfied. Oh Allah, thank you for all the blessings I am living in. Oh Allah, forgive my sins and accept my repentance." His face felt like it was on fire. He raised his right hand and touched it, but it was not his face. It was a mass of swollen, sticky flesh, and his beard was plucked. Over his eyes were swellings the size of chicken eggs. His cheeks were also swollen, spongy, and sticky. Wherever he touched burned. He touched his chest to discover it was not harmed. He realized he was naked except for his underwear. His body was not as bad off as his face. He got up and stood for a few moments, then sat down again.

Suddenly he heard a metallic clanking sound, as if someone was trying to open a padlock somewhere far off, then a chain being pulled through a hasp clanked even more. A creaking door, then footsteps. More than two feet were approaching. Another metal door being opened but closer this time. Then running footsteps and yelling as if someone had been struck. The noise was coming from the right of his position, but he couldn't tell if it was the next room to his or if there was another room between. More punching sounds followed by cries of agony that sounded a bit like comrade Abu Moos's voice. The mullah's heart trembled, a bitter taste in his mouth, and fearful anticipation in his mind. The hitting stopped. The person who had been hit was crying out in pain. A metal door slammed shut and locked. Footsteps again, but moving away this time, and again more clanking noises followed by another metal door being slammed, probably the one he'd heard at first.

The silence was sharper than a knife, there was nothing he could do but continue reciting supplications and wait for salvation.

The pain in his face was getting worse, his breathing sounded like a horse after a race. His heart beat violently, a heat blazed inside him. He was sure he had a fever. During his training, his stamina had improved big time, but now his exhaustion was due to the fever. He got up, dragged his feet slowly across the floor, and stretched his arm out ahead of him, searching for a door. When he located the metal door, he pounded on it with his fists, yelling for help and water to quench his thirst. No answer, so he moved away from the door and sat down again. His breathing was getting worse. It felt as if a huge rock was lying on his chest.

The clanking of the padlock and chain started again.

The mullah stood up, dragged his feet, and stretched his arm out in front to avoid stumbling. He found the door and started banging and yelling again, as the sound of steps came closer. Another clank as a key was inserted into the lock and turned. The door swung open with the squeal of rusty hinges. A gust of wind made the mullah step back as heavy, booted footsteps advanced. No one spoke, but suddenly a sharp stinging pain in his forehead caused him to scream. His face had been hit with a solid rod. Then another blow to his shoulder and one to his belly doubled him over. Each blow made him scream like a small boy. He couldn't tell how many were around him. He didn't know which way to move to escape, so he collapsed on the floor with his hands over his head and his swollen face tucked between his arms to ward off more blows to his face or head. Now the blows fell on his back and arms. One of his attackers dropped what he was using to hit him with, and it sounded like wood when it hit the floor. So, they were using wooden rods. Sticky liquid filled his mouth with a metallic taste. The smell of blood filled his nostrils. Sharp pain now in all parts of his body. Even as he lay on the ground, the hits continued. He could no longer scream, he just took hit after hit and wished his soul would leave his body and return to his creator, Allah.

When the mullah woke up, his eyelids felt heavy, and pain throbbed in his temples. He tried to open his eyes, but after considerable effort, he was only able to see through two tiny slits. He raised his right hand to touch his eyes but found himself handcuffed to something solid. Trying his left hand instead, he touched his eyes and discovered they were swollen shut. Gingerly, he touched other parts of his face, only to find it was even worse than before. His chin and cheeks were covered with a sticky substance that could only be blood. When he realized he hadn't lost his sight, he tried to smile, but his cheekbones hurt too much, causing him to frown, which only made his forehead hurt. Oh God, every inch of his face hurt.

He was lying on a metal cot with no mattress, wearing only his underwear, his body covered with bruises and dried blood. When he turned his head to the right, a sharp pain in his neck forced a moan from his lips. The room was unpainted, the cement bricks exposed, and bright sunlight spilled through the single iron-barred window. From where he was lying on the low cot, he could see nothing except a clear blue sky. There was a trolley with some first aid supplies on it next to the cot and a plastic chair. He held his breath, then released it slowly, hoping that would reduce the pain in his neck when he turned his head to the left. The metal door was rusty, looking as if orange powder had been sprayed on it. The mullah gathered his strength to pull himself up into a sitting position on the side of the bed. Every cell in his body screamed in pain. He lowered himself back down and lay still.

Sometime later, the squeal of door hinges woke him. He opened his eyes and moaned in pain. Turning his head slightly to the left, he could see the man who had entered was wearing a mask, and carrying an M16 on his right shoulder, and a black canvas sack in his left hand. The man strode quickly to the mullah and pulled the canvas sack down over his head. Wherever the mask touched his face, it caused burning pain, making him moan, and struggle to breathe. The mask was pressing on his face, and he tried to pull it up with his free hand, but then the man forced it back down, causing the mullah to scream. Then the man cuffed his free hand to the side of the cot. Now that the mullah's hands were both cuffed, he pressed the back of his head down hard, hoping doing so would reduce the pressure of the rough sack against his face, but it didn't help. The pain only got worse, and now his forehead was sweating, and the sweat ran into his eyes, making them sting.

"You can make it easy or hard, but believe me when I tell you, I will get the information out of you one way or another. It's up to you," a male voice said. The mullah didn't know if it was the same man who'd put the mask on his head or if someone else had entered the room.

"What do you want to know?" the mullah asked, his voice raspy.

"Who are you?" the man asked.

"You don't know who I am? Or you know, but you want to be sure?"

"What is your name?" the man asked, as if he hadn't heard him.

"Shaddad Abu Saif," the mullah answered.

"I see," the man said, "and who do you work for?"

"The Sword of Truth. May I know who you are and what you want from me?"

"You may not," the interrogator replied. He proceeded to ask the mullah numerous questions. When he was done, he said, "I am going to inject you with a sedative now. Don't move your arm or you may break the needle."

The mullah barely felt the sting in his right arm and fell asleep within moments.

When the mullah next opened his eyes, he found himself back in the dark place. He moved his arms and found they were not cuffed, but moving them was painful. He seemed to be on the ground, which was muddy. He wondered how the room could be so totally dark. Usually, his eyes could adjust to the dark and see at least some shapes, but this room was totally different. Maybe he was so deep underground that not a single ray of light could reach him. His body still burned from fever, and he was both thirsty and starving.

A few hours later or maybe only a few minutes, he couldn't be sure, the door opened. A group of men came in and began to beat him with wooden rods like the first time. He didn't have the energy to moan or scream. He curled himself into a ball and took blow after blow without resistance. He just wondered how they could see in this darkness.

30

Zahra

Zahra's last class period was math. She found it pure torture. She tried to focus, and keep George off her mind, at least during class time. But that was like asking her heart to stop beating. Imagining him in front of her and telling him her life story had become her daily routine. She spent hours in her room imagining conversations with him. If she couldn't find the right answer in her math homework, she asked him. If she couldn't find the right words for her literature assignment, she asked him. She would tell him how much she worried about her father, and how much she worried about her mother, who had become like a ghost. Her body was in the house, but her soul was elsewhere. She told him about her dreams and worries. She didn't tell him about her desire to touch his hand, or his beard, or his ears. She thought he had such small, cute ears. She knew to touch a strange man would be a sin, but she could touch her husband when she was married. Of course, it was okay to touch her father's face or hands, but she had never felt what she was feeling towards George with her father or her mom or anyone else. She would never want to make Allah angry at her for committing sins. She just wished she had the courage to tell George all these things in person when he walked her home from school. Even if she'd had the courage to talk more, she preferred to use those few intoxicating minutes to listen to his velvety voice, and for her eyes to be overjoyed observing his lovely smile as he talked with her.

She knocked on the door and waited for her mom. When her father had been around, the minute she entered, her mom would ask her about her classes, friends, teachers, and much more. Nowadays, after opening the door, she would simply turn away without speaking, dragging her feet as she went back to her bedroom.

When Amani opened the door, she was sobbing. Zahra had seen this from her mom a lot lately, but when she heard more crying from inside the house, she looked at her mom's face inquiringly.

"The daughters of Hadiya are here." Her mother always called them Hadiya's daughters because Hadiya was the one who had spent her youth bringing them up despite their destitution, while their father, Mazen, lived in Dubai swimming in a pool of money.

Zahra rushed to the courtyard. Farah, Marwa, and Ro'wa were seated side by side on the sofa in the liwan, crying their eyes out.

"What happened? Is Zakiya ok?" Zahra asked, shifting her gaze between the three girls, afraid to hear something she didn't want to.

"Their father passed away," Amani said.

Zahra gasped. "But how? What happened?"

"A few days ago, he told us he was going to a village in Ghouta to negotiate with an armed group to bring Zakiya back," Farah said. "He never returned."

"But that doesn't mean he's..." Zahra's voice faltered, unable to finish the sentence.

"We went to the neighbor of my grandfather's shop to ask if he knew anything," Farah continued, wiping her eyes and blowing her nose. "He spoke to some people from that village. They told him my father and another man had an accident."

"I'll never forget the sight of his body," Marwa said, her voice trembling, eyes brimming with tears. "It looked like a tank had run over him."

"They sent the body?" Zahra swallowed.

"No, we had to go identify the body before they issued the death certificate," Marwa said.

Tears welled up in Zahra's eyes, but they weren't for Mazen. Her tears fell for the three unfortunate girls, whose mother had passed away before the war. Their grandfather had died only a few weeks earlier, their sister had been kidnapped, and now their father had died. She broke down and cried inconsolably, as she succumbed to her deepest fears, knowing how she would feel if she lost her family. She allowed those horrible feelings, because Farah, Marwa, and Ro'wa were like sisters to her. Her sobs were even louder than theirs.

"You must spend the night here. We will say prayers for your father's soul," Amani said.

"Our father only wanted to find Zakiya," Marwa said, tears streaming from her eyes, drawing two glistening curves down her pink cheeks before dripping on her black blouse.

"We don't even know if she is still alive," Ro'wa said.

"I think she is, and I'm sure she will come back safe to us," Zahra said.

"Why do you think that?" Ro'wa asked. "Since the war started, hundreds of people have gone missing from our neighborhood. Every day we hear they found the body of this man here and that woman there, why do you think Zakiya is any luckier than them?"

"Yes, you're right, we can't assume anyone is luckier than any others," Amani said, "'The reasons are multiple, and the death is only one. When it is a person's time to die, they will die regardless. But my dear Ro'wa, we must stay optimistic and hope for the best. I believe, like Zahra, that Zakiya will come back safely and live happily with you again."

"Do you think it's best for her to come back safe?" Ro'wa said, "Wouldn't it be better for her to die and not know that our father is dead now? Now we are orphans. We must find work and feed ourselves. Our chances of getting married will be zero now."

Fresh tears streamed from Marwa's eyes again.

"My dear Ro'wa, Allah tests his beloved servants. Whatever calamities you have faced or are facing now will alter the scale of your good deeds in the hereafter. Nothing is free with Allah. For Zakiya to come back alive and live with you and help to support you will add to her good deeds in the hereafter. I agree with you that what you are going through is not easy, but it's an honor to be chosen by Allah for testing. If Allah didn't consider you to be people of patience, He would not be testing you."

Zahra looked at her mother, who seemed to be very calm. She was different from how she had been recently. It must be because when someone sees another's calamities, their own calamities become less important.

"Who said you need to work to feed yourselves?" Amani continued. "Your father will inherit money from your grandfather and all of that money will come to you. Also, I believe your father's money in Dubai will come to you."

"We don't want money," Marwa said, still crying, "We want him back."

"Enough," Farah snapped in Marwa's face, "Don't act like babies. Yes, it is unfortunate what has happened, but look around you, is there a home in the neighborhood that hasn't been afflicted by this stupid war? We need to be the daughters of our mother. She was a perfect example of a patient believer. The first thing we should do is to discover what fate has befallen Zakiya. Second, we need to go back and continue our studies at the university. Without our father to support us, we will need our degrees more than ever."

"You really are your mother's daughter," Amani told Farah. "I remember once I asked your mother what her secret was that allowed her to bear all her misfortunes. She told me, 'Every time she felt that life was too hard, she would think of Lady Zainab, the granddaughter of the prophet Mohammad. During the battle of Karbala, Yazid's army slaughtered seven of her brothers, her sons, and all of her nephews. One of them was only six months old, and many of her cousins were killed right in front of her eyes. They took her and the other women and children as captives on camels all the way from Karbala to Damascus. When they brought her with the other women to his palace in chains, Yazid asked Lady Zainab, 'How did you find the acts of Allah toward your brother Hussain?' Lady Zainab raised her head proudly and told him, 'I see nothing but beauty.' And your mother said, 'Despite all the calamities Lady Zainab witnessed, her faith never wavered. So, what are my calamities compared to the calamities of Lady Zainab?'"

Farah, Marwa, and Ro'wa smiled at the memory of their mother.

"Even though we are not Shia," Farah said, "our mother used to go to the Lady Zainab shrine every month, taking our brother Khaled with her."

"Lady Zainab is not only for Shia," Amani said. "She is a role model for all women throughout history, and not only Muslims. All the credit goes to your mom."

Zahra looked at her mother wide-eyed. She never failed to surprise her.

31

Ward

Lying on his bed covered with a blanket and a pillow over his head, Ward pressed his hands tightly over his ears. The whistling of mortar shells was even scarier than his stepmother when she used to scream at him.

What happened to the sky tonight, Ward wondered. Why are so many mortars falling? Usually only a few fell during the daytime, far away from their house; causing the ground to shake after a noise like a hammer falling on a thick rug. But tonight, not only was the ground shaking but every door, window, chandelier, table and chair, tree and flowerpot in the courtyard. His closet and his bed shook; even his father's picture hanging over the door. The noise was the worst. It reminded him of the slapping of the leather belt on his back when his stepmother lashed him as a punishment, but multiplied by a hundred times, as if a giant stepmother was lashing the city. *Oh, Mother of Jesus.*

George was still out. He'd gone to the church when they called for his help.

Ward got up, picked up his foam mattress and blanket, and ran to George's room. While passing through the courtyard, he held the blanket over his head and ran. He dropped the mattress beside George's bed and threw himself on it as if he was jumping into a swimming pool. He didn't know how long George would be gone or he would be counting on his fingers like every other afternoon.

The bang of the outside door startled Ward. He pulled himself up and leaned against the wall, waiting for George to appear.

"I know, no one can sleep under this rain of mortar shells," George said as he took off his pants and wrapped a towel around his waist. Then he pulled off his shirt and headed for the bathroom.

After his shower, George sat on his bed reading a book. Ward simply sat where he was, looking at him. He felt calmer now that George was there. The whistling and thump of the falling mortar shells didn't jangle his nerves as much as before.

Suddenly, all hell broke loose. George flipped off the bed, throwing himself on top of Ward, and gripping him tightly.

Flying debris clattered against the outside wall. Ward imagined a giant stepmother spitting rocks at their house. Each bang caused Ward to squeeze George even tighter. The rain of stones and debris continued for a while, followed by an eerie silence.

George raised his head, looked Ward in the eyes and asked, "Are you ok?"

Ward just nodded. At that moment, he understood why George had acted like that. He hugged George with all his strength, he mumbled, "I lub ou."

George said without raising his head, "I love you too, my hero."

George got up and headed outside, with Ward following close behind. The courtyard, once a haven of peace, now lay in disarray. Its stones were violently displaced and piled against the walls like debris after a storm. The mortar shell had struck the center, leaving a gaping hole where the fountain once stood. Shattered flowerpots, broken plants, and scattered tree branches were strewn across the ground. Every window facing the courtyard was shattered, and shards of glass glistening everywhere.

George looked at Ward and hugged him, "Mother of Jesus, thank you."

"Othor o eeses, ank ou," Ward said and hugged George back.

32

Zahra

As Zahra exited the school the next day, her smile disappeared when she didn't find George waiting for her. The ten minutes she waited for him seemed like an eternity. Every day she had been walking with George through the alleys of old Damascus and talking. Most often in the Bab Thomas area, which was mostly inhabited by Christian families. A few times he'd asked her to join him for coffee in a cafe, but she always refused.

She started walking, but kept looking back every few steps like a bereaved mother looking for her lost child. She hoped she would see him running toward her, saying he was sorry he was late. But she got to the end of the school road where she had to turn right. Still, she waited there for a few minutes before giving up and hastening toward the sisters' apartment. She was so upset she needed someone to talk to. Besides, she didn't want her mother to see her like this, barely able to breathe.

Marwa opened the door, wearing a long black dress, "What's wrong?" Marwa asked the minute she saw her.

"Nothing's wrong," Zahra said and took a seat on the sofa. Farah and Ro'wa came out of the bedroom and sat on the other sofa. Both were wearing black pants and T-shirts.

"You look nervous or something," Marwa said.

"Is it that obvious?" Zahra asked.

"I don't see the usual sweet smile you always have on your face," Marwa said.

"She is in love," Ro'wa said with a giggle.

"Are you ready to talk about it?" Marwa asked.

"You had Falafel for lunch?" Zahra asked.

"Yes, how did you know?" Farah asked.

"I could smell Falafel all the way out by the front gate," Zahra said.

"Don't change the topic, young lady," Ro'wa said and giggled again.

"Yes, I have recently been meeting someone every day after school. We just walk and talk," Zahra said, avoiding the girls' eyes. She looked down at her finger as she traced invisible circles on the sofa cushion.

The three girls cheered and applauded as if they had just heard the happiest news ever.

"Today he didn't show up after school," Zahra said.

"Don't worry, he might just be busy," Farah said.

"He is a teacher, and he finishes work at the same time as I finish my classes," Zahra said.

"He is your teacher?" Marwa asked.

"No, he teaches at Assieh School," Zahra said.

The three girls gasped and said in one voice, "He's Christian?"

Zahra said nothing, just nodded. But the three girls were staring at her as if she had announced she was pregnant.

"How do you know him?" Farah asked.

"He is the brother of the man who tried to rescue me and Zakiya," Zahra said.

"He is a hero then," Ro'wa said.

"No, he is the brother of the hero," Marwa said. The three sisters laughed.

"But what about your family?" Farah asked. "You know your father's position in the neighborhood as the imam of the mosque. Where do you see this relation going? Have you thought about that?"

Zahra sighed, "I have tried to kill the desire of meeting him and talking with him or even just thinking of him, but I have failed." She buried her face in her hands and started to cry.

Farah moved to sit beside her and put an arm around her shoulders, "It's ok Zahra, I am sorry. I shouldn't have asked you that."

"No, you are right. Such a relationship can only lead to a dead end, unless he becomes a Muslim," Zahra said.

"Have you talked about that with him?" Farah asked.

"No, I think both of us are scared to open that topic," Zahra said.

Marwa went and got a small towel and handed it to Zahra to wipe her tears. Zahra took it and laughed, "You don't have tissues?"

"No, my dear, tissues are a luxury we can't afford," Ro'wa said. The three sisters laughed, and Zahra joined them while wiping at her tears.

"What's his name?" Ro'wa asked.

"Shush," Farah said, throwing a sharp look at her sister, then turning her attention back to Zahra, "You don't need to tell us his name if you don't want to."

"It's George," Zahra said, smiling happily.

"Oh, you poor thing," Marwa said, "You really are in love."

"I have never felt so happy. I've never felt so energized. Despite this miserable war, I see everything as rosy. My mom is so worried about dad, but I don't feel worried at all."

"I think you have a mania," Farah said.

"What is mania?" Zahra asked.

"It's the opposite of depression," Farah replied.

"Wow, isn't that great?" Ro'wa asked.

"Not really. It's about extreme feelings of happiness, but the trouble is, most extremes aren't realistic," Farah said.

"What do you think about all of us going to the Grand Mosque to pray for your father's soul?" Zahra asked the three girls.

"That's a great idea," Marwa said, looking at Farah for approval.

"Sure, when?" Farah asked.

"This Saturday," Zahra said.

Farah looked at Marwa and Ro'wa, "I am fine with it. What about you two?"

Both nodded in agreement.

"But…" Zahra paused.

The three girls waited for her to continue.

"Can George and Ward come with us?" Zahra asked then swallowed.

The three girls exchanged glances, then smiled. Farah said, "Yes, of course. It would be nice to meet them."

"By the way, I've been telling Mom I visit you every day after school, but I actually go with George to walk in the Bab Thomas alleys," Zahra said.

The three sisters laughed and assured her they wouldn't betray her trust.

Zahra left the girls' apartment. She now had a reason to check on George, but she still needed the courage to reach his house. She had underestimated the crushing weight of guilt, unaware that it could be heavier than a mountain. But why should she feel guilty in the first place? She had no intention of committing any sin. She just wanted to go and invite him and Ward to come with her to the Grand Mosque this Saturday. But was that truly the real reason? Or was she simply yearning to check on him?

Deep down, she knew that whatever the reason was, going alone to the house of a strange man was what fueled her guilt. The overwhelming feelings she had for him, the joy and excitement she felt every day because of him, while her father was missing, all added to her guilt.

Her heart pounded as she approached the cracked door of his house. The heavy wave of guilt still pressing down on her shoulders. Her mind raced with a whirlwind of thoughts, a mix of fear, excitement, and that gnawing sense of guilt. With a trembling hand, she knocked and waited.

Ward opened the door, "Ao Zawa," he greeted her, jumping and clapping his hands while calling George, "Org, Zawa ier."

Ward's enthusiasm made her smile despite her nervousness. But when she glanced through the door and noticed the devastation of the courtyard, her smile faded. "What happened?"

Before Ward could answer, George appeared, "Hello Zahra! Are you ok?"

He was wearing denim pants and a tight T-shirt. His charm made her swallow her tongue. Ward was mumbling about what had happened, but she was lost in another world.

"Zahra," George said, louder than usual, with a smile,

"Would you like to come in?"

"Oh, no, I mean yes, no I mean no," She stammered, trying to hide her embarrassment. She pointed to the courtyard, or what used to be a courtyard, and asked, "What happened?" She regretted asking because the answer was obvious.

"Last night was our turn to win a mortar shell draw, like most of the lucky families in this country," George said.

Zahra didn't find his joke funny. "Thank Allah, you and Ward are safe."

"I am sorry I couldn't make it to your school today."

"I understand," Zahra said, glancing through the door at the piles of dirt. "I came to invite you to come with us to the Grand Mosque this Saturday."

"Who's us? Did your dad come back?" George asked, his eyes reflecting genuine excitement.

"No, me and the three sisters of Zakiya," Zahra said, but the confused look on George's face prompted her to elaborate. "Zakiya, who was kidnapped when Ward rescued me."

"Oh, okay, sure," George said, rubbing the back of his neck, "Can Ward come with us?"

"Yes, of course," Zahra said, smiling at Ward, "He's the most important one of us."

Zahra was bouncing on her way home, with light and carefree steps.

33

Zakiya

Zakiya pulled the wheeled mop bucket to service room number eleven. It was seven thirty, and she had only one room left to clean before she could call it a day. When she opened the door, a girl was lying on the floor, crying. She stared at her in shock; the girl was so beautiful it took Zakiya's words away for a moment.

"What's wrong?" Zakiya whispered, forcing a smile. She put the rubber wedge under the door to hold it open, since she was not allowed to close a door while she was cleaning any room.

The girl held up what looked like a white pen with a little screen on the side showing a blue line.

"What is that?" Zakiya asked.

"I'm pregnant," the girl said, choking back a sob. Her head bobbing in time to her sobs like a baby crying.

Zakiya gasped, though she didn't know what the relationship was between the white pen and the pregnancy, she did know that for a girl to be pregnant by anyone other than her husband was terrible. Her child would be a bastard, "What are you going to do?"

"I don't know." The girl tried to hold back her sobs, but it didn't work too well. Her crying became even louder.

Zakiya went to the door and closed it, breaking the rules. Then she went back, kneeled, and hugged the girl. She smelled of Jasmin, her hair was honey color, her skin ivory, and she felt so soft. Zakiya fervently wished she had a body like that. The girl hugged her back and asked, "Why is my life so miserable?"

Zakiya pulled her head back and looked into the girl's red eyes. "Your life is not so miserable."

"Are you serious Matchstick?" She stopped her sobbing, as she looked into Zakiya's eyes.

Zakiya looked down, and a tear rolled down her cheek.

"Oh, don't be so sensitive, you know I'm only kidding," the girl said, "We call Nazih, Dick Head, and Mona, Smelly Witch."

They both giggled.

Zakiya wiped her eyes on her sleeve. "I can understand how you feel. If it was me, I would be terrified of having a bastard."

The girl stood up and went to the dressing table and pulled a few tissues from the box to wipe her tears. She glared at Zakiya and snapped, "Either you are stupid or very naïve."

Zakiya froze. Her tongue couldn't find the right words to respond. She wondered why the girl was so angry with her.

"It is not about having the baby or not." The girl's eyes softened, as she approached Zakiya, took her hand and led her over to the bed and sat beside her. "Please promise me you won't mention this to Miss Mona."

Zakiya nodded. "But how long can you hide it?"

"I have to do something, otherwise I'm dead," the girl said.

"Do any of your clients like you? Could you ask one of them for their help?" Zakiya asked.

This was the first time Zakiya had ever had a conversation with any of the girls.

"I know stealing is forbidden," Zakiya said, not looking the girl in the eyes, "But to save your life, maybe you could steal a client's mobile phone to call your family. Surely, they would come to help you."

"The clients are not allowed to bring their mobile phones into the rooms, but even if they did, this villa has a device to block the signal. They make millions from this business; do you think they wouldn't think of a little thing like that?"

"Why don't you give a client you trust, the number and ask him to call your family," Zakiya whispered, glancing at the door.

"Who would be willing to call a family he doesn't know, and inform them that he found their daughter committing adultery? And if they asked him how he knows, what should he answer? Plus, if the client was a scoundrel, I would end up buried at the bottom of the garden like Wima. Her client told Nazih, and Nazih killed her."

Zakiya gasped.

A sudden bang on the door caused them both to jump up in alarm. Zakiya looked at the other girl for directions. The girl stood up and slipped the white pen into the pocket of her robe.

"Open this door now," Nazih yelled.

The minute Zakiya pulled the door open, Nazih's first slap caused her to see glittering stars. The second slap knocked her to the floor. He stepped over her prone body and strode toward the other girl, who was standing there like a statue. He grabbed her by the hair and dragged her kicking and screaming from the room.

Zakiya got up slowly. Two slaps was not that bad a punishment, but the punishment room was far worse.

She rushed to the door and peeked out. Nazih was still holding the girl by the hair with one hand while turning the key to the punishment room door with the other. He threw the girl into the room like a sack of grain, slammed the door, and locked it. The girl was screaming like a banshee in the closed room. Zakiya went back inside, grabbed the broom, and started sweeping industriously. Surely Nazih wouldn't put her together with the girl in the punishment room.

Nazih stepped into the room, strode up to her, and punched her in the side of the head, knocking her to the floor, "You little mother fucking rat."

She burst out crying.

Nazih raised his right foot to stomp on her tiny body, but before his heavy shoe could crush her ribs, Mona was right there, grabbing him by the shoulder and pulling him back. His foot stomped the floor, causing it to vibrate.

"Relax, Nazih, relax," Mona said.

"Shut up you," Nazih snapped back in Mona's face.

"Are you trying to kill her?" Mona yelled back, "She is a working donkey. She is doing the work of three maids."

"She was conspiring with Yasmin to run away," Nazih said, a vein throbbing in his forehead.

"No one is running away while I am in charge of this house," Mona said. Going over to Zakiya, she said, "Your mother's dearest, get up now and finish your cleaning." Grabbing her arm, she pulled Zakiya to her feet.

Zakiya wiped her eyes with her sleeve. She clutched Mona's arm for a moment until she felt steady on her feet, then she picked up the broom and resumed her sweeping. Mona pushed Nazih out of the room, telling him, "You go to reception now, the clients will be arriving soon."

The next morning Zakiya was in the kitchen chopping parsley for the tabbouleh. The sound of the metal gate sliding open caused her to glance out the window. The only reason for the metal gate to be opened was to let a car enter the garden. That would be for one reason only: to bring in new girls. A black van entered the garden, two girls got out and were led into the villa. They were glancing around like cats in a strange alley. Today Nazih will be so thrilled.

She went back to chopping parsley. During the past few weeks, a dozen or more new girls had arrived, and the same number had left this hellish place.

34

Ward

Ward was jumping from foot to foot in the courtyard, repeating, "Ee oin owd. Ee oin owd."

When George came out, he was wearing jeans and a long sleeve shirt, just like Ward, and Ward caught a whiff of his cologne. They were going with Zahra and the three sisters to the grand mosque. Ward grabbed George's hand as they stepped out into the alley. He never felt alone when he was holding George's hand. Not like he had felt when his father left the house and never came back. The emptiness in his heart had caused him to cry every night until his pillow was wet from his tears.

He turned his head to look up at George. Squeezing George's hand he said, "I lub ou."

George laughed and said, "I love you too, Ward."

Ward walked with head held high whenever he went out with George. He liked the way people smiled when they saw them holding hands. He was certain people must like him, otherwise why would they smile?

Only his stepmother didn't like him. She never wanted him to walk beside her or hold her hand when they went to the vegetable market together. She always scolded him in front of people on the street. Once she had screamed at him and called him stupid. Then she slapped his face and told him he was the reason his father had left. But she also told George, he was the reason his father had left. Ward was confused. Was he the reason, or was George the reason? She was like the water in the bathroom taps, sometimes very cold and sometimes very hot. A few times, she locked him in the attic. He got so hungry he ate the dried onions hanging in the attic until George came and let him out. He peed his pants every time she locked him in, but he never messed in his pants, because he was a grown man and must hold it until George came back.

One day, his father called. She screamed and screamed and screamed over the phone and called his father names. Terrible names. She told him she was going to kill herself and kill Ward and George if he didn't come back. Ward started to bawl and George tried to calm him down. He was so scared. George took him to eat ice cream, and when they got back, she was hanging by a rope around her neck in the attic. He would never forget her vacant eyes, like the eyes of the doll in a horror movie he'd watched with George. He had so many nightmares after that day. For many nights, he would carry his mattress to George's room and sleep on the floor beside his bed.

When they reached the grand mosque, Ward spotted Zahra right away, but he had never met the other girls who were with her. He squeezed George's hand when they stopped in front of the girls.

"Hello Ward," Zahra said, smiling.

"Ao Zawa," he said, staring at the three girls.

"These are my best friends, Farah, Marwa, and Ro'wa," Zahra said, pointing to each of her three friends in turn.

"Ao, Fa'wa, Mawa, oa'wa," Ward said. His wide smile exposed his teeth and upper gums.

As they walked up to the huge wooden door to the piazza of the mosque, Zahra said, "Girls, this is the hero who rescued me and tried to rescue Zakiya."

They all smiled and thanked Ward for his bravery.

Ward paused, and said to George, "Wa' if ey fine ou we ristian an kin us?"

George laughed, and said, "Don't worry Ward, I'm with you, if anyone tries to kill you, I'll stop them."

Ward jumped up and down and clapped his hands when the girls and Zahra laughed at George's promise to protect him. *They like me.*

They all took off their shoes and placed them in the plastic bags they were given at the gate for the purpose, then entered the huge piazza, where a flock of pigeons were pecking grain from the marble. Ward ran ahead and jumped into the middle of the flock. The startled pigeons fluttered up all together and rose a few meters, then landed again not far from where he was standing. Ward ran to where they'd landed, causing the pigeons to fly up again and land in another spot. Once more Ward ran to that spot. George grabbed his hand, preventing another jump, and said, "If you keep disturbing the pigeons, someone will come and kick us out."

Ward meekly followed George and the girls. They didn't enter the place of prayer because the men's area was separate from the women, and they didn't want to be separated. All of them sat down on the marble floor, their backs against the wall, with a full view of the vast courtyard. A few children were running and following the pigeons as Ward had done. Ward wanted to get up and run with them, but George grabbed his arm just in time and asked him to stay seated.

"Did you know that inside the mosque there is a

shrine to the prophet Yahya, which in your religion is the name for John the Baptist?" Farah asked.

"Really?" George responded, "But John the Baptist lived before the Islamic era."

"This place is as old as history itself," Farah said. "It wasn't a mosque then, or even a church. It was a temple, built a thousand years before Jesus was born. The Arameans built a temple dedicated to their god, and then when the Romans invaded Syria, they converted it to a temple for their god. Then, around four hundred years after Jesus was born, this place became a cathedral, then three hundred years later, when the Umayyad state was established with Damascus as its capital, the caliph al-Walid converted it to a mosque."

"You know your history," George said.

"The eastern minaret used to be called the minaret of Jesus, because it was said at the end of time, when the antichrist rises up, Jesus will descend from the sky to that minaret to fight him," Farah said.

Ward looked up at the roof of the mosque, where a dome rose from the middle of the long-gabled roof, forming what looked like the head and wings of an eagle.

Farah pointed to the left. "Over there is the shrine of the head of al-Hussain bin Ali, the grandson of the prophet Mohammad. Some historians say it was buried there and some say it was only put there temporarily when they brought the decapitated heads of the warriors from Iraq to Damascus, so the caliph could celebrate his victory."

"The head of the prophet's grandson was brought to the Caliph?" George asked.

"Every year the Arfad commemorates the event,"

Zahra said.

"The Arfad?" George asked.

"The Shia sect. We Sunnis call them Arfad," Farah said.

"The objectors?" George said.

"Yes exactly," Ro'wa said, "Arfad always object."

"What was the reason the Caliph killed him then?" George asked.

"Because he refused to pledge his allegiance to the Caliph," Farah said.

"And because of that, the Caliph cut off his head?"

The girls nodded.

"Who was the Caliph then?" George asked.

"Yazid bin Mu'awiyah," Zahra said.

Ward contemplated the four girls, as they and his brother sat in silence for a few minutes. It was his first time inside the mosque. He and George often walked along the outside of its high walls, but he had never dreamed it was so beautiful inside.

On their way home, he held George's hand and didn't let go until they stopped to buy ice cream.

At the gate to the sister's building, George said, "Next week my class will be making a trip to the convent of St. Thecla in Maaloula, mostly female students will be coming with me and Ward. Would you like to come with us?"

Ward jumped up and said, "Ou ust tum, Ou ust tum."

Zahra smiled and said, "Yes, I'd love to."

The other three girls didn't share Ward and Zahra's excitement.

"We'll let you know," Farah said.

Then the three sisters and Zahra entered the building. Ward took George's hand, and they walked home together.

35

Mullah Abdullah

The mullah hadn't missed his five daily prayers since he'd reached puberty unless he had no choice. Normally, he would hear the Azan, (call to prayer), each day and pray. In the camp, there had been no Azan, but he would calculate the approximate time for each prayer by observing the position of the sun in the sky.

He didn't know how long he'd been in this dingy, pitch-black chamber, since there was no view of the sun, so, he couldn't even figure out when it was morning or night, and he didn't have a watch to know the time of day. He assumed the cup of water and piece of bread they threw in for him was once per day. He had counted up to nine times he'd received bread and water. After that, he lost track.

He was always super alert and vigilant, like a stray cat, for any small noises outside. The clanking of the padlock on the far door was like an alarm, setting his muscles to shivering, and his body sweating. The clicking of the footsteps of the men carrying their wooden clubs were like nails being hammered into his bones. The few seconds it took for them to move from the outer door to his were excruciating. When they came to beat him, by the time they left, he would be nothing but a quivering pile of flesh covered with bruises and blood. If they went instead to beat the other man, by the time they'd finish torturing him, the mullah would be lying on the floor, barely able to breathe.

The mullah knew it was all a test from Allah, and he must not lose his faith if he was going to pass it. But there were moments when he wondered if it was not a test but only punishment. He would immediately force himself to erase such thoughts from his mind.

The clanking of the padlock pulled his mind from the swamp of his thoughts. Steps were approaching, his body started trembling, he dragged himself into a corner, and curled up to make himself as small as possible so he would expose less body area to the blows. He heard the door open with a clang. It was his turn today. He shut his eyes, covered his face with his arms, and put his hands over his head, so only his back and buttocks would bear the brunt of the blows. His body trembled while he waited for the pain to start. Maybe if they slaughtered him now, no blood would leak out, because he felt so dry inside.

But no blows came. Strong arms pulled him up and covered his head with a sack before they dragged him out. He tried to focus on how many corridors or flat spaces they passed and how many stairs they climbed, but it was all blur. All he could remember was the pain in his feet that banged against each step as they dragged him along. Finally, they picked him up and threw him on the floor like an old mattress.

His head cover was snatched off. The mullah snapped his eyelids shut immediately; the light was so bright his eyes needed time to adjust. He heard laughter, and squinted enough to see he was in a large hall, like an Arabic-style Majles, or sitting room, with mattresses and cushions placed around the walls. There in front of him was a real throne, on which the real Shaddad Abu Saif rested, half sitting, half laying. On either side of him were half-naked boys wielding long white feathers and fanning the man's head. *This man thinks he's Pharaoh.*

Shaddad Abu Saif wore a cobalt blue turban with three maroon gems on the front and a golden-colored dish dash. Over his shoulders was a blue velvet cloak. *This man plays the Caliph perfectly. Could he truly believe himself to be the Caliph of Allah on Earth? Oh, man.*

The mullah was thrown down on a tarpaulin so the filth on his body wouldn't soil the Persian carpets. For a few seconds, he was lost in the beauty of the brilliant colors of the carpets.

"How do you want to die?" Shaddad Abu Saif asked.

The mullah was shocked by the question, but he didn't have enough energy to respond.

One of the soldiers kicked him in the gut. And ordered, "Answer the caliph."

The mullah moaned and struggled to breathe, his voice was hoarse, "I don't want to die."

"Yes, of course, you'd rather be a slave to the infidels," Shaddad Abu Saif said with a wry smile.

The mullah said nothing, just stared at Shaddad Abu Saif. The same soldier slammed the butt of his rifle against the mullah's head, snarling "Lower your gaze in respect to the Caliph."

The mullah moaned in agony again. The pain was like being hit on the head with a hammer. He rubbed his head to ease the pain, and immediately his hands were covered in warm blood. He didn't dare raise his head to meet the Caliph's eyes.

"Let me make it easier for you," Shaddad Abu Saif said, "We can peel your skin while you're alive like the Japanese did to their prisoners in World War Two, or we can impale you like the Ottomans did to kill their traitors, or we can tie your limbs to four cars and drive them in four different directions like the Chinese did to kill traitors in the old days, only they used oxen. Or maybe we could roast you within a hollow metal bull like the ancient Greeks used to execute their traitors. Or we could just decapitate you like we did to the traitor before you."

The mullah was speechless; he had no energy to argue, but even if he'd had the energy, he knew it would be pointless to argue.

"Did you think Allah would allow the infidels to defeat his righteous servants?" Shaddad Abu Saif asked.

The mullah was too terrified to answer. He just kept staring at the blood dripping from his head onto the tarpaulin.

"You, you bastard, lived as a slave to your infidel government in this life and now you will be in hell forever in the hereafter. In both life and the hereafter, you are servile. Did your government inform you how we killed the previous traitor like you? We slaughtered him after we slaughtered his family before his very eyes."

One of the soldiers came forward and pulled the mullah's head up by his hair and screamed, "Bastard! Answer the Caliph."

The mullah said without daring to look at the Caliph, "Yes, they told me how you killed them."

"But did they tell you how we knew he was a traitor?" Shaddad Abu Saif asked. "Of course they didn't tell you."

He laughed and other men in the room laughed with him.

The mullah avoided looking directly at him. "No. They did not," he said.

"One of the army officers sold us the information, just for the money," Shaddad Abu Saif said.

Shaddad Abu Saif could be playing a game with me. It would be so easy for him to lie.

"You don't believe me, do you?" Shaddad Abu Saif said. "It doesn't matter, because we are always the winners, and Allah willing, we will take over the government and slaughter all traitors like you. Allah will help us, as we are the true servants of Allah."

The mullah raised his head and looked at Shaddad Abu Saif for a moment, then he asked, "How did you know about me?"

"The same way we knew about the one before you," Abu Saif said and his laugh echoed in the mullah's ears.

Two masked men in leather vests, who looked like gladiators, approached the mullah, covered his head with a black sack, and pulled him up, grasping him under the arms. They dragged him back the way they had come and threw him into the dark room.

He lay down, still rubbing his head, which was still oozing blood. He rubbed his sticky, bloody palm on the ground to dry it in the dust and dirt. He wondered which was filthier, his body or the ground. The ground was covered with dirt, but his body was covered with various shades of blood mixed with dirt and dust. His hair was full of dirt mixed with sweat.

He performed Tayammum, which he substituted for ablutions in the absence of water. He didn't know in which direction Mecca was, so he prayed in all four directions, at times he assumed to be prayer time. He didn't perform all the physical movements because he was too tired, he just recited the verses and nodded his head.

His prayers helped him to keep from going totally crazy, and they helped to remind him that Allah would find a way for him to leave this place alive and continue to look for his kidnapped daughter. Tears streamed from his eyes involuntarily when he remembered Zahra. He only wished to stay alive long enough to rescue her. She deserved like any child in Syria to live a safe and happy life.

The beatings stopped after that, but his nerves had become too agitated to allow him to calm down. Every time the padlock clanked on the outer door, his body trembled, and he automatically moved to curl his body up in the corner.

Darkness became a part of him. His very soul was soaked in darkness. His dreams were dark and foreboding, as were his every thought. Time seemed slower in the dark. The last time he'd seen Amani and Zahra seemed like months, years, decades, even. He busied his mind with sweet memories of Amani's smile and Zahra's laugh; the warmth of their daily family routine; having breakfast together as a family, dropping Zahra at her school, fetching her back from the school after his noon prayers in the mosque were distant memories. Their family connection was the only thing that prevented his heart from shattering, as had happened to so many people because of the war. His eyes streamed tears, as he sobbed like a young boy who had lost his most precious toy.

The door opened, and whoever came in pulled him

out of the room after they put the sack on his head, as usual. He wondered how these men could see in the inky darkness. Maybe they wore night vision glasses. From the distance and the number of steps his feet banged over as they dragged him up, he knew they were taking him to the room with the cot and the window.

They cuffed his left wrist to the side of the cot but didn't pull the sack off his head, and they didn't leave the room. Something that felt like rubber touched his arm. Then he realized it was a gloved hand. He prepared himself for the sting of an injection. A slight gasp escaped his lips when the sting came.

36

Ward

The van pulled out of Bab Thomas Square with nine girls onboard, including Zahra, plus George and Ward.

Ward whispered in George's ear.

George turned to Zahra and asked, "Why didn't Farah, Marwa, and Ro'wa come with us?"

"This morning, I went to their apartment and begged them to come with me, but they said they didn't want to. So, I left my stuff with them, and I told them I'll be back later to get it, since my mom thinks I am spending the day at their apartment."

Naturally, Zahra was the only one wearing a headscarf, but the other eight girls were eager to meet her. During the hour-long drive to Maaloula, they asked her tons of questions about Islam and Muslims. Ward just sat quietly, observing and listening.

The village of Maaloula sits at an altitude of 1600 meters, in a narrow opening between two tall, rocky hills. The van stopped in the garage at the bottom of the mountainside and the group continued to the village on foot. Ward held George's hand the whole time. George didn't object or show any sign of annoyance. Zahra smiled when she saw their hands. The group passed between the houses of the village until they reached the majestic pass between the hills.

"Sa ala Cra," Ward said as he crossed himself. The

eight schoolgirls and George did the same.

Zahra looked at George.

"St. Thecla's Crack," George said, gazing up at the stone hills.

The hills looked as if the land had suddenly risen hundreds of meters.

"This is one of the oldest Christian villages on earth. The people here speak the Aramaic language, the same language Jesus spoke," George said.

"Do ou ow ory of Sa ala," Ward asked Zahra.

Zahra swallowed, and said, "Yes."

George raised both eyebrows and said, "Really, you know the story of St. Thecla?"

"Oh, no. Sorry. I meant to say no," Zahra said. "Do you know it?" she asked.

"Of course, it is one of the classics of Christian literature," George said, pointing at the convent, "The convent was built in a cave where St Thecla spent her life worshiping God, until her death at the age of ninety. She was the daughter of a well-known pagan family. Her father forced her to become engaged to a pagan man, but she broke the engagement and ran away, announcing her desire to be a Christian nun. She was sentenced to death, and the Roman soldiers chased her until she reached the bottom of this mountain." He pointed at the opening between the two hills. "She prayed for God to save her. The mountain split apart, and she ran through, avoiding the soldiers. She hid in a tiny cave in the rocks. She was so thirsty, she prayed again and God bestowed His blessing upon her once more. Fresh water gushed out from between the rocks, and she drank her fill. She spent the rest of her life in that cave, and later, the convent was built on the site.

Her grave is inside the convent."

As the group entered the gap between the two hills, a cool breeze sprang up. The light became dimmer, and some areas were only wide enough to walk in single file. The inner sides of the two hills on either side matched exactly, as if the two hills had simply been pulled apart. The space between them would connect like Lego blocks.

About a hundred meters into the gap, they reached a place where it widened out, and there before them was the legendary convent of St Thecla. It was built entirely out of white stones and protruded from the side of the mountain like an eagle's nest.

At the gate stood a nun dressed all in black. Only her face and hands weren't covered. Her tender face and warm smile framed pale blue eyes that seemed to penetrate one's soul.

Zahra smiled and told George, "If it was not for the huge golden cross hanging around her neck, I would have mistaken her for a very conservative Muslim woman."

"She ot oslen," Ward told Zahra.

George laughed and looked at Ward. "Yes Ward, Zahra knows she is not Muslim."

"God be with you," the nun said as she approached and shook hands with all of them in turn. When she reached Zahra she said, "You are most welcome, my child," as she pressed Zahra's hands between her own.

"This is Mother Pelagia Sayyaf," George told Zahra. "She is the head nun of the convent, with twelve nuns under her supervision."

"Ma fen Zawa," Ward said to Mother Pelagia.

"I see you have a nice new friend," Mother Pelagia said

to Ward.

Ward jumped up and down and clapped his hands in delight.

"Zahra, what a lovely name," Mother Pelagia said.

Just then, the church bells began to chime. "You arrived at just the right time. Mass is about to start, let's go inside."

Mother Pelagia guided them into church. The burning incense made Ward's head swim. He smiled broadly as he inhaled deeply.

After George, Ward and the eight girls had said their prayers at the altar, Mother Pelagia took them to the ancient cave where St. Thecla was buried. Crystal-clear water streamed out of the rocks, and a tree spread its leafy branches over the spring.

"This is a miracle tree because it has remained green ever since it grew beside the grave of St. Thecla," George told Zahra, pointing at the tree.

Before they left the convent, Mother Pelagia and four of the nuns brought hot tea with freshly baked orange sponge cake.

Ward ate and talked at the same time.

When they'd finished their tea, they left the convent and climbed to the top of the hill where they could look down on the village of Maaloula and the convent of St. Thecla. They spread a blanket and took nuts and lemon juice from their packs and chatted gaily, mostly asking Zahra about her life.

Ward was happy that Zahra was with them, and most importantly, that she was having a good time. He savored every second in this holy place. He enjoyed watching the girls, chatting, laughing, and enjoying his new friend Zahra. Ward wished his father could be there to see how happy he and George were now.

When the sun's rays no longer reflected off the church bells, they became dull, like a flame going out. The merry group descended the hill and filed back through the gap. Ward held onto George's hand as they made their way to the van, then they all returned to Damascus.

37

Zahra

Zahra climbed the dingy stairs of the three sisters' building two steps at a time. Arriving at their door, she pressed the doorbell several times, expecting the three sisters to open it with wide smiles.

When the door opened, the person standing there was the last one she expected to see. Her mother.

Amani moved aside, allowing her to enter. The three sisters were sitting on one of the sofas, their faces pale and unsmiling.

"Where were you?" Amani asked.

Zahra looked at the sisters, "You didn't tell her?"

"I am asking you, Zahra," Amani said, "We brought you up to be honest. I shouldn't need to ask anyone else to get the correct answer. Where were you?"

"I was in Bab Thomas," Zahra said, avoiding her mother's eyes.

"With whom?"

"With George."

Amani gasped, "Alone? Where? At his house?"

"No, no, we just went to the church."

"What?" Amani yelled, "And why didn't you tell me you were going there?"

"Would you have agreed if I'd told you?"

"Of course not," Amani snapped, "I feel I don't know you anymore. Your father disappeared trying to find you because he thought you were kidnapped. I don't know if he is alive or dead, and you are going out with a stranger. Is that how I brought you up?"

Amani turned to the three sisters. "She won't be coming to see you again unless I am with her." They all nodded and looked down as if their teacher was scolding them.

"Let's go." Amani opened the door, and Zahra followed her. All the way down to the ground floor, Amani didn't say a word. Once they were in the street, she said, "From now on I will drop you at your school and pick you up afterward every day. You will not leave the house unless I am with you."

When they arrived home, Amani went to the liwan, removed the telephone from the table in the corner, and said, "Bring me the telephone from your room."

Zahra obeyed and brought her pink telephone, handing it over to her mother. Now the only telephone was in her mother's room. She said, "I'm sorry, mom."

"You should be," Amani snapped.

The next day after school, Zahra exited the building to find her mother standing at the school gate. Grabbing her mother's arm, she mumbled, "Let's go home." She didn't want her mother to meet George.

"Hello madam," George's voice came from behind them.

They both turned, but Zahra dared not raise her head to look at him. She wished he would get the message.

"I see you are a man of chivalry," Amani said, "Please stay away from my daughter."

Zahra fervently wished the earth would open up and swallow her at that moment.

38

Ward

Ward opened the door as George was inserting his key in the lock. "Boo," he yelled.

"Ward, how many times have I told you not to scare me like that?"

"Ori, ori Oj," Ward said, a genuine look of contrition on his face.

"Today, Zarah's mother told me not to talk with or try to meet Zahra anymore," George said, as he dropped onto a plastic chair.

Ward sat down in front of George, on a wooden box near the edge of the hole where the fountain had been. "Wa ou anna do?"

"I have to find a way to contact Zahra," George said.

"Ee eo er ouse an kin er othor," Ward said, driving his right fist into his left palm. The slapping noise echoed in the courtyard.

"That's no way to talk, Ward. We definitely don't want to kill her mother," George said sternly.

"Ee idnab er an ring er eir," Ward said, expecting George's approval.

"For heaven's sake, Ward, no. We don't want to kidnap her and bring her here, either."

Ward pressed his lips together and frowned. George got up, and sat beside him on the wooden box, putting an arm around his shoulders, "You are my hero buddy, but I just need a simple solution to get to speak with Zahra. There'll be no killing or kidnapping, OK?"

Ward hugged George, "Ok Oj."

The next morning Ward got up and prepared breakfast, then knocked on George's bedroom door.

George came out wearing a light-yellow shirt and dark blue silk tie and black pants. He sat at the table, as Ward brought him an omelet, hummus, Makdous, Zaatar and Yogurt cream, and a pot of black tea. To top it off, he brought him warm pita bread.

"Do you know the Shagoor High School?" George asked as he ate ravenously.

"Ia cool?" Ward shook his head no.

"Ok, you'll come with me, and I'll show you where it is," George said, licking olive oil off his thumb.

"Ou ut me ia cool?" Ward asked as he tossed a sizeable chunk of omelet into his mouth.

"No, I don't want to put you in the school, I just want you to deliver a letter to Zahra when she comes out of class. Her mother doesn't know what you look like, like she does me. The letter will be inside a book, so if her mother is with her, you just pretend the book fell from her bag and you picked it up for her. She is clever enough to understand what you're doing."

Just then, the phone rang, so George got up and picked it up. "Yes."

Ward watched George's eyes as he listened to the voice on the other end. He swallowed the bite of Zaatar, took a sip of tea, then got up and walked to the sofa beside the phone. George put the receiver down and stood staring at the wall behind Ward.

"Wa?" Ward asked.

"The terrorists attacked Maaloula and burned and

demolished most of the church and kidnapped Mother Pelagia Sayyaf and all the nuns from the convent of St. Thecla," George said. He picked up the phone and called the school, "Hello, Mr. Antwan." Mr. Antwan was the principal of the school where George taught. Ward had met him once.

"Yes, I know. The secretary of the community just called to inform me," George said, "No, I won't be at school today. I am going to Maaloula now. Yes, ok, thank you." George put the phone down and looked at Ward.

"There is money in the drawer in dad's bedroom if you need it. You only leave the house when you need to buy food, ok?" George said. "I will call you from Maaloula."

Ward started to cry. "Ont ia, ont wan ive ere aon."

"No, I am not going to die, and you are not going to be living here alone. I am just going to Maaloula to help the Christian families to flee the area. We don't want them to be killed. Don't worry. I will come back, I promise."

George left the house but forgot to give Ward the book.

Ward spent the day checking all of George's books, but he couldn't find the one with the letter to Zahra.

39

Mullah Abdullah

The mullah opened his eyes, blinked a few times, and looked around without moving his head. To his surprise, he was lying on a proper hospital bed, his body was clean, and he was wearing a blue hospital gown. His left arm was handcuffed to the bed rail, his right arm connected to a saline drip. Several wires running from a beeping machine were connected to his chest, and a green blip on a monitor showed that his heart was functioning normally.

It was a small room with a narrow space on the right side of the bed, occupied by the beeping machine and a medical supply cart.

He raised his right hand and patted his head to discover he was bald. He lowered the hand to his face. His beard was growing again, though not as abundantly as before.

A nurse wearing a surgical mask opened the door, regarded him for a moment, then left. A few minutes later, she came back, followed by a doctor wearing a white coat and a stethoscope around his neck. He was tall and blond with disturbingly blue eyes. The pair were not talking Arabic, but the mullah wasn't sure if it was English or some other language. The doctor put his stethoscope in his ears and moved the chest piece over the mullah's chest in the area of his heart and listened, then moved it to the middle and listened some more.

The doctor gently took hold of the mullah's hand and gestured with a slight flip of his head for him to sit up and lean forward. Then he moved the cold metal disc to several locations on his back and listened again. The doctor gestured for the mullah to open his mouth, then flicked on a small pocket torch and shone it in the mullah's wide opened mouth. Using a tongue depressor, he pressed down on his tongue so he could see the back of his throat.

After that procedure, the doctor spoke to the nurse again in a language that was complete gibberish to the mullah. The nurse answered with a few words, scribbled something on the clipboard at the bottom of the bed, and they left the room.

A short while later, two strong male nurses came in with a gurney, uncuffed the mullah, put him on the gurney, then wheeled him down the hallway, with closed doors on the right and a blank white wall on the left, into an open elevator. One man stood next to the gurney, while the other waved a plastic card in front of a panel of buttons. It made a beeping sound, then he pressed a button, the door closed, and he turned back to face his colleague. The mullah couldn't see which number he'd pressed.

When the lift stopped, the door slid open, and the nurses pushed the mullah out into another hallway that looked much like the one outside his room. To the far left was a shiny steel door. One of the nurses pushed it and held it open, while the other guided the gurney through.

On the count of three, the two nurses lifted him from the gurney onto a cold metal table. The coldness seeped into his bones, causing him to shiver. They proceeded to put him through a head-to-toe CT scan.

After the scan was complete, the same two nurses took him back to his room and cuffed his left arm to the bed. No one said a single word to him the whole time.

Then a male nurse brought him breakfast on a stainless-steel tray. A few hours later, the same man came back to take the empty tray and brought him lunch on another tray. The mullah assumed the second one was lunch, since it had soup and rice and salad. He knew the first one was breakfast because it consisted of milk and a boiled egg.

There was no clock in the room, but the mullah knew it was three days after the CT scan by keeping track of the activities of the doctors and nurses. On the third morning, a nurse came in and gave him two injections. He didn't bother to ask what they were for, first of all because he wouldn't understand the answer anyway, and second, he felt much better after the injections.

They served three meals a day. The first time they served him meat with his food, he asked what the meat was, but the answer was in a language he didn't understand, so the mullah didn't bother to ask again. He didn't eat the meat because he was afraid it might be pork. When they noticed he didn't eat the meat, they stopped bringing him meat, but he was happy and ate the food voraciously. It was hospital food, but compared to the bread and water they'd given him when he was in the dark room, it was incomparably better.

Gradually, his bruises faded, and his strength returned. His nerves became less jumpy. Despite no one talking to him in his own language, no one hit him with wooden rods either, plus he was eating wholesome food that he didn't have to pick up off a dirt floor. His body was clean, not reeking of sweat and feces. Most importantly to him, he could now perform his prayers with a clean body, but still only nodding as before.

The mullah awoke to the sound of bullets. It wasn't nearby but muffled rapid fire shots, probably from an automatic or semi-automatic rifle. Definitely not handguns. He couldn't tell if the sound was coming from above or below his room. Since the room had no windows and thus no sunlight, he didn't know if he was on an upper floor or below ground. The gunfire wasn't getting any closer, but it increased to a shower of bullets.

There were no sounds in the hallway outside his room, so he assumed it was nighttime. The gunfire continued for quite a long time and the mullah was deep in thought when suddenly everything went quiet. The total silence was a sharp contrast, the stillness almost creepy.

He thought there had to be a nurse on night shift, and he wanted to call out, but then he thought even if there was a night shift doctor or nurse willing to talk to him, he wouldn't understand them, anyway.

The mullah initially assumed the people in this hospital were good because they took care of his health and didn't torture him. But why was he still handcuffed to the bed as if he was a murderer, and why didn't they talk to him at all, as if he was an experimental animal in a laboratory? The flying bullets must mean something. If he was still in the hands of the bad people, then the people fighting against them must be good. But then he wondered, what if the bad people win? He was still contemplating what worse could happen to him when he drifted off to sleep.

***

"Hello," someone called out from another room. It was Arabic. The mullah, like a lost boy finding his mother, shouted back, "Finally, someone who speaks Arabic."

"Every hostage here is Syrian," the voice came back loud and clear. "Where are you from?"

"I'm from Damascus," the mullah said, his heart beating faster, "and you, brother?"

"I didn't know they were kidnapping people from Damascus these days. May Allah curse those infidels; they are the worst of Allah's creations."

"They didn't kidnap me from Damascus," the mullah said, but then he quickly thought it was too dangerous to give more details.

"Where did they kidnap you from?" the man in the other room asked.

The mullah lied, "Aleppo, and you?"

"Me too. They kidnapped me in Aleppo."

"Aleppo's are people of great generosity," the mullah said, "I am sure those evil people are not from Aleppo."

"What about you, brother? Where are you from in Damascus?"

Should he tell the truth? He decided against it. "I'm from Mazzah." Then he asked, "Do you know the reason for all the shooting a while ago?"

"Hopefully, the government army has discovered this location and has come to rescue us. Is it your first time talking to someone in this place?"

"It is the first time even speaking in this place, what about you?"

"No, there was a woman in your room before you," the man said, "But they took her away before you came. I think they operated on her and extracted her organs."

"Glory be to Allah," the mullah said, as he thought, what a coincidence. "But are you sure they took her organs? Are you sure this is a place for such things?"

"I heard them," the man said, in a lower voice.

"But they don't speak Arabic," the mullah protested.

"Who doesn't understand English nowadays?"

The mullah made no comment.

"Today is supposed to be the turn of someone called Shaddad Abu Saif," the man said. "By the way, how should I address you, brother?"

The mullah's heart skipped a beat, and he said, "I am Shaddad Abu Saif."

40

Zakiya

A week later, Zakiya was on the first floor cleaning the common toilet of the living room.

"Good morning," a sweet voice said from behind her.

Zakiya turned to see who it was. Her heart beat faster. She swallowed and said, "Good morning, Yasmin."

"You know my name?" Yasmin said with a surprised smile.

"Yes, of course," Zakiya said as she stood there holding the toilet brush.

"I need to use this toilet," Yasmin said, "I don't want the flushing sound of our toilet to wake up the other girls."

Zakiya quickly stepped out of the toilet stall. "Of course, please go ahead."

When Yasmin came out, she stopped to wash her hands, and Zakiya said, "I am so sorry for what happened last week."

"Don't worry about it," Yasmin said, as she looked at herself in the mirror and curled a lock of hair around her finger, "It wasn't your fault, Matchstick."

"I have an idea," Zakiya whispered.

Yasmin turned to look at her.

"Mona has a mobile phone," Zakiya said, "Why don't we steal it and make a call?"

"Matchstick, have you ever had a mobile phone

before?"

"No, we didn't even have a landline in our apartment." Her ears were hot.

"Unless we kill Mona and cut off her finger, we won't be able to use her mobile phone. You can't even turn her phone on without a password or a fingerprint."

"But don't you want to run away?" Zakiya said, then immediately shook her head, "I'm sorry, how dare I even ask you such a question?" She went back into the bathroom to finish cleaning it.

"Matchstick, of course I want to run away, but how? I need to be realistic. Unless you have a plan for us to run away together, it's pointless to even talk about it."

Zakiya nodded and resumed cleaning.

"By the way, what is your real name?"

"Zakiya."

"Nice to know you, Zakiya," Yasmin said and left.

Zakiya smiled. If excitement had weight, she was as heavy as an elephant at that moment. She'd made a new friend.

Zakiya went to the kitchen, made a cup of coffee, and took it to Mona's room. She knocked and waited.

"Your mother's dearest," Mona said from inside, "Come in."

Zakiya opened the door and entered. The stench of cigarettes exuded from every piece of furniture in the room and lingered in the air like a trapped ghost. She put the tray on the coffee table beside the red velvet, high-backed chair Mona was sitting on.

"Sit," Mona said.

Zakiya sat on a chair to the right of Mona without speaking.

"Masha Allah, now you know how to make coffee,

Lebanese style," Mona said between sips.

"Thank you for teaching me," Zakiya said.

"Your mother's dearest, do you think I am a bad person?" Mona asked while holding the lighter to the tip of yet another cigarette.

Zakiya just shook her head.

Mona started coughing. "I must stop smoking." Zakiya was used to hearing this comment every time Mona coughed.

"What's for lunch today?" Zakiya asked.

"Don't change the topic, and don't worry about lunch, Nazih ordered kebab."

"Ok, Miss Mona." Zakiya looked at the closed door.

"My brother thinks I am a bad person because I do this kind of work," Mona said, "As if I am the prostitute."

Zakiya didn't know where to put her hands. First, she put them on her lap, then on the chair cushion on either side of her.

"Look at me," Mona said, raising her voice.

Zakiya looked up and forced a smile.

"Do you think I'm bad?"

Zakiya shook her head.

"That's crap, and you and I both know it. You're about as stupid as the cushion you're sitting on," Mona said. Her cigarette tip blazed as she took a drag. Then she blew out a cloud of smoke and started coughing again. She waved her hand for Zakiya to leave.

Zakiya left the room and closed the door. From outside the door, she whispered, "Yes, you are a crazy bitch."

Later in the kitchen, Zakiya was preparing Tabbouleh, while Mona and Nazih were smoking and chatting.

The front gate bell rang, and Nazih left the kitchen to

fetch the kebab from the gate.

Zakiya turned and asked Mona, "Which city are you from in Lebanon?"

"You think I am Lebanese?" Mona laughed.

Nazih entered carrying two heavy boxes, and barked at Zakiya, "You stupid shit, don't you see me carrying boxes here? Come and take the one off the top." She ran and took the top box and put it on the marble counter.

Mona, still laughing, said to Nazih, "She thinks I am Lebanese."

Nazih spun around and slapped Zakiya. "You are trying to find out where she is from. You think you can run away?" Then he cursed her mother, which made her cry.

"Relax, relax," Mona said, while she drew circles around her right ear with a finger.

Zakiya was hurt more by her gesture than all of Nazih's slaps. *This woman thinks I am stupid.*

"You! Don't allow her to talk to you. Give her a kick every time she asks you a question like that," Nazih told Mona.

Zakiya finished setting the table with her eyes full of tears.

***

The next day Zakiya and Mona were making Warak Enab, meat and rice wrapped in grape leaves. Savory chunks of spiced lamb were already simmering in a pot on the stove, filling the kitchen with a heavenly aroma. Eventually, the meat would be put at the bottom of the pot under the rice wrapped in grape leaves, and cooked together. Zakiya was combining ground meat and rice in a bowl, while Mona laid out the prepared grape leaves on the counter. Zakiya hadn't eaten Warak Enab since her mother passed away.

Zakiya put the bowl of spiced rice and meat on the counter. She and Mona started wrapping the grape leaves around spoonfuls of rice and meat mixture. The wrapping technique was not easy for Zakiya, but after trying a few times and observing Mona, she managed to get the hang of it, even though her wrappings were still not as tight as Mona's.

Out of the blue, Mona said, "I am Syrian, from Aleppo, you know?"

Zakiya dropped the spoonful of rice and meat mixture as she stared at Mona in surprise, "But you speak such good Lebanese."

"That's because you don't speak Lebanese yourself, so you think mine is perfect. The Lebanese dialect is not so difficult to learn. Didn't the girls tell you I am Syrian?" Mona asked.

"No, I never talk to the girls," Zakiya said, picking up another spoonful of rice and meat mixture to wrap.

Mona continued, "My father owned a clothing factory. We exported garments to Iraq and Turkey and made a fortune. Then the war started and armed gangs raided our factory, stole all the machines, burned the building to the ground, and killed my father with a bullet to the head."

Zakiya listened without looking at Mona, and Mona talked without looking at Zakiya. Both were watching what their hands were doing.

"My mom had heart failure after my father died and two weeks later, she died. My brother joined up with the animals who killed my father. He said they were only seeking freedom. They brainwashed him. He grew a beard and put on the same stupid clothes the fighters wore. Then he wanted me to marry one of his leaders, an old man who already had two wives, and I would be the third. I refused. He didn't want me to stay alone at home while he was with the fighters, so he sold our house. He took the money and forced me to stay at my uncle's house. My uncle has three children, all of them working here in Lebanon, and through one of them I got this job with Nazih."

"Did you know what kind of work Nazih was doing?"

"I didn't have any choice. It was either marry the gang leader or run away," Mona said with a sigh.

"Don't you worry sometimes about the girls getting pregnant?"

Without looking at her, Mona said, "We give them pills to prevent pregnancy. So don't worry, and don't talk about things that are none of your business, understood?"

"Yes, Miss Mona, but they taught us in school that the pill doesn't always work."

Mona raised her head to look at her. "Anyone who gets pregnant in this house will have an abortion, then we'll send her to work as a whore in a cheap hotel."

"Ok Miss Mona." *But aren't they whores here?*

41

Mullah Abdullah

The mullah woke up to the sound of footsteps in the corridor. Not one or two people approaching, but several, and all of them were running. He pulled himself into a sitting position.

The door to his room flew open, smashing against the wall. Two soldiers with M16s and helmets bearing Iraqi flags on the side, barged in.

"Keep your hands where we can see them," one soldier shouted, pointing his M16 at the mullah's chest.

The mullah raised his right hand, but the handcuff on his left hand clattered on the bed rail, drawing the soldier's attention. Raising a walkie-talkie, he said, "The hostages to be freed are handcuffed, we need keys immediately, or a technician to cut them off." He spoke Arabic in an Iraqi accent. *The freed hostages.* A wave of elation washed over the mullah. Finally, they were here to set him free. He raised his head and with a trembling voice said, "All thanks and praise be to Allah."

The soldiers left the room, leaving the door open.

The mullah could hear the excited voices of prisoners in the other rooms. Finally, a soldier arrived with a bag full of keys, and tried a couple that didn't work, but the third one opened the handcuffs. Rubbing his chafed wrist, the mullah rose from the bed and in bare feet followed the soldier out of the room. The door of the room next to his stood open, but when he peeked inside, he could see it was already empty.

One by one, other men wearing hospital gowns left their rooms and followed the soldiers. They headed to the big lift, and they all filed inside. Along with the three soldiers, the mullah counted seven men, all of them younger than himself. One of the soldiers waved a plastic card over the panel, then pressed the G button and the lift doors slid closed.

When the doors slid open again, it was to reveal a room with brightly colored carpet and fancy velvet chairs. If the room had been empty, it would seem like the living room in a fancy villa, but now it was full of soldiers and officers. Some were talking on walkie-talkies, some on mobile phones, and still others telling the new arrivals to hurry.

The mullah's bare feet sank into the soft carpet as he hurried toward the exit. Outside, a garden surrounded by a high wall, which was half demolished in some places, and bullet holes in others.

Several army vehicles and four black vans waited outside the wall. As the mullah and his companions came out, two vans that were already full drove off. One of the two remaining vans moved forward, stopping in front of them, the side door slid open, and a soldier hurried them inside. The van's engine purred softly.

The mullah kept his eyes on the road ahead as the van passed through a suburb with villas on both sides of the road.

The freed prisoners were discussing the bad luck that had led to their fate, which seemed to be the fate of so many people in Syria lately. The mullah ignored the conversation. He was much too intoxicated with the hope that now he would be able to proceed with his goal of finding Zahra.

***

The mullah finished the last scraps of the delicious Iraqi meal they'd served him in his new hospital room. He got up and raised his arms high over his head in a stretch, enjoying freedom he hadn't had for so long. *Amani will tell me how long I've been away.* An enormous lump welled up in his throat as he wondered how Amani had been doing on her own. Her days must have been as difficult and gloomy as his, especially if she'd thought he was dead all this time, and that no one would rescue Zahra.

The door opened and a young lady wearing a dark blue suit entered. Speaking perfect Arabic, she said, "Hello sir, my name is Sara, and I am here to convey your personal details to your embassy and help you return to your country."

"Ok, sister Sara, thank you," the mullah said while he avoided staring at her.

She sat down and opened a laptop before asking him, "Do you remember your name?"

In a panic, the mullah didn't know how he should answer. Should he tell her his real name, or should he maintain his cover and give his new name? Finally, he said, "Abu Saif. Shaddad Abu Saif."

He watched as her long fingers tapped the keyboard and then froze, motionless as she stared at the screen as if the devil himself had appeared on her screen. She turned and looked at him for a few seconds, then back at the screen again. She started to say something, but instead took her mobile phone from her jacket pocket and dialed a number. Holding the phone to her ear, she closed the laptop, stood up, and left the room in a hurry.

A few minutes later, four soldiers came in, cuffed the mullah's hands behind his back, covered his eyes with a black velvet blindfold and dragged him out of the room.

The mullah was neither scared nor surprised. He knew immediately giving them his fake name had been a mistake. After a much shorter drive than before, they put him in a room with a mirrored window, a metal table, three folding chairs, and a camera on a tripod in the corner. They uncuffed his hands from behind his back and cuffed him to a ring in the middle of the metal table, then left the room.

He looked at the reflection of the man sitting cuffed to the table. He stood up and tried to get closer to the mirror, but the cuffs pulled him back. He didn't recognize the man in the mirror. His beard had been reduced to a few tufts of hair. Between his eyes were two deep furrows. The skin beneath his eyes was dark and puffy. Multiple scabs covered his forehead, cheeks, and neck. He could see his scalp through the short hair on his head. He looked like a murderer from a sixteenth-century mystery novel.

Two men entered and greeted "Salam Alaikum."

"Alaikum Assalaam," the mullah replied with a wide grin. It had been a long time since he'd heard the Islamic greeting.

Both men wore gray suits with black neckties.

"Who are you?" one of the two men asked.

"Abdullah al-Allab," the mullah said.

"You are Shaddad Abu Saif!" the second man said.

The mullah exhaled slowly, then said, "No, I am not Shaddad Abu Saif, I was kidnapped by Shaddad Abu Saif."

The two men looked at each other, then the first one asked, "Why did you say in the hospital you were Shaddad Abu Saif?"

The mullah explained to them he was an agent on a special mission related to the real Shaddad Abu Saif.

Both men jotted down notes. They didn't ask any more questions, just thanked him, and left the room.

The only sound in the room was the ticking of the clock on the wall behind him.

A man in civilian clothes entered the room carrying papers and ink. He put them on the table, uncuffed the mullah, and took his fingerprints. He cuffed the mullah back to the table, then, taking out a plastic bag and a pair of tweezers, he said, "I need two or three hairs for the DNA test." Without waiting for the mullah's approval, he plucked three hairs, one from his head, one from his beard, and one from an eyebrow, carefully placing them in the plastic bag. He sealed it and left the room without another word.

A few minutes later, a soldier came in and took the mullah to a cell with a cot and an empty bucket.

The only light in the cell was from a single yellow bulb in the ceiling. The dirty walls were covered with names and dates scratched into the surface, as if being in this cell was something the occupants needed to remember or remind others of.

The time passed slowly, and the mullah used the drinking water they'd brought him to perform his ablutions, then he prayed. He spent his time in the cell supplicating to Allah and pleading for only one thing; to leave this place safely and rescue Zahra.

Five days passed before the door of his cell opened and a man in civilian clothes entered and closed the door behind him.

The mullah rubbed his eyes like a bewildered child and looked again. There in front of him was General Zafer al-Abyad, the reason for everything that had happened to him so far in this operation.

The mullah stood up and glared at the general, took a deep breath, then pointed at his face. "Do you see what they did to me?"

The general was wearing a light blue t-shirt over dark blue pants and carrying a honey-colored leather bag. He took two steps forward and threw his arms around the mullah, "This is what genuine heroes look like."

The mullah didn't hug him back.

The general stepped back, looking at the mullah's ravaged face, "Please tell me what happened," he said, as he sat on the end of the cot.

The cot squealed as the mullah sat on the other end. He told the general as much as he could remember about what had happened to him. The general took notes now and then, in a notebook he took out of the leather bag.

"You should be proud of yourself," the general said, "You served your country. That is the most noble action you can do to bring you closer to Allah."

Look who is talking about being close to Allah, the mullah shook his head, "Yes, I am glad to serve my country and be closer to Allah. What brings you here?"

"I came by plane," the general said.

He thinks he's being funny, "Seriously general, why are you here?"

"I came to tell you what your next mission is?"

Seriously. The mullah opened his mouth, then closed it again. He covered his face with his hands for a few seconds, then crossed his arms over his chest and stared at the general, "I almost died."

"That's why you are a hero," the general said, taking a cigar out of his leather bag and lighting it with a match, throwing the matchstick on the floor.

Oh, Allah your mercy, even here he wants to smoke. "Do you want me to ask for an ashtray for you?" the mullah asked, pressing his lips together in reproach, but he smiled eventually when the general laughed.

"No, I have one," the general said, as he took a small tin can with a cover out of his bag and set it on the cot beside him. "I am here for two reasons."

"I am listening," the mullah said, still with his arms crossed.

"Let me start with excellent news. We have gained intelligence which will lead us to the sex slavery and human trafficking branch of the Sword of Truth. You will be able to see your daughter soon."

The mullah dropped his arms, opened his mouth, stood up, but then sat down again. He said, "That really is good news. But what if my daughter was not kidnapped by them?"

The general blew a thick cloud of aromatic smoke. *This cell is so small, soon I won't be able to see the general's face clearly.*

"Don't you, in the Friday ceremony, tell your congregation to keep their faith in Allah strong? Just put your trust in Allah and pray that soon you will be reunited with your daughter."

The mullah rolled his eyes.

"My second reason is to tell you about your next very important mission."

The mullah turned his head to the side and closed his

eyes, like an angry child.

"Listen now," the general said, "I don't need to remind you how many families you've saved, or will continue to save by beating those terrorists."

He turned back to face the general, "What if I die on the mission, who will rescue my daughter then?"

"This mission is not as dangerous. Plus, if anything happens to you on this mission, your daughter will be under my protection."

"Do I have the option to refuse the mission?"

"We are sending you back to Damascus on an Iraqi Airlines plane. Your mission will be on that same plane, so I don't see any reason to refuse it. You are going back to Damascus, anyway."

"What do I have to do?"

"On that plane, a very big deal is going down between a high-ranking leader of the Sword of Truth and another party. We know who the leader of the Sword of Truth is, but we don't know who the second party is. Your mission will be to tail the leader and discover who the buyer is."

"Buyer?"

"The deal is the sale of a large shipment of heavy weapons ammunition," the general said.

"What? Wait, you said I have to find out who the buyer is? So, the Sword of Truth is not the buyer, they are the seller?"

"Yes, you must know by now the Sword of Truth's only purpose is to raise money, nothing more."

"Well, those people — correction, not people. Those beasts who captured and almost killed me were fanatics who think they are the soldiers of Allah on earth."

"Those are mere puppets of the organization," the

general said. "They are made to believe they perform the operations on the ground in the name of religion."

"But how are they sellers? Are they producing weapons now?"

"No, they seized a large shipment of ammunition from our army."

"Wouldn't it be possible to learn from the passengers' manifest who the buyer could be?"

"Yes," the general said, "This is how we know who the leader of the Sword of Truth is. But also on the plane, will be officials from both governments, Iraq's and ours. Our intelligence says the buyer will be someone from one of the two governments. All the officials have clean records. That's why we need someone to identify the buyer."

"So, during the trip, I just have to identify who the buyer is, that's all?"

"You will take photos and record their conversation."

"You want me to record the meeting with the buyer without being noticed?" The mullah could no longer see the general's face clearly. The air was so saturated with the heavy smoke, he was becoming lightheaded. He inhaled deeply and smiled weakly.

"Not him, her," the general said, "It won't be that difficult. One of the buttons on your shirt will be a camera. You only need to be sure they are both directly in front of you."

"Her?" the mullah said. *An easy mission, he says.*

"Your flight will leave tomorrow morning. The plane is a Boeing 737-800. Its capacity is a hundred and fifty passengers over three classes. On your flight, the total number of passengers will be 47, no more. There will be two male pilots, and four female flight crew." The general took a pile of clothes out of his leather bag, and put them on the cot between him and the mullah, "Here are your shirt and pants."

He held up the polo-type pullover with three buttons below the collar. He pointed to the center button of the three and said, "This button is a micro-camera. Its lens covers 180 degrees, so you don't need to move a lot to be able to capture them while they negotiate the deal. Here is the instruction pamphlet in Arabic so you can familiarize yourself with its operation."

The mullah grabbed the shirt, brought it closer to his face, and squinted at the button. It looked like any cheap plastic button and matched the other two perfectly.

The general took out a yellow envelope and laid it on the bench, "Here is your passport, your flight ticket, and boarding pass. The flight time from Mosul to Aleppo, sorry, to Damascus won't exceed seventy minutes, so you have to be very vigilant."

The mullah put the shirt down and grabbed the yellow envelope, looking inside. He took out the passport and opened it.

"Shaddad Abu Saif?" he asked.

"Technically, Mullah Abdullah died in the mosque explosion, remember?"

"So, I will never have my real identity back?"

"Not to worry, all of that will be corrected in time. I didn't have time to issue a passport under your real name. Don't worry, I will take care of all that as soon as you're back with your family."

The mullah sighed.

The general continued, "One more thing," he took a picture out of his bag and handed it to the mullah, "This is a photo of the woman from the Sword of Truth."

The mullah took it and glanced at it, then raised his head and looked at the general, "Are you serious?" The photo showed an uncovered woman.

"Yes," the general said, and blew a thick cloud of smoke. "Why does that surprise you?"

"I just thought they would at least pretend to be following Islamic doctrine," the mullah said.

"It hurts, doesn't it? They are tricking simple people in the name of religion, but unfortunately, those people can't see the bigger picture. They believe they are on the virtuous side fighting the malignant side."

"Yes, it hurts, mostly someone like me," the mullah said.

"Just don't be deceived by the shiny glitter of some people or be misled by their sweet words. The world is full of evil."

"I can't do that. The Islamic doctrine teaches us to assume that all people's intentions are good and not to judge them before they commit actions that prove otherwise."

"Good luck with your methods," the general said.

"It's not my method, it is the divine rules which allow people to live coherent and happy lives rather than living in anxiety and fear of the people around them."

The general stood up and picked up his leather bag. As he did, the cot squealed as if out of relief, "Oh, I didn't expect to see you with bare feet, so I didn't bring shoes." He stepped out of his own shoes and bent to remove his socks, tucking them inside the shoes. As he straightened up, he said, "The socks are clean, don't worry." He stretched out his right hand to the mullah.

The mullah stood up. He needed a couple of moments for his head to stop spinning, then he reached out his right arm and shook the general's hand, "So after I reach the airport in Damascus, I can just go home, or do I need to meet someone to hand over the camera?"

"The camera is connected wirelessly to a satellite. We will know immediately who the buyer is while you are still in the sky. I will be there to meet you when you arrive, don't worry." He banged on the metal door for the guard to come and open it.

"General, is my seat on the plane next to that woman?"

"No," the general said, as the door opened. Some fresh air flowed into the cell from outside, and some of the smoke escaped.

Before the guard closed the door behind him, the general turned and said, "Be sure to study her photo carefully. You will understand why your seat is not next to hers."

The mullah picked up the photo. No matter how hard he stared at it, he still didn't know why he wouldn't be seated next to her. Not a clue.

***

The mullah sat in an aisle seat, the last one on the right side. Behind him was the galley. The passengers poured in and stowed their carry-on luggage in the compartments above their seats. He was still wondering how he would figure out where the Sword of Truth woman was sitting. He knew he didn't have the full seventy-minute flight to find out, because she and the buyer would need time to negotiate the deal. Or had the general said they had already negotiated and just needed to sign the contract? Maybe they would only need a few minutes together? If he located the woman, it wouldn't be difficult to figure out the rest.

From behind him in the galley came the clatter of metal compartments being opened and closed as the stewardesses busily stowed things away before takeoff. The speakers crackled to life above him, and a flight attendant announced in very clear Arabic that the door was now closed, welcomed them to the flight, named the two captains, let them all know the safety briefing would start soon, and warned them they should pay close attention. Then she repeated the whole thing in English.

One stewardess stood in the middle of the plane, another at the front, with the curtain to first class closed behind her. The mullah stared at the one in the middle. She was of average height, with white skin, and black hair cut to just below the ears. She wore only light makeup. The mullah wanted to turn his head to avoid looking at her, but there was something familiar about this woman. What! He swallowed hard. It was the Sword of Truth woman.

Thank you general. I have to tail a working stewardess, which will be nearly impossible. The mullah rubbed the back of his neck as he calculated the possibilities of her closing the arms deal without him being able to witness it. She could just do it while serving a passenger his meal. She could whisper to him or leave him a note, or they could meet out of his sight in the galley in first class with the curtain closed, where he would never get a picture. He drew a deep breath and decided to just forget about his mission. What was the worst that could happen? He would just tell the general he didn't get close enough for a photo.

The flight took off at nine forty-five, and when the seatbelt lights went off, some of the passengers unbuckled their seat belts. Everything appeared normal. There was no activity among the stewardesses yet, and the galley behind him was quiet. He looked at the time on the screen at the end of the cabin to see it was five minutes past ten. No meals had been served yet.

Suddenly the plane dropped for a few seconds causing screams to erupt. The fasten seat belt light started flashing, so the mullah buckled up quickly, his heart hammering in his chest. The toilet signs switched from green to red, the screen at the front showing the plane's route was now black. The plane tilted to the right at a dangerous angle. Some of the overhead compartments on the left side flew open and a few pieces of luggage tumbled out. More screams. A girl was crying. When the plane leveled out, some of the men stood up, trying to see what was going on. But then the plane dropped again, more rapidly this time. Three of the men who had been standing were flung forward as if propelled by an unseen vacuum at the front of the plane. Their screams were lost among the terrified cries of the other passengers. The mullah started to cry out in fear, like everyone else. A deafening clatter erupted as metal cubical drawers were torn loose from their moorings in the galley behind the mullah. Suddenly, the plane stopped dropping and started to ascend at a sharp angle.

There was no announcement to reassure them, or even explain what was happening. The mullah's tongue was like a piece of dead wood in his mouth. He thought his heart would fail soon if it kept hammering at this rate. His hands clutching the armrests were deathly white. Kids cried, women screamed, men shouted, begging Allah for mercy. The cabin moaned and creaked as if it, too, was screaming.

The mullah kept repeating the two testimonies every Muslim must say before death, "Ashhad An la Ilaha Illa Allah, Ashhad An Muhammad Rasoul Allah. I bear witness that there is no god but Allah. I bear witness that Muhammad is the messenger of Allah." There would be no chance of ever seeing his wife and daughter again. Tears streamed from his eyes.

Gradually, the plane returned to the horizontal. Lights came back on in the cabin. The fasten seat belt signs stopped blinking. The screens lit up again, saying the time was seventeen minutes after ten. People ceased their screaming, but some of the women and kids were still crying.

A stewardess's voice erupted from the speakers, "We are heading to Aleppo for an emergency landing, please remain in your seats and keep your seat belts fastened."

One passenger didn't comply and left his seat, heading toward the cockpit, and a few other passengers followed him. The stewardess yelled through the loudspeaker for them to remain seated, but they didn't listen.

The mullah's head was tumbling like the plane had only a few minutes ago. People were quieting down so the announcer could be heard ordering the passengers to stay seated, when one of the men came back shouting that a pilot had been shot dead in one of the first-class seats, causing people to scream and shout again. Some were using their mobile phones to call whoever was waiting for them at Damascus airport, reporting that the plane had been highjacked.

42

Zakiya

Zakiya took a moment to admire the shine she'd just put on the floor in the reception area. It was usually a taboo area because Nazih occupied it most of the time. She dipped the mop in the wheeled bucket, wrung out the excess water, and went to clean the common bathroom. Every morning while everyone in the villa was still sleeping, Yasmin came down to use the common toilet, Zakiya waited a few moments in anticipation. Yasmin reminded her of her friend Zahra, the mullah's daughter. She was similarly pure of heart and friendly.

"Good morning." If ears could smile, Zakiya's ears would have grinned broadly when she heard Yasmin's voice.

"And a very good morning to you," Zakiya answered. Then she got a look at Yasmin's face. "Oh, what's wrong?"

"I feel nauseous," Yasmin said, forcing a smile. She wore a knee-length pink night dress. Her legs were like ivory columns.

"What month are you in now?" Zakiya asked.

"I'm not sure, maybe the third."

"What do you plan to do?" Zakiya asked, glancing around at the door to Mona's room every few seconds.

"I want to get an abortion," Yasmin said.

"No!" Zakiya put a hand to her mouth, "It's a major sin

to kill the baby."

"Are you serious?" Yasmin asked, "What about having sex every night with five different men? Isn't that a major sin?"

"Still, the baby in your belly is a human, and killing it can't be compared to adultery," Zakiya said.

"You are right, but if I don't kill it, Mona and Nazih will kill me when they find out I'm pregnant," Yasmin said.

"What about telling Mona?" Zakiya asked, "Don't you think she would be able to help?"

"She can't be on both sides," Yasmin said, "Either she is with Nazih or with us. Who do you think she will choose?"

"We have to find a way to leave this place so you won't have to kill the baby."

"Before I knew I was pregnant, I hoped the day would come that I could escape this hell," Yasmin said, "But now, I am too ashamed to go back to my family, pregnant with a bastard child."

"My mom used to say, 'Patience is a virtue, and every time you feel a situation couldn't be worse, it means salvation is near,'" Zakiya said.

"What worse could happen? I am barely eighteen with a baby in my belly outside of marriage and I don't even know who the father is."

Zakiya didn't respond. Yasmin was right.

Yasmin went back up to the girl's sleeping room without using the toilet.

43

Zahra

Zahra was no longer allowed to be alone at all, especially outside the house. Her mother dropped her off and picked her up from the school every day. Every day when they reached home after school, Zahra went up to her room, closed the door, and spent her time alone until the next morning. She went down to have her lunch with her mother without speaking. Her mother was in no mood to talk anyway, not even enquiring about her day, ever since the day her father went to the police station and didn't come back.

Zahra was careful to avoid provoking or hurting her mother. She still felt the searing pain in her heart since the day her mother had forbidden her to see George. She understood her mother's concern. What she didn't understand was her own feelings and how she could justify her actions, which, before she'd met George, she had considered forbidden.

One Friday, she asked for permission to visit the three sisters. Amani didn't object, but simply got dressed and went with her.

In the sisters' apartment, the atmosphere was fraught with anxiety. They appeared worried and careful with each word that left their mouths. Zahra simply didn't have the energy or desire to talk anyway, so Amani and the three sisters were quite surprised when Zahra stood up and announced she wanted to leave. While she was kissing the sisters goodbye, Zahra pressed a crumpled letter into Marwa's hand. On the outside of the sealed envelope, she had written a note to Marwa asking her to pass it along to George at his school whenever she had a chance.

The next day, Marwa came to her house for a visit and while Amani was busy in the kitchen preparing coffee, she told Zahra that the principal of the school told her George hadn't shown up for work for the past two weeks.

Zahra received the news like a slap on the face. She didn't drink her coffee and just sat silently staring at the coffeepot. Marwa didn't ask her what was wrong, but Amani asked more than once, "Are you ok?"

"I am just fine," Zahra said and stood up. "I am sorry Marwa I'm not feeling well. I'm going up to my room."

Zahra spent her days distracted, and her nights tossing and turning. Her imagination swirled with questions about the reason for George's disappearance, and hoping he was ok. She wondered how she would be able to go on with her life if he was hurt or injured. The uncertainty was like a noose around her neck, squeezing to the point of cutting off her breath.

She forced herself to smile when she sat with her mom for breakfast or lunch, but her mom's worried looks were obvious. She commented more than once that she must eat more because she was losing weight. Zahra would answer with a wan smile, then return to her room and shut the door.

At school, she was just a body in the classroom without a soul. Her teachers stopped asking her questions because she was always too distracted to answer.

Day and night, all she longed for was to see or hear from George.

44

Mullah Abdullah

Once the plane landed and taxied to a stop, the mullah unbuckled his seat belt, and shifted to the window seat, to peek out. They were not at the Aleppo civil airport. They were surrounded by a vast area of open ground. Dozens of trucks were approaching, leaving clouds of dust billowing behind them. All the trucks bristled with men carrying rifles, who jumped down the minute the trucks stopped and swirled around the plane like a swarm of wasps.

Neither the mullah nor any of the passengers dared to stand up or move. A bearded man entered the cabin with his M16 cocked and ready. He screamed, "Everyone, put your hands behind your heads and leave the plane, now! Keep your eyes on the ground. If you raise your head, you die."

The passengers started filing out.

The sudden ta ta ta tat of the M16 caused all the passengers to scream and drop to the ground.

The same bearded man shouted, "He died because he raised his head. I told you to keep your eyes on the ground. You raise your head, you die. Now MOVE!"

The passengers scrambled to their feet and stepped over the dead man.

The mullah couldn't move for reasons beyond his comprehension. Two armed men entered the cabin and walked down the aisle. One hit everyone who was still sitting, with the butt of his rifle, while the second one was ready to fire if any passenger tried to resist. Blood gushed from the passengers who were hit and spattered on the seats. The mullah was still sitting when they came to him, and the blow to his head made him scream in pain. Blood was running down the side of his face. He stood up, the searing pain in his head blinding him. He stumbled a few times before reaching the door. Outside, the passengers were on their knees, their hands behind their heads. One of the armed men kicked the mullah behind his knee, causing him to tumble forward. Sand and gravel filled his mouth when he hit the ground face first. His head still throbbing in pain, he didn't get up right away, but the armed man shouted at him while aiming his M16 at his head. He got onto his knees slowly, his hands behind his head, blood dripping from the corner of his mouth, his mouth full of sand and blood.

Two men exited the plane carrying the body of the pilot and threw it on the ground in front of the kneeling passengers. It rolled in the dirt once before coming to rest face down. Three more armed men came out of the plane, pushing the three blindfolded stewardesses and the other pilot. They were forced to join the rest of the passengers on their knees. Out of the corner of one eye, the mullah could see the last one to leave the plane was the stewardess who was supposed to close the ammunition deal. In one hand she held a silver pistol, and in the other hand a walkie-talkie. She was talking, but the mullah was unable to hear what she was saying.

With much shouting and poking with their rifles, the gunmen forced the prisoners back on their feet and made them walk two by two with their heads bowed, staring at the ground. As they shuffled away from the plane, the mullah turned his face slightly without raising his head, and glanced back at the plane.

Some men were pulling crates out of the plane's cargo bay and loading them into a truck.

What are those crates? Then the answer came as he spotted the shape of a gun painted on the side of the crate.

Ammunition.

The armed men searched the passengers one by one, men and women. They took all of their mobile phones, wallets, passports, IDs, and everything of value they found in their possession. Then they ordered everyone to remove their belts and shoes before pushing them onward toward an empty hangar. The mullah was feeling faint from the strong odors of feces and urine. He gagged and covered his nose with his sleeve. His mouth was still dirty and tasted of blood. Clouds of flies buzzed around them, attacking like tiny kamikazes. The dried blood caked on his face only attracted the persistent flies more.

Hours passed in the dingy hangar, or at least it seemed like hours to him, because of the throbbing pain in his head. It was as if a hammer was pounding on his skull from the inside with each heartbeat. Some of the passengers moaned in pain. Some were crying. Others prayed loudly, asking Allah for mercy and salvation. Some remained motionless, with eyes closed, lost in their own pits of sorrow.

The deadbolt on the side gate slid back. The hinges squealed as the gate was pulled open, and an armed man entered with a passport in his hand. He screamed,

"Misbah Abdu," and one of the seated men stood up. The armed man grabbed him roughly by the shoulder and hustled him out, closing and securing the gate again.

A few minutes later, a gunshot exploded nearby. A few of the women screamed, and the children cried.

The same armed man came back and shouted, "Akram Khalaf." No one stood up this time, so the man, holding the passport up, moved from man to man, comparing each one to the photo. When he found Akram, he kicked him in the face and dragged him outside. A few minutes later, another gunshot was heard outside.

A child with his parents was crying and begging for water. The father went to the gate and banged and asked for water. Two men opened the gate and answered him with blows from the butts of their rifles to his face. The man dropped like a stone, blood spurting from his face like a smashed tomato. His son ran over and threw himself on his moaning father, crying piteously as he clung to him.

It was getting hotter in the hangar, making the mullah dizzy with nausea. Amani and Zahra came to his mind. He wondered if he would ever leave this place alive and have the chance to rescue Zahra. He looked up and whispered, "Oh Allah, please either help me leave this place alive or send someone from your side to rescue Zahra."

The gate opened again, and three men entered, holding handguns. One of them shouted, "There is a secret agent among you who works for the Syrian government. I will start counting. Every time I reach three, I will shoot one of you until he comes forward."

"One." The armed man said.

Everyone was looking right and left, some objected loudly, they were not even Syrian. The mullah looked from face to face, trying to guess who could be the agent.

"Two," the armed man yelled.

Some of the women pleaded loudly for the agent to surrender himself. The mullah was still scanning the surrounding faces. *I should speak up and say I am the one, I should not be the reason for the death of anyone.*

"Three," the armed man yelled, raised his pistol and flicked off the safety. He grabbed the boy, who was still hugging his bleeding father. The boy's mother screamed and took hold of his legs, trying to pull him away. The other two men kicked her in the chest, and she fell over backward, screaming for the agent to show himself.

The mullah stood up and shouted, "Stop! I am the one you want."

***

Outside the gate, the mullah inhaled deeply, filling his lungs with fresh air, as if he had not been able to breathe inside. The armed man cuffed his hands behind him and led him to a one-story building surrounded by barbed wire and sandbags. On the roof was a heavy machine gun, with a man standing behind it. They entered the building, a wide hallway with four metal doors, two on the right, and two on the left. The sound of voices was coming from the only open door, the second one on the left.

The air in the room was thick with smoke. Four men and the stewardess sat on chairs around the room. Small tables in front of them held drinks and ashtrays. They directed him to sit on a plastic chair in the middle of the room.

"What is your name?" the man sitting to the left of the stewardess asked him. He had a bushy mustache but otherwise a clean-shaven face.

"Shaddad Abu Saif," the mullah said. All the men burst out laughing as if he had cracked a joke.

"Today is the last day of your life. You are about to die," the same man said, as if he was announcing he was about to have lunch. "So, you have nothing to lose. You can just tell us the truth. Who are you, really?"

"Shaddad Abu Saif," the mullah said.

"And I'm Aladdin," the man said, and they all burst out laughing. Then he held up a hand, and they fell silent, "Let's play a game on your last day on earth, before you join your traitorous ancestors in hell." They all laughed again. The mullah sighed.

"I'll tell you what. I will tell you anything you want to know if you tell us the truth," the man said.

"If I am dying today anyway, so why should I care about that?" the mullah asked.

"Curiosity is an instinct in the human brain," the man said, "Oh, wait, you don't have a human brain." They laughed again.

"Ok, I agree to play along with whatever truth game you want." The mullah said.

"Ok, here is my question," the mustached man said, "Do you still think the earth is flat?" More laughter.

"Forget it," the mullah said and stared at the wall, "You are not being serious."

"Ok, ok," the mustache man said, "Let's start with who you are?"

"I am Abdullah al-Allab, the Imam of a mosque in Damascus. I am well known as the mullah." He paused before saying, "I don't need to know who you are, but I am curious about something else. If you promise to tell me, I will tell you everything you want to know."

"What is it you want to know?" the stewardess spoke this time.

The mullah forced himself to smile while looking at her, "Is it true that you sell Syrian women for sex slaves?"

"Why do you want to know that? Didn't you say you're a mullah?" the man with the mustache said, "Do you think you will have an opportunity to have sex with one of them?"

Everyone in the room laughed.

"He is womanizing mullah," said a man from the back, and his silly comment amused them even more.

What is the point of knowing the answer to my question if I am going to die now? No, I should not give up, I won't die unless Allah wills it. It's not up to this bunch of murderers.

The mustached man flicked a lighter and lit a cigarette. His sucking and blowing were interspersed with coughing and some insulting curses about the mullah.

"Ok, ok, I promise to tell you whatever you want, if you promise to tell us the truth," the man with the mustache said. He cleared his throat and spat on the ground, "Or you know what? Just to prove to you that you're dead anyway, I will tell you whatever you want to know, whether you're honest or not, it doesn't matter." He looked at someone standing behind the mullah, and said, "Samer, when you were in Lebanon, you were in charge of one of our pleasure villas there, were you not?"

"Yes, the one in the apartment building on the

corniche in Beirut, we had seventeen whores in that facility."

"But you know where the other facilities are?" the mustached man asked.

"Yes, of course, we used to exchange whores, so our clients could test out new flesh from time to time." He chuckled.

"Can you tell this mullah where the other facilities are? Maybe by some miracle, he will stay alive and want to try some of them."

Everyone laughed.

Controlling anger is a virtue. Controlling anger is one of the most important virtues. The mullah smiled.

The man came around in front of the mullah, "Seriously, do you think you will have a chance to go and test them? You are already dead." He looked at the others and said, "Or maybe, this superman thinks he will go back to his government and tell them about the villas." He looked at the mullah again, "You pitiful, stupid piece of shit, you don't even know the people you are working for. Do you know that half of your government officials go to those villas to fuck the girls?"

More laughter.

Oh, Allah, grant me patience. The mullah's hands were ice cold.

"Just tell him," the mustached man said. "He is stupid enough to fight for the wrong side, and he is dying today, anyway."

"Ok, the best flesh was in the villa at Sycamore Gardens, and of course, the apartment I was in charge of." He turned to the mustached man and said, "Maybe after he dies, he will visit them." They laughed again.

The mustached man swallowed his smile, and put on

a stone face before saying, "Now, tell us what shit your government put you in."

The mullah told them everything.

After he stopped talking, the stewardess said, "You really think you can rescue your daughter? Wow, how much you must trust your god. I think your god will disappoint you this time, because you are not leaving this place alive."

The mullah didn't reply.

"I don't know for what purpose your general put you on this plane," the stewardess said, "But I can assure you, whatever reason he told you, is a blatant lie."

"So, what is the difference now?" the mullah asked.

"At least you will die knowing the truth," the stewardess said.

"The truth that he lied to me?" The mullah asked. *Why am I asking, isn't it obvious that he lied to me?*

"No, the truth is that you lost your life fighting on the wrong side," she said. "Let me prove it to you." She stood up, took a folding knife from her jacket pocket, and walked over to the mullah.

The mullah turned his face away, waiting for fresh blood to start leaking from his face. Instead, she cut the third button from the top off of his shirt, laid it on the table, and smashed it. She went back to the mullah and looked him in the eyes.

"As you can see, there is no camera or recording device in it, it is just a normal plastic button." She went back to her seat. "The ammunition your general told you about was on the same plane you were on."

The mullah lowered his gaze and exhaled, "How did you know there was an agent on the plane?"

"We didn't know, it was just a lucky strike. We always

know whenever the government puts a donkey like you on the plane because they don't know that half of their officers are in our pocket. This time, the general you spoke of was very careful not to let anyone know about you, so none of our agents in your government would know it was you. We expected you to play the hero on the plane and try to sabotage the hijacking plan, but you were a pussy. You didn't dare show yourself.

"I think your cowardice saved your life on the plane, because we would have killed you immediately if you had tried anything. Killing one of the passengers is the best technique to make the others shit in their pants and shut up."

"Would you like to know how we will kill you?" the stewardess asked.

"I don't really care."

She looked at the men around her and asked, "What do you think?"

The suggestions came fast. "Let's just shoot him," one said.

"Let's decapitate him, take pictures, and send them to his government," the one behind the mullah said.

"Or let's just run over him with a tank," the mustached man said.

"Better yet, let's bury him alive," a man next to the mustached man said.

***

They took the mullah's clothes off, leaving him in his underwear. Then they cuffed him to a wooden post in the middle of a dirt yard, like a chicken ready to be slaughtered and drained of its blood. The cuffs cut into his wrists as the weight of his body tore at his shoulder muscles, causing his neck to feel as if it was between two balls of fire. Only the tips of his toes touched the ground.

The hostages from the plane were all ordered out of the hangar and made to surround him in a semicircle. The mullah avoided looking directly into their eyes, so he didn't have to see their pity for him or their fear for the situation they were in. The rebel soldiers and stewardesses were not in attendance. Instead, a group of men with long beards and scary gazes were there to carry out Sharia law. Or at least that's what they believed they were doing. All were carrying M-16s. One of them held a huge knife, bigger than a dagger but smaller than a sword. Another was setting up a video camera on a tripod.

The mullah wasn't scared, just confused. *I spent all of my life serving Allah, preaching the doctrines of Islam, helping poor people, taking care of orphans and widows. I avoided lying or cheating or gossiping or even criticizing other people. I never committed adultery or even looked at other women with forbidden desire. I treated my wife, Amani fairly, and always respected her. I brought up Zahra on nothing but noble principles. Is it possible that Allah will let me down? Or is it possible now is my time of death?* He remembered the verse from the holy Quran in the chapter of the prophet, Younus, **'When their time arrives, they cannot delay it for a moment, nor could they advance it.'**

Oh Allah, all I wanted was to rescue Zahra from the hands of the evil ones, bring her back home, and let her live a normal life like other teenagers everywhere. Oh Allah, why does she have to go through such a cruel experience? Why must she be kidnapped and punished for crimes she didn't commit? Pain pierced his chest. He didn't want to cry, so he swallowed hard and closed his eyes.

If it was not written in the divine records, that it was my destiny to die now, even if all armies on earth aimed their weapons at my head, I wouldn't die. However, if now is my time to die, then now at the time of my death all I should think of is asking Allah for forgiveness and wishing to be among the lucky people who will go to heaven in the hereafter. He started to repeat the two testimonies, "I testify that there is no god but Allah, and I bear witness that Muhammad is the messenger of Allah."

One of the armed men told the cameraman to start recording, then he raised his M-16 and fired a short burst into the air. Then the armed man faced the camera, and with the mullah hanging from the post on his right, he held the M-16 high and started talking to the camera. He pointed at the mullah and said, "This apostate of the religion is the same age as my father, but the difference between him and my father, is that my father joined the Jihad and was martyred for the sake of Allah, this one will be killed for the sake of infidelity and blasphemy." He shook the rifle as each word left his mouth. His Arabic was that of one for whom Arabic is a second language. He looked around at the hostages and told them, "Brothers and sisters, your men are going to die, anyway. Your fathers, your brothers, your sons, it is written that all of them will die. Thus, you must choose for them to die in the path of truth. Otherwise, they will die struggling for the sake of this mundane earthly life. Or they will die in shame like this apostate.

"Nowadays crusaders, infidels, and the Rafizah (Shia) send their men to war. By Allah, they are not braver than we are. No, by Allah, we are the martyrdom and death in the path of Allah's lovers. We are the death huggers, we are the beasts who attack the death in the war, we are the grandsons of Khaled bin Alwaleed and Salahuddin al Ayyubi.

"I beg Allah to accept my father, brothers, and children as martyrs for his sake. And I beg Allah to bring me with them into heaven, rather than with this apostate of the religion," He inserted the muzzle of his M-16 in the mullah's mouth and pulled the trigger. Nothing happened. He threw it on the ground and grabbed another from a man next to him, shooting a round in the sky to be sure. As if his bullets had opened the gates of hell, the sharp whistles of mortar fire erupted, followed by the heavy thuds of explosions.

One explosion nearby plucked the wooden post from its roots and hurled it, taking the mullah with it. As the post struck the ground and rolled over and over, his body repeatedly hit the ground, dashing him against the stones, bruising and cutting him mercilessly. Finally, he landed on the ground amid piles of sand mixed with fried flesh and boiled blood, he couldn't see anything due to the mud covering his eyes, but the smell of burning flesh was a memory he would never forget.

45

Zakiya

A week later, Zakiya was cleaning the toilet when Yasmin came in wearing yellow pajamas. Zakiya bounced up from her scrubbing and said, "Good morning, Yasmin."

"I have a plan," Yasmin said, clutching Zakiya by the arms.

"What is it?" Zakiya caught the elation in Yasmin's voice and shook her arms up and down.

"I will abort the fetus and put it in a plastic bag with a written letter asking for help, and the trash company will find it and call the police," Yasmin said.

Zakiya's smile evaporated, "Didn't we agree to find a way to escape without killing the baby?"

Yasmin sighed, "Put yourself in my place, what would you do?"

"I would never kill the baby, it's a living being," Zakiya said.

"The soul enters the fetus after the fourth month, so technically we are not killing a living being."

"We?!" Zakiya raised her eyebrows.

"Yes, we. You're going to help me abort," Yasmin said, "You just need to hit me in the belly as hard as you can a few times."

Wide eyed, Zakiya looked down at her own skinny body, then at Yasmin's healthy full figure. "What if you have bleeding after the miscarriage? Assuming I could even hit you hard enough to cause a miscarriage, which I seriously doubt."

"Do you have a better plan? I am still using sanitary pads even though I don't have my period, just to keep Mona and the girls from suspecting anything, but I'm not sure how much longer I can keep it secret. If I'm going to run away, I don't want to be pregnant."

"But who says we'll be able to run away even if we succeed? What if no one noticed the fetus, or what if they notice but don't know where they picked it up from?"

"Matchstick, either you come up with a better plan or shut up," Yasmin said, turning her head away. Zakiya could tell she was trying to hide her tear-filled eyes.

"I truly want to help, but I can't hurt you," Zakiya said.

"This plan won't work unless you agree to be part of it, because you're the one who collects the trash," Yasmin said, her voice quivering, still not looking at Zakiya.

Zakiya swallowed.

"Think how many girls will be able to go back to their families if we succeed," Yasmin said. "I really wish, from the bottom of my heart, to be the reason for Nazih and Mona to rot in prison."

Zakiya glanced at the door to Mona's room and said, "When do we do it?"

"Tomorrow."

***

That afternoon the black van showed up with a delivery of new girls, and the smile on Nazih's face was wider than his belly. This time, three new girls descended from the van, as well as a nurse.

The nurse spent over two hours in the hall with the girls, then another two hours in a room with Mona and Nazih. Zakiya was in the kitchen when Mona called her.

"You go down to the basement now. Don't come up unless I call you."

"What about cleaning the service rooms?"

"Don't worry about it. The girls will do it. Don't come up unless I call you, understood?" Mona waved her hand for Zakiya to go.

Zakiya nodded and went to the basement.

That night, Zakiya tossed and turned, thinking about Yasmin's plan. What if Yasmin died when Zakiya hit her? Or what if she bled to death? That would make her a killer. Zakiya buried her face in the pillow and cried. The alarm went off while she was still agonizing over the possible consequences of her actions.

She got up and performed her ablutions and prayers. In the mirror, she could see dark circles under her eyes. She staggered up the stairs like a drunk and started her cleaning chores in the service rooms. Next, she cleaned the living room and reception area, then started in the common toilet. She was vigilant for every small sound, knowing Yasmin would appear at any minute.

But Yasmin never came.

46

Mullah Abdullah

The first thing the mullah noticed was the sharp smell of disinfectant and the depressing stench of blood. When he opened his eyes, all he could see was a colorful mist. He squeezed them shut, then opened them again, but still, it was as if he was looking through misted glass. He blinked a few times, then sighed and kept them shut. He lay there listening to the sounds around him. Nothing that any human would want to hear. Moans and groans from many unfortunate men like himself who had experienced the searing fires of war.

As he raised his upper body, throbbing pain stabbed his left arm and forced him to drop back. He groaned, his breath wheezing in his chest. With his right hand, he rubbed his closed eyes, then opened them again. He could see a little better. Still not as clear as normal, but he couldn't help smiling. He was still alive. He closed his eyes again.

Loud screaming woke the mullah up. Someone was shrieking in pain. He raised his head slightly. A young man with both legs amputated below the knees writhed in agony in a bed next to his. Stark white bones were exposed. The mullah looked around, he was in a hospital ward, with ten beds including his, all of them occupied by injured men. He was able to see more clearly now.

A nurse ran toward the screaming young man and injected another dose of morphine into his IV. As she was leaving the room, she noticed the mullah was awake and looking at her.

"Bed seven's awake," she called out as she left the room.

A doctor entered. The mullah assumed he was a doctor by the stethoscope around his neck, but he could have been mistaken for a butcher.

"I'm Captain Faisal," he said, as he checked the clipboard hanging at the end of the bed, "What's your name?"

"Oh, nice to see you, doctor." He must decide quickly what name he should give. "Sorry, I mean Captain. I mean Sir."

Captain Faisal laughed, "They brought you here because you were injured in an aerial bombardment, which caused the explosion of a huge amount of ammunition, causing many people to be burned alive. You are one of the lucky ones." He flipped a paper on the board, "You have a lot of bruises, a concussion, and a broken arm. Other than that, you're strong as a horse."

"Where am I right now?" the mullah asked.

"Sorry, I forgot to tell you. You're in the military hospital in Aleppo." He put the board back and left the room quickly when a nurse called him from outside the ward.

The mullah lay his head back on the pillow and smiled. He decided to use his real name from now on. No more hiding or lying.

The room was quiet now that the screaming man with the amputated legs was sleeping. On his other side was another injured man, his face completely covered with gauze except for a slit for his mouth. His body quivered, almost bouncing on the bed, then suddenly blood burst from the slit propelled by violent coughing and gagging, making it clear that he was choking. A nurse rushed into the room and helped the bandaged man to sit up and spit blood and sputum in a bucket next to his bed, then she gave him an injection before leaving the room.

"Excuse me, Sister," the mullah called out.

She looked at him, "Yes, Uncle."

"When can I leave?"

"We haven't tended to your broken arm yet. After we put a cast on it, you can probably leave. Is there anyone from your family around to help you?"

"No, my family is in Damascus."

He thought she looked at him rather suspiciously before walking out.

A few hours passed before the doctor found time to put a cast on the mullah's arm. During those hours, the nurses gave him something for pain whenever it became unbearable.

Captain Faisal came with the tools and materials to make his hand splint, "Salam Uncle," he said.

Uncle! Do I look so old that everyone calls me uncle here?
"Salam Doctor Faisal."

"Don't look at me or at your arm while I'm applying your cast," Faisal said.

The mullah turned his head and said, "Ok."

"You still haven't told me your name?" Faisal said as he started working on the mullah's arm.

The mullah groaned a little, forcing himself not to pull his arm back, "It's Abdullah al-Allab."

"Uncle Abdullah, I think you are from Damascus, am I

right?"

"Yes, that's right."

"You were one of the lucky ones. Many of the hostages from the plane either died shortly after they arrived or were taken straight to the morgue."

"So, you knew we were hostages?"

"Yes, the orders were for us to send all the ambulances we have to ..." Faisal paused. He worked for a few seconds silently. Only the mullah's groans didn't stop. Then Faisal continued, "... to where the bombardment happened. They brought in all the hostages."

"Thanks be to Allah."

"So, what took you to Mosul in these difficult times?"

Is he just trying to distract me by talking randomly, or does he really want to know? "They kidnapped my daughter, and I would go to the moon to rescue her, not only to Mosul," the mullah said, then turned to look at Faisal's face.

Faisal was frozen in place, holding the mullah's arm and staring at him. "And were you able to rescue her?"

"Not yet, but I asked Allah to help me, and not dying is the strongest evidence that He is helping me." Again, he turned his head away.

"Do you know where she is," Faisal asked, "Excuse me for saying so, but how can you be sure she is even still alive?"

The mullah opened his mouth to speak, but no sound left his lips. Suddenly, his tears started streaming.

"I am sorry, uncle," Faisal said, "But in this war we are witnessing the worst things humans can do to their fellow humans."

"She is in a pleasure house in Lebanon," *What makes me so sure that she is there? Wouldn't it be better if she is dead than working as a whore?*

"Are you sure?" Faisal asked, standing up and patting the mullah's shoulder. "Insha'Allah Your arm is going to be ok."

"When can I leave?"

"In a few days. We will let you know when you're ok to leave. Right now, the road to Damascus is not passable, anyway. You must wait for the army to drop you back in Damascus, probably by helicopter."

"I will not be going to Damascus, I am going to Lebanon, to Beirut, to find my daughter."

"Do you have your passport or ID with you?"

"No."

"So how will you go to Lebanon?" Faisal asked before rushing out again in response to a nurse shouting his name.

The situation was chaotic in the hospital, many of the injured people entered screaming in pain but left as mute carcasses. A week passed and every day, the mullah asked the nurses and Faisal when he could leave. The response was always the same, he must wait. He finally gave up asking, but on the morning of the eighth day, with his arm in a sling, he left the hospital. No one tried to stop him.

The hospital was on a heavily trafficked street. Cars, vans, buses, and motorbikes polluted the air with not only exhaust fumes but also an ear-splitting racket. In any other situation, breathing such polluted air would irritate him, but today, even inhaling poison couldn't upset him. His smile was wide, and his breathing deep. He almost bounced with every step. He was going to rescue his daughter.

"Uncle Abdullah, Uncle Abdullah," someone was

yelling.

The mullah turned to see Faisal running after him, so he turned and walked back towards him.

"Where ......are ....you...... going?" Faisal said between gasps for breath.

"I think you need my empty bed more than I do," the mullah said.

"What are you talking about?" Faisal said.

"I must go. The sooner I arrive to rescue Zahra, the better for her."

"Your daughter's name is Zahra? My mother's name is Zahra."

"Yes, the name of the daughter of the prophet."

"So, you are going to Lebanon to rescue her?"

"That's right."

"Can you tell me how you plan to get there?"

"I trust in Allah that He will help me," the mullah said, avoiding Faisal's eyes.

"Allah said 'First think, then trust.' To start with, you have no official papers and even walking around without an ID is a fatal mistake. Every few hundred meters, there's an inspection point where they will ask for your ID. Second, you have no money for a bus or a car."

The mullah smiled. "I have survived worse than that."

"Tell me what you're going to do?"

"I don't know yet. I only know one thing: Allah helped me to survive situations that were fatal for others. He will help me now and I will rescue Zahra."

"Do you hear what you are saying?"

"Son ..." the mullah paused for a few seconds, then turned and started to walk away.

"Wait, Uncle," Faisal ran and stood directly in front of

the mullah to prevent him from getting away.

"Wait for what?" the mullah asked.

"My brother Sarmad manages a small trading business between here and Lebanon," Faisal said, "I called him, and says he can help you get to Lebanon."

"Your brother is a smuggler?"

"Well, kind of."

"Without money or papers, he can smuggle me?"

"Yes."

"How?"

"Is that important right now? Or do you just need to get to Lebanon?"

"Yes, of course, but why are you helping me and why would your brother put himself at risk to help someone he doesn't even know?"

Faisal sighed. "My sister was also kidnapped, and we don't know if she is still alive or ..." Faisal stopped and looked down, "Come back with me to the hospital. My brother will pick you up there. It is too dangerous to walk around like this with no ID unless you want to spend your night in prison."

What do you know about spending the night in prison? The mullah thought, as he followed Faisal back to the hospital. His broad smile never left his face. He was clueless but still alive, as he looked up at the sky and said out loud, "Thank you, Allah."

47

Zahra

Zahra went to the principal's office and asked for permission to leave school, explaining that her period had started unexpectedly and she didn't have any sanitary pads with her.

But Zahra wasn't actually on her period. She just wanted to leave school early and go to George's house. As usual, the heavy guilt pressed down on her, but she had learned to bury it deep inside. Now, she added the guilt of deceiving the principal to the burden she already carried, pushing it just as deep.

When she reached George's house and knocked on the cracked door, she noticed an eerie silence in the alley. No one answered. She knocked again and pressed her ear against the wooden door, but there was still no noise inside. She had to find out what had happened to George and Ward. The principal wouldn't let her leave early again, and her mother would surely get suspicious if she came home early more than once. Zahra glanced around, then walked to the neighboring house and knocked.

An old woman, dressed in black opened the door just a crack, revealing part of her wrinkled face. She remained silent, waiting for Zahra to speak.

"Salam aunt," Zahra said, forcing a smile. "Do you know where your neighbors, George and Ward, are?"

The woman shook her head, muttered a quick "No," and shut the door.

Zahra sighed, standing alone in the middle of the deserted alley. No passersby, no bicycles, no cars, it was as if the place had been abandoned. *What am I doing? It's too dangerous to be here alone.*

Zahra walked toward the Maryamian Church on Bab Sharqi Street. When she arrived, the gate was closed. She pressed the intercom and waited for a response. At least on this street, she could hear the noise of everyday life–it was a semi-commercial area.

The gate opened with a loud, grating creak. A pastor stood in the doorway, his smile not reaching his eyes.

"God be with you, my daughter," the pastor said.

"Salam, Father," Zahra said, "I just need a few minutes of your time."

"Please," the pastor said, though he didn't move or invite her in.

On her way to the church, Zahra had thought of the best excuse – a plausible reason for why a Muslim girl might ask about a Christian young man. In times of war, it was risky to give out someone's whereabouts to strangers.

"My father's friend used to tutor me after school," Zahra said. "But he disappeared suddenly, and we're worried. I went to his house, but no one answered the door. He often mentioned that he volunteered here at the church, so I thought you might know something."

"Who is this teacher?" the pastor asked, his smile now replaced by a frown.

"His name is George; he teaches at Assieh school," Zahra said, then swallowed.

"I'm sorry, my daughter; I don't have any information

that could help you. Perhaps you can find another tutor," he said, beginning to push the gate closed.

"No, it's not about finding a new teacher," she insisted. "We still need to pay him a large sum of money."

"I don't know which George you're referring to," the pastor said.

"He lives on Zukak Tanyus, and he has a brother with special needs – his name is Ward," Zahra said.

"Oh, everyone knows Ward," he said, "Just ask your father to bring the money, and I'll make sure it reaches them."

"Thank God! They're alright?" Zahra asked. "Would it be possible to deliver the money myself? Because..." She hesitated, then added, "My father was injured by a mortar shell, so it would be difficult for him to bring it."

"Unfortunately, there's no way for you to meet them personally," the pastor said. "The church has arranged for both George and Ward to seek asylum in Germany. They're already in Lebanon, waiting for their documents."

A wave of dizziness washed over her, and she steadied herself by holding onto the gate. The pastor's eyes narrowed as he noticed her reaction.

"You can leave the money with me, and I'll make sure it reaches George," he said, before slamming the gate shut with a deafening clang.

Zahra went home. Her mother's eyes widened when she saw her. "Are you alright?" she asked.

"I've got a bad stomachache. I just need to rest," Zahra muttered, heading to her room. She closed the door, collapsed face-down on her bed, and began to cry.

***

A few days later, while Zahra was walking home from

school with her mom, a girl approached them and said, "Hello Zahra."

With a moment of concentration, Zahra recognized her as one of the girls from their trip to Maaloula, though she couldn't recall her name.

"Hello," Zahra greeted her, kissing her on both cheeks.

"How are you, Zahra?" The girl asked with a warm smile.

"I am fine, how about you?" Zahra replied.

"I'm good," the girl answered. "I'll visit you at home soon, as I promised." She hugged Zahra tightly and slipped a crumpled letter into her hand. "I'm in a rush," she said, before hurrying off.

Zahra tucked the letter into her pocket, trying hard to contain her excitement as she continued walking.

"Who was that?" her mother asked.

"One of the girls from the trip to the church," Zahra answered, surprised when her mother didn't ask any more questions.

Later in her room, Zahra unfolded the paper. It was from George, confirming what she already knew – that he and Ward were in Lebanon, preparing to leave for Germany. But what made her heart race was the Lebanese phone number written at the bottom of the letter.

***

Zahra waited until Friday, the weekend, and seized the chance while her mom was in the bathroom. She sneaked into her mother's bedroom and dialed the Lebanese number. She knew the call would show up on the phone bill, but she didn't care. All that mattered right now was talking to George.

"Hello," he said.

Her head felt lighter when she heard his voice on the other end, though he sounded congested, as if he had a cold.

"Salam George. Why didn't you tell me you're going to Germany?"

"Oh, Zahra, it's wonderful to hear your lovely voice. How are you?"

Zahra's cheeks burned. "I don't have much time; my mom will be out of the bathroom soon," she said, glancing at the door.

"I am sorry. I didn't want to cause any trouble by coming to your house. We only had two days to pack and move to Lebanon."

"Do you know when you're leaving for Germany? Is it soon? Do you think we can meet before you go?"

"I am not sure when we're leaving, but we're not allowed to return to the country. We've registered with the UN refugee agency here, and the church is working hard to push our case. For Ward's sake, they're speeding things up."

"Okay," Zahra said, still glancing at the door. "I just want to say one last thing."

"Me too, I wanted to say something but...." George trailed off.

"What is it?" Zahra asked. "You go first... then I'll tell you mine."

"No, you go first," George said.

Zahra searched within herself for the courage to say what was on her mind. She found it, and so much more, but it wasn't a lack of bravery that made her hesitate. It was the fear of regret. Once the words left her lips, there would be no turning back. They would pierce his heart like an arrow. But this might be the last time they would hear each other's voices. Shouldn't she tell him the truth? Or would saying it just complicate things? Maybe it was better to hang up now, keeping the heartache to herself and sparing him any further pain.

"Zahra," George said softly, "What is it?"

"I just want to say..." She paused as she heard the bathroom door creak open, "I love you," she whispered, then quickly hung up.

48

Mullah Abdullah

Sarmad drove a BMW with dark tinted windows, not a new model but still with the style and energetic soul of German vehicles. The mullah sat in the passenger's seat and listened as Sarmad instructed him. "You won't leave the car at the borders or inspection points. I will get you through them all, but you must not ask me how I do it. Deal?"

The mullah nodded seriously, and said, "Yes, sir." They both smiled.

The BMW pulled over in front of a barbershop. The mullah looked at Sarmad, noticing his hair was short, and his beard neatly trimmed.

"Have you looked in a mirror recently?" Sarmad asked, as if he'd read his thoughts.

The mullah flipped down the sun visor and looked in the mirror. He was staring at the face of a farmer, and an old farmer at that. "I don't have money for a haircut," the mullah whispered, without looking at Sarmad.

"Don't worry, I will pay," Sarmad whispered back, "Just keep your mouth shut in there. No matter what subject the barber talks about, you just listen. Don't speak."

They got out of the car and went into the shop. In the large mirrors at the front and rear of the shop, the mullah saw the reflection of Sarmad in his stylish black suit and shiny shoes entering the shop followed by a homeless old beggar wearing a torn shirt and scruffy pants, one arm in a cast held up by a sling, with shaggy hair and straggly beard. He was grateful that Sarmad dealt with the barber. His own face was red the whole time and he could barely raise his eyes to look at the barber while he was cutting his hair.

As they got back in the car, Sarmad looked at him with a wide grin. "Now we need to get you some new clothes to match your good looks." He put the car in gear and sped off like a bullet.

***

At the Syrian border, Sarmad said, "You stay in the car." Then he took a plastic file folder and left the car. Half an hour later, he came back with an officer, who sat in the back seat while Sarmad got in the driver's seat. They left the Syrian border and entered the Lebanese border control. The officer and Sarmad left the car without a single word. In a couple of minutes, Sarmad came back alone and drove on toward customs.

After they'd passed through Lebanese customs, the mullah couldn't remain quiet any longer, "You are a powerful man."

Sarmad made no comment, just kept driving until they reached the outskirts of Beirut.

"Now tell me where you want to go in Beirut?" Sarmad said, looking straight ahead, and changing gears as if he was on a racetrack.

"I want to start with the Sycamore gardens," the mullah said.

"Do you think you will find your daughter there?"

"I am not sure. I have several potential places to check out."

"You know you'll need money to do that?" Sarmad changed gears and stomped on the gas pedal. The engine roared, and the mullah was pressed against the seat back.

"I know, and I don't have money," the mullah said, "but Allah has brought me this far, I think He will send me the money to rescue my daughter."

Sarmad exploded in a fit of laughter. He drove without further comment until they arrived in a quiet area with many villas. Sarmad said, "Here we are at the Sycamore Gardens. Do you know which villa?"

"Unfortunately, I do not," the mullah said, "but you can drop me here, and I'll continue on foot."

Sarmad pulled over, and the mullah stepped out.

"Uncle," Sarmad called from inside the car.

The mullah bent his head to look at Sarmad. Sarmad's hand was stretched out to him, between his fingers was a thin bundle of dollars. The mullah plucked them from his hand, saying, "I told you Allah would send me the money. But don't you worry. Allah will pay you back for your good deed, even if I can't find you when this is over, to pay you back."

"I am not worried, I will find you and take my money back," Sarmad said, before driving off like a lunatic.

When the car disappeared at the end of the street, the mullah counted the money. Five hundred dollars. He slipped the money into his pants pocket.

***

The mullah walked down the street between the villas of the Sycamore Gardens. The only sounds were the birds tweeting and flitting from branch to branch of the sycamore trees. The intertwining tree branches allowed only a few of the sun's rays to pass between the permanent green leaves to trace bright spots on the ground. The sun would set in two or three hours.

A man was washing a car in front of one of the villas. *What a waste.* The mullah headed towards him. The hose was pouring water on the ground while the man was scrubbing the wheels. He contained his annoyance and forced a smile. "Salam brother."

The man replied in a Lebanese accent without raising or turning his head from what he was doing, "Salam."

"Do you know which one of these is the pleasure villa?" the mullah asked.

The man looked up at him, his eyes wide in surprise. "Old man, aren't you ashamed of yourself, looking for girls at your age? Get out of here before I give you a soaking."

The mullah said nothing. He didn't blame the man for his reaction. He knew if he was in that man's position, his reaction would be even worse. He kept walking, eying the enormous villas on both sides of the street. All the villas had high metal fences which allowed views of lawns and gardens. So far, he'd passed only one villa with high walls, like a fortress. He walked and walked and walked, his gut twisting with hunger. He hadn't eaten since the day before at the hospital.

He kept walking, looking for someone else to ask, but no one appeared. From time to time, a car passed him.

Finally, he stopped for a rest and stood contemplating the sycamore trees around him. Clusters of sycamore figs grew in bunches from the very bark of the tree trunks. The area was like a piece of heaven. "Praise Allah," the mullah said.

A taxi slowed down and honked the horn to attract his attention. He waved a hand for the driver to stop and darted forward. *Tourists ask taxi drivers for these sorts of details all the time.*

"Hello brother," the mullah said, leaning in with his hand above the door on the passenger side.

"Hi brother, where do you want to go?" the driver said, he was an old man with white hair and a long neatly trimmed gray beard.

The mullah stared at the driver, his white hair and long beard rendered him speechless for a moment. Then he stood upright and swallowed. *Is it possible this solemn looking old man would know about the villa?*

The old man's next words ended his hesitation. "What do you want, old man? Tell me how I can help you."

The mullah leaned again into the open window, intending to tell him to leave, but the driver winked at him with a sly smile. The mullah sighed and said, "I'm looking for a villa around here to have a pleasant time, do you understand me?"

The driver laughed and said, "Get in."

The mullah got in, but the driver didn't move. He said, "I will drop you at the villa, but it will cost you fifty dollars."

The mullah swallowed and nodded.

The driver held out his hand, palm up, "Money in advance, please."

The mullah gave the driver a hundred-dollar bill.

The driver threw it on the console as if it was a piece of trash and stepped on the gas abruptly. A few minutes later, he pulled up at the same villa the mullah had passed earlier, the one with the high walls.

The car stopped, but the mullah didn't get out. He pointed at the hundred-dollar bill.

"Oh, brother, I don't have change. However, let me give you some advice."

"What's sort of advice?"

"Your accent is Syrian. They won't let you in if they know you're Syrian."

"Why don't they allow Syrians in?" the mullah asked while staring at the high walls.

"I don't know. Maybe because all the girls inside are Syrian," the driver said.

The mullah turned and looked at the old man. Such a charming face, "Maybe I could pretend I'm deaf and mute."

The driver laughed, "You have a sense of humor, brother."

Is he mocking me or is he serious?

"Or I could make the arrangements for you to go in for the other fifty dollars." The driver pointed at the hundred dollar note.

"Ok, it's a deal."

"Ok, wait for me in the car. They know me here and trust my clients." He winked at the mullah again and left the car after picking up the hundred-dollar bill and shoving it in his shirt pocket.

The mullah could see the driver talking on the intercom to the left of the gate, but couldn't hear what he was saying. The driver turned and waved for the mullah to join him.

The mullah wiped his sweaty hands on the back of his pants and swallowed hard before walking to the gate. An electronic motor activated for a moment, opening the gate only wide enough for one person to pass through at a time. The driver went in, and as the mullah followed, he noticed the garden was tidy and the lawn had been recently trimmed.

They entered the villa into a large room with a huge oval table surrounded by chairs. On the left side, a middle-aged man with a large belly and shiny black hair sat behind a desk.

"Welcome my friends." The man behind the desk stood up and stretched out his hand to shake with the mullah. The mullah looked at the man's hand in front of him but didn't respond. The driver made a noise in his throat. The mullah immediately shook the man's hand, then pulled his own hand back as if it had been touched by fire.

"One hour, three hundred fifty dollars," the man said.

The mullah took out the money and handed all of it to the man.

The man counted it with a wide smile and placed it in a drawer, handing fifty dollars back, then handed the driver a ring binder with photos of the girls printed on glossy paper. The mullah and the driver sat down at the oval table and opened the binder. The mullah flipped through all the photos quickly until he'd seen them all.

"Didn't find your desire?" The driver asked, "Would you rather have a boy?"

The mullah closed his eyes for a moment. He wanted to spit in the driver's face, but he controlled his temper.

He flipped through the pictures again, but this time to choose a girl. He chose the most worn paper in the ring binder. He wanted to be sure she had been in this villa long enough to know what was going on.

The man behind the desk had been watching closely. Without the driver or the mullah saying a word, he raised a receiver and pressed a button. After a few seconds, he said, "Ask Jori to come down."

Jori was everything the mullah didn't like in a woman. She was exactly the opposite of his Amani. Her smile was fake, she wore shorts barely covering her fat bottom, and a sleeveless shirt knotted above her navel. She reached out to shake the mullah's hand. He froze, looking at her hand as if he was looking at a snake. He stretched his arm out, but as soon as she touched his hand, he pulled it back.

She turned to go, and he followed. As she climbed the stairs ahead of him, her bottom was on a level with his eyes, so he focused his gaze on the steps his feet were stepping on. A short distance down the hall from the top of the stairs, she opened a door with the number eight on it and waited for him to enter.

She followed him in and closed the door, pointing at the clock. "It is six twenty, I will come back in ten minutes so you can have a quick shower. At seven ten, I will leave you to take your after shower." She left the room.

The minute she went out, the mullah bounced up as if he was sitting on a hot stove. He stood in the middle of the room and looked around with disgust. There was the bed where the sin of adultery was committed; the closet where the woman's clothing was. Two chairs sat in front of a small table and opposite them a flat screen TV hung on the wall. This must be where these lost souls sat and spent their time between sinning. Jori came back and looked at him, still standing there.

"Do you need more time?" she asked, "You must take a shower, otherwise I can't do anything with you."

"No, I am not here to do anything with you," the mullah said, "I am a happily married man."

"Most of our clients are married," Jori said while

pulling down her shorts.

The mullah turned his head away and stared at the wall and said, "Please, you are my daughter's age, I won't touch you, please put your clothes back on. If you have anything else to cover your body, I would appreciate that as well, so I can talk to you."

The mullah heard the swish of her shorts, then he turned back to face her. She opened the closet and took out a large white towel, wrapping it around her middle, covering her stomach and navel.

"Are you from Homs?" he asked.

"Yes, how did you know?"

"From your accent."

"Usually my clients are Lebanese, or maybe Syrians, but too ashamed to admit they recognize us." Jori's eyes were full of pain. She didn't need to explain. He understood what she must have gone through before she came to this place. Her eyes spelled out her sorrow.

"My daughter is the same age as you. She was kidnapped."

Jori moved to sit on one of the chairs and motioned for him to sit on the other.

"I am looking for her," the mullah said as he sat down. "She has fair skin and dark hair, her cheeks are pink like flower petals, her eyes pure and full of honesty, she has a sweet voice and is full of joy and laughter. When she moves, you expect flower petals to drop all around her. She has a kind heart and polite manners. She is the reason for our existence. Me, and Amani, her mother. My house with her in it is heaven. Without her, it is hell. I no longer have a reason to...." He covered his face with his hands and sobbed.

"You are describing half of the Syrian girls before the

war," Jori said, and then paused. The only sound in the room was his crying.

He raised his head, wiping his eyes with the tissues Jori pulled from a box on the small table. "Do you have a photo of her?"

"No, I don't," he said, "But her photo was not among the pictures of the girls down in reception."

"Were you there when they kidnapped her?" Jori asked.

"No," he said with a choked sob.

"What happened to your daughter has happened to many girls in Syria. We lost our house in Homs and we were fleeing to Lebanon through the Jawsiya crossing in the Qusayr region. It was nighttime, and the road was dark between the villages. We were hundreds of families walking toward the unknown, mostly women and children, with only the clothes on our backs and carrying enough sorrow to dry up all the seas and oceans on this earth. I don't know why the van stopped next to me that night. Two men jumped out, picked me up, and threw me in the van. They left all the other girls and chose me. My mom was screaming and crying. I will never forget her voice; the voice of a helpless, oppressed woman." Jori started to cry.

"Where is your father?" the mullah asked.

"My father was in the army reserve. I don't know where he is or where my mother is now. Whether they are still alive or dead. If they are looking for me, or have given up? I don't know." She sighed.

The mullah looked at the door when he heard footsteps in the hallway. He stood up and went to the window. He peeked out from behind the curtain to see the yard filled with armed men.

"Do you think you are being rescued?" the mullah asked Jori.

She stared at him, then in two jumps was at the window, too close to the mullah. He smelled the lilac scent of her shampoo and stepped back.

They both spun around to look at the door when it opened with a bang, hit the wall and bounced back. An armed man stepped in, pushing it open again with his machine gun. Behind him were enough armed men to arrest a tribe. The first man shouted, "Put your hands behind your head and come out slowly."

49

Zakiya

Zakiya was cleaning service room number nine. She had skipped room number eight because there was a client with the girl in there. Her days had become colorless since the day Yasmin disappeared. She thought maybe they'd shifted her to another villa. When she asked Mona about it, the only answer she got was a slap in the face. It was the first time Mona had slapped her.

The curtain was open. The blue of the sky tinted by the golden rays of the setting sun. She walked to the window and slid it open. The breeze caressed her cheeks. She inhaled deeply. A movement behind one of the sycamore trees caught her attention. She gasped and rubbed her eyes. Three, six, nine. Nine ropes were dangling from the top of the garden wall and men in black uniforms with guns were descending into the garden. Maybe there were more ropes on the other walls. They wore black helmets and vests. She read one man's vest. "Lebanese Special Forces." She quickly closed the curtains and observed through a tiny opening between them. One of the men waved a hand, signaling the others to move. They were all bent low, aiming their guns ahead of them while they advanced toward the villa.

Zakiya's breath quickened as she peeked through the open door from time to time from where she stood.

Nazih was in the reception area, Mona in the girls' common room checking on them. *Finally, Nazih and Mona will get what they deserve, thank you Allah, thank you. So many men and guns. This is so great. May Allah bless the Lebanese Special Forces.*

She didn't dare to leave the room, so she hid behind the closed curtain and kept her ears alerted for movements outside the room. The footsteps of the men were soft but audible. At any other time, they would have been horrifying steps, but today she listened to them as if they were her favorite melody.

Footsteps drummed on the stairs. Doors banged open.

Loud voices outside room eight. A kick, and the door exploded inward, men yelling at the client in the room, "Put your hands behind your head and come out slowly!"

A male voice from inside the room said, "Ok, ok, take it easy."

The client's accent was Syrian. She knew that soulful tone. It was as if his voice had invisible threads pulling her from where she stood, toward the door.

His eyes met hers. He had an arm in a cast, and his reddened chin was visible through his beard. The beard was shorter, with much less hair than before. His face had aged, as if this person was the father of the mullah she knew.

The minute he cried out her name, she could no longer remain where she was. Despite warning shouts from the armed men around her, she ran and threw herself on the old man and started sobbing. She hugged him so hard.

Three armed men tackled him, forcing him to the floor. One of them grabbed the arm without the cast and handcuffed him.

Instead of letting go, Zakiya fell with him. One of the men tried to pull her away, but she clung to the mullah even harder, pressing her face to his chest and crying the entire time.

"Is Zahra here with you?" the mullah asked.

She pulled back and looked at him, his face calming her soul, "Did they kidnap Zahra too?"

"Weren't you together?"

The men in black were pressing the mullah's head to the floor.

"They didn't kidnap her when we were together."

Other men were yelling at the girls to come out into the hall with their hands behind their heads. One by one, they herded the girls down the stairs.

The three armed men who had handcuffed the mullah pulled him up from the floor and forced him down the stairs. Zakiya refused to let go of him, and so she descended with him, clutching his arm tightly.

There were many more men in black on the ground floor, some were talking on mobile phones, some busy arranging the girls in a line against one wall, and still more surrounding Mona and Nazih, who were securely handcuffed and forced to lie face down on the floor. Several vans and police pickups were in the garden, their red roof lights flashing.

Zakiya was put in the same pickup as the mullah, and they were driven away from the villa together.

50

Mullah Abdullah

In the back seat of the black and white Lebanese police truck, the mullah turned to Zakiya and said, "Tell me what happened?"

There were armed men in the front seat and more in the truck bed behind them. It was now late at night and the lights of the city reflected off the shiny cars on the streets of Beirut.

Zakiya told him everything that happened from the moment she was taken until he called her name only a short time ago.

"You see..." the mullah said, but the pickup had come to a stop, and he turned to look out. They were in an enclosed yard full of police cars and pickup trucks. The back door opened and armed men ordered him to get out. He climbed down and Zahra followed right behind him.

A young woman with a broad smile approached them and said to Zakiya, "Sweety, come with me."

"No, I won't leave the mullah," Zakiya snapped and stepped closer to him.

"She is from the rescued girls," one of the armed men told the young woman.

"Why did you bring her to the station, she must be taken to the rehabilitation center."

"She was stuck to him like glue," the armed man said,

pointing at the mullah.

"My daughter, do not worry," the mullah told Zakiya, "I will make sure we go back home together safely."

His words were like a magic spell. Zakiya released her grip and went with the young woman, who immediately began asking her questions. He wondered if he would be able to fulfill his promise.

The mullah was taken to an office with five desks. Four of them were occupied by uniformed Lebanese men and women. Two were busy chatting and two were staring at their computer screens. The mullah sat beside the fifth desk. A maid brought a cup of coffee and a glass of water and set them in front of him. The mullah looked around him, *is this some kind of joke?*

A clean-shaved man wearing the same black uniform as the others, with gray hair and saggy cheeks, entered the room.

"We should lock you up in prison," he said as he took a seat behind the desk. "But we have orders from above to treat you kindly and wait for a Syrian official to pick you up and take you back to Syria. I assume it's so you can rot in prison there."

The mullah didn't speak, and didn't touch the coffee, he just drank the glass of water. He didn't have the energy to talk. He just wondered who the official might be. He bent his head with his chin on his chest and soon dozed off.

A tap on his shoulder woke him. "Time to move," an armed man said.

The mullah looked around. None of the five uniformed men were still in the room. He followed the man who'd awakened him, out to a police truck with the engine running. As soon as he climbed into the back, the door slammed, and the truck sped out of the compound.

"Where is the girl who came with me earlier," the mullah asked the armed man.

"Which girl?"

"She refused to leave me until I promised her we would go back to Syria together."

The armed man made a call and questioned someone on the other end of the line.

"They took her to the rehabilitation center. She must go through medical examinations and then the police will question her before they return her to Syria," the armed man said.

When they reached the airport, the armed man accompanied the mullah like a shadow, right to the door of the plane, where he passed a sealed envelope to the purser. "In Damascus, a military escort will be waiting for him, you just need to hand him this envelope."

"Ok," she said with a nod, then she led the mullah to his seat and helped him fasten his seat belt. When the plane was full and had taxied to the runway, she came again to the mullah and asked him to follow her. She led him to a seat in first class.

Thirty minutes later, the plane had landed and was taxiing to the terminal of Damascus International Airport. As soon as the steward opened the plane door, General Zafer al-Abyad stepped on board.

The mullah stood up and stared at the general's outstretched hand, then looked at the general's sly smile.

The general approached and hugged the mullah. "Syria is proud to have a hero like you."

The mullah didn't reply or hug him back or even shake his hand.

***

The mullah sat in the passenger seat of General Zafer al-Abyad's Mercedes 600, with cars behind and in front of them as escorts.

The streets were empty at such a late hour. They passed an inspection point shortly after they left the airport and took to the highway. Of course, the guards just saluted the general and let him pass.

Silence hung heavy in the car. The mullah hadn't spoken a word since they left the airplane, and the general hadn't said a word either, other than the initial greetings. Within the mullah swirled a torrent of rage against the man next to him. He turned and looked at the general's impassive face and thought. *Is ruthlessness a prerequisite for leadership? Are there any who rise to power with the well-being of their people at heart? Or is this generally the norm? A man willing to throw anyone to the wolves to achieve his goals?*

"You're probably wondering why the Lebanese Special Forces arrested you in the villa in Sycamore Gardens," the general said, while he flipped his unlit cigar from one side of his mouth to the other.

"For now, I just want to reach home and make sure my daughter is safe."

"She is safe and healthy, and sleeping in her own cozy pink bed."

"For Allah's sake," the mullah said, "How do you know that her bed is pink?"

"We know everything in this country," the general said, then laughed, "No, I am joking. It was a lucky guess. Don't all girls like pink?" Taking his eyes off the road for a moment, he looked at the mullah with a sly smile before looking back at the road, "So all you cared about was how I knew her bed was pink. You're not concerned about how I knew she was safe at home."

"At this point, I don't care how you knew," the mullah said, looking at the trees standing along the sides of the road like black ghost sentries. Then he looked at the general. "But I do doubt your reassurances. From what's happened to me recently, I realized you must sometimes say things you're not sure about."

"I never say things I am not sure about," the general said. "But regarding your daughter, it only took one call to her school to learn she's doing ok and attending her classes."

"You could also be sure about false information," the mullah said, "like the weapons deal supposed to happen on the plane."

"There is always the possibility that information we receive is incorrect, especially in a time of war. That part is beyond my control, but in your case, there was no wrong information."

"I almost lost my life three times in the last few weeks, were you sure of the outcome of that?"

"You were aware of the risk you were taking, and you're not considering how many innocents you rescued in the last few weeks?"

"But were you aware that I was going to die?" the mullah asked.

"You are the religious man among us. Do you think I can be sure about your life or death? Don't you teach your congregation that death is pre-ordained, and no one can change their fate?"

"You know what I meant by my question," the mullah

said. "I won't insist on an answer, I just want you to know that I feel you were not honest with me. You were concealing something, or worse, you pushed me to risk my life."

"Let me tell you a story. During World War II, the Nazis invented a cipher device called Enigma. At the time, it was a brilliant encryption machine which allowed secure communications between all the branches of the German military. However, British intelligence built a copy of the machine and were able to intercept the German's top-secret correspondence and decrypt it. They were extra careful not to let the Germans know they had the Enigma machine. One day during the war, a controversial thing happened. The enigma machine decrypted a message that said the Germans intended to bomb the city of Coventry. The leader at that time, Winston Churchill?"

The general looked at the mullah for a moment, but the mullah shrugged his shoulders, showing he didn't know who the leader was then.

The general turned his eyes back on the road and continued. "He had to decide between two critical plans of action; either evacuate the city and risk letting the Nazis know that British intelligence had cracked the enigma codes or keep quiet and continue cracking the codes that would help them defeat the Nazis." The general paused, waiting for the mullah to speak, but he was still processing the information.

"What do you think was the correct decision for Churchill to make at that moment in time?" the general asked.

"He should have evacuated the city." The mullah knew if he gave any other answer, he would be justifying the decision the general had made to put him in mortal danger.

"Maybe," the general said. "You think that, because you are not looking at the bigger picture."

"I don't think a good leader would risk the lives of his people that way." The mullah was clutching the edges of his seat tightly.

"Many historians think exactly like you, but don't you think the hundreds or maybe thousands of casualties burned by Nazi fire might save the world from a much larger risk? If Germany had defeated the Allies because of the loss of the advantage the Enigma machine provided, Hitler had plans to conquer the entire world, not only Europe. He could have developed nuclear bombs and started dropping them at will."

"Still, you can't justify that action at that time," the mullah said. "He couldn't know for sure if Germany finding out about the Brit's Enigma machine would result in defeat. Germany might have found out and yet the Allies might still have defeated Hitler. You are only assuming the decision was the right one, because we now know they won the war."

"I didn't say the decision was right or wrong, I am just saying sometimes sacrifices are worth it to improve the chances of winning."

"What should I understand from this story?" the mullah asked.

"You don't get it, do you?"

"So, I was the scapegoat?"

"No. You are still alive."

"But was I supposed to be?"

"Because of you, we raided the stronghold of Shaddad Abu Saif and Abu Moos, and captured hundreds of terrorists and tons of weapons. Because of you, the Iraqi forces raided the remote hospital, the Sword of Truth used for the human organ trade. Because of you, we found the location of the hijacked airplane and saved hundreds of families from being killed by the stolen weapons. Because of you, we helped the Lebanese Special Forces capture the branch of the Sword of Truth involved in sex slavery."

"But how?" the mullah asked, "The plan of Ain Alward didn't work out. The plan in the airplane didn't work out. I went alone to the Sycamore Gardens. I don't see how I helped."

"Do you remember the microchip they embedded in your tooth? They told you it was a device for some kind of transmission. Actually, it was a GPS microchip. We planted it in you, so we'd know where you were at all times."

The mullah inserted a finger into his mouth and touched his tooth. He said, "So what about the plan to replace Shaddad Abu Saif, was it all a fictional plan?"

"Not at all," the general said, "But unfortunately we were sold out by the officer who was interrogating the real Abu Moos at the Ain Dewar border checkpoint. While one of the officers was interrogating Shaddad Abu Saif about the alleged bribery, the officer in the next room was selling us out to the enemy."

"How do you know that?"

"When the plan didn't work out, we started an investigation to see where things went wrong."

"I hope this officer will drink from the same cup the crazy animals in Ainal made me drink out of," the mullah said.

"That officer is enjoying the glitter of gold in Europe

now. He ran away," the general said, glancing at the mullah before looking back at the road, "But don't worry. He will burn in hell in the hereafter." He laughed with no response from the mullah.

"But if you knew where I was through the GPS microchip, why didn't you rescue me from the hands of the monsters in Ainal?"

"The place where they imprisoned you had GPS jammers which prevented us from locating you, but when they moved you to the hospital in Iraq, we spotted you and informed the Iraqi government."

The mullah's feet and hands were so cold. "So, I was supposed to be the scapegoat in the second half of the plan, when you came to see me in Mosul."

The general's silence was enough answer to prove his point.

The general reduced his speed and took exit 44D to enter the city. The mullah stared out at the streets, deserted except for the guards at the inspection points.

"Why me?" the mullah asked. "Didn't you have agents already planted in their organization?"

"You had motive," the general said. "Your resolve to save your daughter was stronger than most motives, which the terrorists could have used to get you to switch sides. Many others did so before you. You wouldn't trade your daughter's freedom even if they offered you a plane full of gold."

The cars entered the narrow alley of Shagoor, and before the mullah got out, he asked the general to help in bringing Zakiya back to Syria as soon as possible.

∗

The guards from the other two cars walked the mullah to the door of his house. He knocked, since he didn't have his keys. After the third knocking, he heard Amani's voice timidly from behind the door, "Who?"

"It's me." He didn't need to say more. The door opened wide. Amani stood there with her hand over her mouth, crying. She'd lost weight, and her face had more worry lines. Stepping forward and closing the door behind him, he took her in his arms and stood there, holding her, as she let out all her sorrow. He hugged her tightly, welcoming the warmth he'd missed for so many months. The warmth of the only female he was allowed such intimate contact with.

"I called hundreds of times to tell you to come home, that Zahra is ok," Amani said. "Thank you, Allah, for bringing him back to me, alive."

"Is she sleeping?" he asked.

"Yes, she has school tomorrow."

The mullah just wanted to take a look at his daughter. He wanted to be sure she was okay. He wanted to tell her how much hell he had gone through to rescue her. He wanted to tell her he'd almost died a few times while trying to find her. He wanted to tell her how much he loved her, how important she was to him. He wanted to reassure her she would always be safe as long as he was still alive. But he didn't want to disturb her sleep.

As they walked arm in arm from the hallway out to the courtyard, he stopped to gaze at the lime tree and the pots of basil. He approached the Jasmin tree and inhaled deeply, closing his eyes and savoring the pleasant aroma. He hadn't realized how much he'd missed each and every pot and tree in this courtyard. It was so quiet and peaceful here. It was home.

After he'd taken a shower, he went up to wake Zahra for the dawn prayer. He knocked on her door and listened to the rustle of blankets being pulled back, joints cracking, a muffled yawn, then the door opened.

"Papaaa!" she screamed and threw herself on him. He hugged her and kissed her forehead, and they both started crying.

She was much thinner than when he'd left, her cheekbones more prominent. She pulled back to look at him and said between her tears, "Papa, thanks be to Allah, you are safe."

**

The mullah was in the courtyard carrying a watering can, moving between the plants to water them. He was wearing a brown woolen dish dash. The air was filled with the buttery aroma of his favorite roasted chicken dish. Farah, Marwa, and Ro'wa were with Zahra in the kitchen, preparing lunch. The general had called the mullah in the morning and told him that Zakiya would arrive around noon. The mullah asked him to bring her to his house and he would later drop her at her own apartment. It took the general three days to bring Zakiya back to the country, not due to his lack of authority, but because they kept her in Lebanon until they completed their questioning and gave her a thorough health screening. The morning after his arrival, the mullah and Amani went to the girls' apartment and informed them Zakiya was okay and would be coming home soon. The three girls were very excited, despite still mourning their father's death, which had been devastating news to the mullah, but the girls' excitement was contagious.

Zahra seemed to have an aura of guilt around her every time they sat together. She was still excited to have him home, but she avoided looking at him directly.

He assumed she felt guilty because she was the reason he went through such tribulation. He didn't need to tell her or Amani what he endured. His changed demeanor was enough evidence that he went through seven hells, and it was only because Allah didn't want him to die that he was still alive. He himself had a bit of guilt for feeling satisfied when he noticed Zahra's guilt. Was it because her guilt was proof of how much she loved him, or was it because he was emotionally immature and needed signs of reassurance from the people around him?

The doorbell cast a spell of silence over everyone in the house. The clatter of utensils stopped in the kitchen. The chatter and laughter of the girls stopped. Even the chirping of the birds ceased momentarily. Amani went to open the door, as Farah, Marwa, and Ro'wa stood at the end of the hallway waiting to see who would enter the house. When Zakiya stepped in through the door, the three of them ran and hugged her. They were all crying tears of joy. With a lump in his throat, and tears starting, the mullah wiped his eyes quickly when Amani came back, leaving the four girls to their joyful reunion. He admired Amani's empathy. A few minutes later, Amani led them all out to the liwan.

Amani and Zahra carried the lunch to the table in the liwan, and all of them sat down to have their lunch. The clacking of spoons and forks on the ceramic plates and bowls filled the air as everyone ate in silence. From time to time, the mullah glanced at Zahra and wondered what caused her to be so pensive. Zakiya was the only talkative one at the table. Her three sisters were not as animated as they had been previously, maybe because of their father's death.

"Why are you all wearing black?" Zakiya questioned her sisters.

Farah looked at Marwa and Ro'wa.

"What?" Zakiya asked.

Then Ro'wa said, "Father passed away."

Zakiya gasped.

"Father came back from Dubai when he found out about what happened to you," Farah said. Then she told Zakiya what had happened in Haj Adel's shop, the porters' story, the circumstances of the death of Haj Adel and then the unfortunate death of their father.

The mullah was plagued by the details of Haj Adel's death, and the later events which led to the death of Mazen. *Is it possible my next mission will be to bring justice to Haj Adel's family?*

After lunch, the mullah told Amani and the girls what had happened to him from when he went to the police station, intending to ask about Zahra until he reached Sycamore Gardens in Beirut.

When he finished, the six females around him were staring at him as if he had been resurrected from certain death.

"... in the last three days since I arrived home and after Zakiya in Beirut told me what had happened with her, I was reflecting on what could be the reason all this happened to me. The only logical explanation is that Allah heard Zakiya's prayers and not only saved her from the evils that surrounded her, but also sent me to rescue her and bring her back safely to her sisters."

Amani recited verse 186 from the second chapter of the holy Quran, "'When My servants ask you 'O Prophet' about Me: I am truly near. I respond to one's supplication if they call upon Me.'"

"But why was Zakiya rescued by you, and yet thousands of others are still kidnapped?" Farah asked.

"As in the verse Amani just mentioned, when we call upon Allah, He will answer us. However, we often don't know when that answer will come. We may feel lost in the twists and turns of our destiny, thinking things aren't getting better despite our prayers. It's not that our prayers go unanswered; we just may not fully grasp what's truly best for us. In His wisdom, Allah always guides us to what's best. So, even if something seems unpleasant in our limited understanding, it may actually be what's best for us or those around us.

"Everything that happened is a lesson for me that I must totally surrender to Allah and not allow my worries and anxieties to control my life, because Allah is sufficient for me. I want you to understand that even though your father and grandfather have passed away, Allah is sufficient for you, and He will always send people, like me, to support you.

"Before I returned, your father's lawyer from Dubai contacted Amani to discuss how to gradually transfer your funds. When I arrived, I called her, and we went over your options. She reassured me that you are wealthy girls. Your father left millions for you in Dubai. She also mentioned that your father's business partner suggested you move to Dubai to live with her. I told her I would discuss it with you.

"As for your inheritance here in Syria, I'll follow up with your uncle Basem to make sure you receive what's due to your father from your grandfather. And if you choose to stay in Syria, I'll be here to take your father's place, and Amani will take your mother's place."

"Although the villa I was at in Beirut was intended

for sin and adultery, I never felt closer to Allah than I felt there," Zakiya said, "I always remembered the verse from the holy Quran 'Those who were warned, 'Your enemies have mobilized their forces against you, so fear them,' the warning only made them grow stronger in faith and they replied, "Allah ˹alone˺ is sufficient ˹as an aid˺ for us and ˹He˺ is the best Protector.'" 3-173

"You are totally right Zakiya, Allah looks inside of us, no matter when or where we are, if we ask Allah sincerely, we will be answered," the mullah said. "Allah listened to your innocent prayers and moved armies to rescue you. And that reminds me of verse 82 in chapter 36 'All it takes, when He wills something ˹to be˺, is simply to say to it: "Be!" And it is!'"

ACKNOWLEDGEMENT

As I sit to write these words, I am overwhelmed with gratitude for the journey that has led me to this moment. This book would not have been possible without the love, support, and encouragement of so many wonderful people.

To my family and friends, thank you for standing by me through the late nights, the moments of doubt, and endless drafts. Your belief in me kept me going when I questioned whether I could finish this.

To my editor, your keen eye, thoughtful feedback, and endless patience have elevated this book to heigts I could never have reached alone. I am forever gratful.

To you, my readers. You are the final and most important part of this journey. If this story has touched your heart or captured your imagination, I humbly ask you take a moment to leave an honest review. Your thoughts and opinions mean the world to me and help other readers discover this work.

Above all, I extend my deepest gratitude to Allah. It is through His blessings that I found the strength and time to bring this book to life. Every moment of inspiration, and every ounce of energy that sustained me during this journey, is a gift from Allah, and I am forever humbled and thankful.

ABOUT THE AUTHOR

Hussin Alkheder

A native of Damascus, Syria, first drew breath in the vibrant city. His formative years were spent navigating the winding alleys of Al-Shagoor street, where he attended the venerable old primary school, imbibing the essence of his cultural heritage.

Over the span of twenty-three years, Hussin's roots remained firmly planted in Damascus, forging a deep connection with the city's rich tapestry of traditions and history. However, destiny beckoned him to explore beyond his homeland's borders, and he eventually embarked on a new chapter in his life, finding himself drawn to the bustling cosmopolitan marvel of Dubai.

For eight transformative years, Hussin luxuriated in the embrace of Dubai's multicultural milieu, absorbing its myriad influences and forging connections with people from all corners of the globe. Yet, this ceaseless thirst for cultural exploration continued to pull him, propelling him further eastward towards the captivating realm of Shanghai, China.

In Shanghai, Hussin delved into the mystique of far eastern cultures, immersing himself in the vibrant urban landscape and unraveling the secrets of this ancient civilization. As he roamed the bustling streets and serene temples, the profound allure of Asia left an indelible mark on his soul.

With an enriching array of experiences and a kaleidoscope of cultures etched into his being, Hussin found himself propelled towards a newfound passion - the art of storytelling. His creative spirit culminated in the masterful creation of his debut non-fiction novel, "The Victorious Blood," a literary testament to the triumphs and tribulations of Imam Hussain 's journey, painted with vivid strokes of truth and wonder.

Thus, the life of Hussin Alkeder traverses continents, cultures, and literary realms, as he pens a literary odyssey destined to captivate the hearts and minds of avid readers across the globe.

BOOKS IN THIS SERIES

Mullah Abdullah

Daughter Of Damascus

BOOKS BY THIS AUTHOR

The Victorious Blood: Will Show You What Happened In Karbala Thirteen Hundred Years Before.

Four Ladies : From The Middle Eastern Storyteller, Comes A Collection Of Short Stories Influenced By Four Major Cities That He's Lived In; Damascus, Dubai, Kuala Lumpur And Shanghai.

Printed in Great Britain
by Amazon

55695187R00202